SOLID STATE CONSPIRACY

BOOK TWO

I0659919

WRITTEN BY

J.SILVERSTONE

NEYTIRI
PRESS

Published by NEYTIRI PRESS
www.NeytiriPress.com

Printed in the United States of America.
ISBN: 978-1-7352987-1-9

Solid State Conspiracy is a work of fiction. Names, characters,
places, and incidents either are the product of the author's
imagination or are used fictitiously, and any resemblance to
actual persons, living or dead, business establishments, events,
or locales is entirely coincidental.

SOLID STATE CONSPIRACY

J.SILVERSTONE

THRILLER

NEYTIRI
PRESS

"THE ONLY REAL TIME
IS THAT OF THE OBESERVER,
WHO CARRIES WITH HIM
HIS OWN SPACE AND TIME."

~ ALBERT EINSTEIN ~

TABLE OF CONTENTS

CHAPTER ONE

They stopped the forced feeding three months ago. She still hasn't had any food or water.

How does she survive?"

"Says she can convert light into energy and store it in her body - like a plant."

"You've got to be kidding."

"No, I'm not."

Detective James Parker sat in the passenger side of a gray unmarked police car flipping through files on his laptop. He tried swallowing the excitement in his voice, but he wasn't succeeding.

His partner Sergeant Richard Boyle has been in the department for over thirty years and close to retiring. Pissed to be stuck with an ambitious rookie studying for a law degree who's taking every case too seriously is making Boyle's thin patience, thinner.

"A precedent was set," Parker continued. "Her lawyer, James Scanlon - know him?"

Boyle grunted.

"Big time!" Parker continued, ignoring Boyle's reaction.

"Scanlon brought in evidence that people can exist without food, citing an Indian woman who had not eaten for 55 years, another in Canada who started fasting in 1923..."

"They must have been skinny," Boyle grunted, patting his ample stomach bulging over the brass buckle of a cowboy belt, engraved, C.O.P.

Parker scrolled to another file.

"The background on this case is interesting. The state Supreme Court overturned a lower Court decision to continue intravenous feeding against the patient's will. It's all here in the transcript. Wanna see it?" Parker turned the laptop toward Boyle.

"Whataya nuts? I'm driving. Read it."

Parker cleared his throat.

"The Supreme Court ruling in the case of Jenny Webster, declared unanimously that she has a 'fundamental right' to refuse food or drink."

"Ha!" Boyle snorted, "rights..."

Parker went on. "After due deliberation, Judge Robert Gray wrote that for self-determination to have any meaning, it cannot be subject to the scrutiny of anyone else's conscience or sensibilities. It is the individual who must live or die with the course of treatment chosen or rejected, not the State."

"Yeah?" Boyle was skeptical.

Parker raised his eyebrows and smiled.

"She's been in that hospital without eating for three months." He paused, waiting. Again Boyle didn't take the bait, so he continued.

"According to the reports she's healthy as a horse."

Boyle frowned. "I don't believe it."

"It's in the document."

"Bullshit. Someone's slipping her something. You've got a lot to learn!"

Parker shook his head. "I don't know. When I first met her, she had something special about her."

"Sure. She's a hot looking piece of ass."

Boyle gunned the gas pedal of the late model Chevrolet, swerving around a corner and barely missing a young woman pushing a baby stroller. Parker didn't seem to notice as he searched to get his bearings as the car slammed to a stop in front of a two-story apartment that hadn't seen a paintbrush in more than ten years. On a dusty lawn in the front, a gaggle of rumpled old people sit on aluminum folding chairs, gossiping in the paling sun. Parker checked the address against the warrant in his hand. He hadn't expected Jenny Webster's apartment to be in a place like this.

Feeling conspicuous as he climbed out of the sedan, Parker felt six pairs of curious eyes turning to stare as a gust of wind revealed the gun holstered beneath his jacket. Boyle nodded confidently to the group as Parker marched stiffly past them, his eyes straight ahead, his neck prickling with the old people's stares. Across the street two young boys, their pale skinny legs bruised and scratched, kick fiercely at each other as they play soccer on the sidewalk.

Boyle opens the front door using a passkey. The elderly audience gaze knowingly. They know who these men are. Cops. They shift in their plastic webbing, watching the action like a television screen.

An old woman with skin like crumpled tissue paper pushes her loose teeth back against her gums with a practiced finger as she hisses to the rotund woman in the next chair.

"It's that girl on the second floor."

"She hasn't been here for awhile," the round woman agrees.

"That's why."

Boyle puffs his way up the stairs to the second floor and follows a much trimmer Parker down the peeling corridor to apartment 2A.

"I can't believe this fasting shit," he wheezes as he fumbles through his master keys. "She's got to be getting something, pills, water-someone's passing her something."

"Not according to the hospital," said Parker, wrinkling his nose against the sour cooking smells permeating the hallway.

"Hospitals," snorted Boyle. "What the hell do they know? I knew a guy once - cat burglar. Climbed out of a hospital window every night for two weeks. Hid his loot in the Director's office." He chuckled. "One night the guy broke his leg trying to climb back in. I read him his rights while they set the bone."

A child screams in the apartment across the hall. A woman's shrill voice yells back. There's the sound of breaking crockery.

"Nice neighbors," observes Parker as Boyle jams a key into the lock. The door opens.

"Jesus H. Christ," breathed Boyle.

"What?" asks Parker.

Boyle doesn't answer but walks straight in. The apartment is sumptuous. Elegant furniture perfectly placed on polished hardwood floors. Shafts of pale sunlight filters through oriental window screens highlighting with light the potted ferns and palms that cast geometric shadows on the glossy white walls. A white marble Parsons table holds a sleek lap top placed precisely in the center, flanked by brushed aluminum trays holding papers on either side. Floor to ceiling bookshelves cover one wall and a mass of elegantly framed lithographs cover another.

"Why in the hell would she live in a neighborhood like this?" Parker whispers as he surveys the exquisite room. "I've only seen places like this in magazines. Museum mounted Picassos in working class rent control. There's a paradox here, a huge contradiction."

"Cheap rent," inserts Boyle. "She makes decent, but not great money as a reporter. She had lost the millions she made as a model before her accident in the Himalayas. That's how she became so famous. People were getting updates about her while she was in a coma. It was one of those glamorous and yet terribly serious public incidents in which everyone knew about it and many were covering her fight to survive. Why and how she became a trouble making reporter afterward is beyond me. It was reported her financial manager who was handling her money while she was in a coma, had invested everything she had with Bernie Madoff. And you know what happened to the people who had everything with him. So if that was true, the furnishings are probably gifts from her boyfriend - her late boyfriend."

Parker shook his head. It doesn't fit.

Boyle picked up a book from the coffee table and frowned. "Take a look at this," he said handing it to Parker. "Tantric Art; a Guide to Ecstasy. Some kind of porn. Keep it as evidence."

Parker started to say something, thought better of it, and put the book in a plastic bag he unfolded from his briefcase.

There was a slight thump from the bedroom. Parker put the briefcase down and moved toward the bedroom door, drawing his gun.

"Where you going?" asked Boyle irritably.

Parker didn't answer. The bedroom was like the rest of the apartment - stylishly furnished with a thick piled carpet and a king - sized bed. Parker looked up, fascinated by the folds of a huge and delicate canopy that hung from the ceiling like a softly billowing tent.

"Nice place for an orgy." Boyle was standing beside him. "Can you imagine what this cost?" he shook his head at the opulence of it all. "I could have put my kid through college with what's in this place."

I didn't know you had a kid," said Parker.

"I don't." Boyle turned on his heel and made for the kitchen.

Parker wandered to the window and squinted through the blinds. Down in the street, a bag lady was pushing a shopping cart piled high with debris gathered from everywhere. Parker turned and surveyed the room again. As with the rest of the apartment, everything was perfectly placed. Silk pajamas lay on a pillow, folded as if for a shop window display. On the opposite pillow sat a porcelain doll, smiling vacantly in a state of blue eyed, wide eyed welcome. Suddenly he frowned. His eyes had fixed upon a small water glass that was lying on the carpet close to the night table. Could this have caused the noise which had drawn him into the room? Parker almost laughed at himself for thinking it. There was no breeze in here, and all the windows were closed. The noise had probably come from next door.

"Seen enough?" yelled Boyle from the living room. "Time for lunch."

Parker turned to see Boyle entering the bedroom with a crystal jar of almonds in his hand.

"Lunch?" he echoed.

"Yeah lunch, that stuff you eat off plates when you're hungry. What are you staring at?" asked Boyle, lifting the jar to his lips and shaking almonds into his mouth.

"Isn't that against regulations?"

"Perks of the job." Boyle chuckled. "She won't miss'em. She's gonna be in that Clifton Sanitarium till we cart her off to prison."

Parker watched as his partner munched. "It's a pretty expensive place isn't it?"

"So," shrugged Boyle, "her boyfriend paid for it. Maybe it was the hospital bills that killed him," he guffawed.

"You know," said Parker. "I really don't understand this. How can we charge a woman with murder when she is locked away in a hospital room thirty miles from where her boyfriend dies, with no access to phones or internet? It doesn't make sense."

"Look," said Boyle. "The D.A. thinks she did it, her fingerprints were there, and we have to find out how."

"It's crazy," said Parker. The charge can't stick."

"It'll stick. I don't know how she did it," said Boyle, "but she did, believe me."

"But how?" Parker's brow furrowed with exasperation. "She never left the sanitarium. And the place was burned. How did they find fingerprints?"

"Oh for Christ sakes," growled Boyle, finishing the almonds. "Don't you get it? It's an alibi."

"Some alibi! She was locked in a hospital room."

"Okay, so it's the greatest alibi ever. I've got a nose for these things. She did it and she's not going to get away with it."

"With what? They're not even sure how he died. He was too incinerated to do a complete autopsy."

"She sets up the alibi by asking the hospital attendant to call the police..."

"That's no reason to pin a murder rap on her."

"So, you tell me, how did she know this Jenkins guy is going to die?" challenged Boyle. "Do you think she was clairvoyant or something?"

Parker stared at the carpet.

"Come on, you're out of your depth. You need to eat. Food's good for the brain." Boyle turned back into the living room and opened Parker's brief case, methodically tipping the contents of the aluminum trays into the case and closing it.

"Wait," said Parker, crossing to the computer and picking it up. "There's evidence in here."

"Right," said Boyle, defiantly. "I was going to do that."

Parker stared back at him and snapped his case shut.

"We passed a place on the corner," said Boyle moving toward the front door. "Italian food. Cheap."

Parker glanced around the room for the last time, and then slowly followed Boyle out of the apartment.

When the front door had clicked shut, only the soft ticking of a bedroom clock disturbed the silence. Then, a slight shadow flitted across the bedroom wall. Someone was moving beyond the half opened door. A woman's hand was picking up the fallen glass and replacing it neatly beside the lamp on the night table.

CHAPTER TWO

"Jenny," the gray-haired man is talking to me softly and patiently.

"Jenny, please."

Sunlight is filtering through the barred window of the small visitor's room, painting a primitive mask of dark and light stripes across the face of the man sitting in front of it. I think I look the way he's used to seeing me, though my straight blonde hair is cut very short. I keep my hands folded primly in my lap, like a submissive nun awaiting benediction.

"Jenny," he said again, "will you please talk to me?"

I stay silent. I used to call him Uncle Jimmy as a child, but now I only think of him as a title, "my attorney".

"Jenny, we're been here almost two hours," he was saying. "How can I help if you won't say anything?"

He got up and moved to the window, trying to control the exasperation I know he feels. He had known me since I was a baby. My father was one of his best friends. Uncle Jimmy had watched me grow into an adult and watched my rise to fame then the strange path I took to become a journalist. Yet here I am, in a sanitarium about to be indicted by a Grand Jury for murder and I have to stay silent. Uncle Jimmy's refusal to accept what I say upsets me.

"Jenny," he turned to me. "I'm going to say it again, what you've told me and the authorities is preposterous."

I won't answer. It isn't necessary. He has already made up his mind what to think.

"Can't you see why we're all concerned?" The moment he uttered the word "concerned" I watched him withdraw it. A mistake. Too formal, too pompous. He shook his head self-deprecatingly. "Guess I'm sounding like a lawyer," he sighed.

I start to smile but he uses that softening as an opening and takes a few paces toward me then squats stiffly beside my chair. "Jenny, you have to trust me," his voice cracks.

Slowly I turn my head. "Please," he was saying, "please let me help you." The potted flower on the coffee table caught my attention. It was wilting, bending, probably from the tension the attorney was creating. I tried to comfort it, send it soothing vibrations, but the flower was not responding. It stayed bowed and unmoving.

The attorney stiffly pulled himself up and went to the small writing table where he sat down and drummed his fingers on the leather top. "I don't know how much more we can do today. I'm not getting through to you. Can you understand my dilemma?"

Why should I answer him? I already told him everything he should know. He just doesn't want to accept it. When the Voices want to communicate with him, they will come through me and talk.

The hair on the nape of my neck is starting to prickle, even tickle a bit. The part I had shaved off is growing back. I wanted to shave it again, this time all over, but the nurse had taken the razor away even though I had tried to explain I needed a smooth head to receive transmissions. She had laughed.

Which reminds me to smooth back the hair at the top of my head to stay receptive. I can't see the attorney very clearly, only the black and white stripes of light passing through and over him.

He pushes his chair back abruptly. "Look Jenny, you could not have been with Tim when he died. He was in the mountains and you were in this hospital miles apart. There was no way you could have been in two places at the same time. You had a dream, and by improbable odds, it came true. That's it. Now stop telling that story."

Longingly I look out the window. The sun is starting to set.

"Tell me, Jenny..." His voice is rising with impatience. "Did you think you saw Tim die when you were sleeping?"

I have to close my eyes. He hadn't believed a word I had said.

He cleared his throat. "I know you didn't kill him."

My hands grip the sides of the chair. I'm shaking with anger. I had been with Tim to oversee, to help him through to the other side. I told him that many times. Why does he choose not to believe me?

Uncle Jimmy leans close, his elbows on his knees, his hands folded in front of him, pleading. "You saw him in a dream, a movie in your head."

Staring at him drives him off the chair and to the window. The reflected light wipes out his features. All I can see is the darkened outline of a human head, like the silhouette picture I used to have as a child. I had loved that picture - three dimensional with black felt figures pasted on top. For hours I'd lie in bed at night watching the figures run up and down their black-felt stairway. The attorney turns to me. I can no longer see his face, only his swollen arthritic hands.

"According to the doctors you're suffering extreme trauma from the rape. I wish I could have gotten you to sign yourself out. Now, they're getting a court order to keep you here while the Grand Jury is investigating. I wish you hadn't ignored me. It could be too late."

Closing my eyes I inhale deeply to calm myself. He had not absorbed anything and was resisting the possibility there might be a reality other than the one in which we're living. He even denies the potential for that.

"You want to play crazy," his voice has a tinge of exasperation," I'm beginning to think you are for staying in this place and throwing your life away." He crumbles a paper.

I shiver.

Scanlon softens. "I understand you may need some help, but you don't have to be locked away. There are better, more private ways of dealing with these fantasies of yours than being shut in here." His voice is hoarse. "If you keep up this crazy act, you're going to be lost." Voice breaking he takes a deep breath.

I don't want to explain my beliefs to him again. The Voices aren't taking over and if I have to do it, I get too emotional. He hadn't believed anything I said about the conspiracy either. He does not want to.

"All right Jenny," startling me as he sits down beside me. "If you're going to continue your little game, I don't want any part of it." His narrow eyes peer over his glasses.

Maybe I should try to explain once more. An inner jolt shakes me, warning me to be silent.

The attorney slouches in his chair and swings it side to side. "They're putting together a competency hearing." He sounds weary. "If you are declared incompetent you may have to stay in the hospital for a very long time." He sighs.

I feel myself tighten. He has totally dismissed my belief that one can never be locked away, because one can always soar away in spirit.

"You can be flip," he was saying more loudly, "because you know underneath it all you can have your freedom. But once the Court sends in their own state appointed doctors for evaluation, they may declare you 'non compos mentis' then it's a whole other matter."

I shudder. He leans closer. I want to draw away but I'm frozen.

"If that happens there will be people deciding your fate who are not as gentle or considerate as we have been, and you won't be able to stay here. This is top of the line. I hope you never see the inside of a state mental hospital."

I have. It's horrific. I'm riveted.

He smiles with the discomfort of one who rarely smiles. "I've known you a long time. When your father made me Executor of his will, I took the trust seriously and vowed I'd care for you as if you were my own daughter." His voice softens. "Jenny, I will help you."

His words are compelling.

"You may have stepped beyond the comfortable boundaries of what society calls sanity, but I believe that one person's insanity is another person's reality. Who is to say where we should draw the line? I don't have that answer. But the State thinks it does."

He rose and came uncomfortably close. I shrink away. He keeps talking. "I know sure as hell you didn't kill Tim. You're hurting yourself by saying the things you do. You're also hurting others who care."

I look at the floor. If anyone wants to be hurt, they're doing it to themselves. I only want to be myself, not another person's version. If people *cared*, they'd open their eyes and not try to force me into a pre-fabricated mold.

He shook his head sadly. "Look..."

I have the power to leave. A piece of paper that says I can or cannot do something means nothing. I'm free. I can leave my body and return to it.

He's looks increasingly sadder.

I smile at his fear of insanity. Some of the "craziest" people in the hospital are some of the best I've met. The least craziest. Less crazy than this Attorney sitting next to me whose wife goes from one cosmetic surgery to another, whose daughter lives for trendy clothes and night clubs, and whose son deals drugs from the family estate's guest house.

Scanlon keeps talking. "The minute you lose your legal rights, it will be disaster. Also, I think you better start eating something."

I straighten my back. Months ago I had told him about the Yogis who stay closed in caves for years without food. Although he first resisted, when I threatened to get another lawyer, he used my information and got the court order to reverse the intravenous feeding. I smile. He probably didn't think I would last this long.

He grabs his cold cup of coffee and drains it. "You're a talented young woman. This is a waste. I ask you to save yourself and your answer is to smile and stare. All that talk about voices, your Guides, leaving your body, and now this fasting business." He shakes his head. "I'm glad to see you're getting nourishment from somewhere."

My body tightens again.

Scanlon starts to speak but I can only see his lips. Moving. No sound is coming from them.

I feel his concern. It touches me. Are the Guides trying to teach me something? Do I have to go back to the outside world to test my new knowledge? What if I forget it once I'm there?

An inner vibration begins rattling me. Thoughts are spinning. The hospital is easy. It's filled with kindred souls. Why do I have to go back to the chaos of society? Is it the circle of fate, the law of life that makes one repeat past mistakes and experiences?

Closing my eyes the planet Earth falls away from me. I can see skyscrapers, cars, factories, clouds of pollution, circling in a perfect blue and white sphere, spinning nearly uncontrollably in the openness of deep space.

I'm at the edge of a diving board leading toward that planet. I don't want to jump off. I'm terrified if I do, I'll fall into an endless void. I never want to be helpless or ignorant again. CHANGE! CHOICES. What if the change plunges me into the darkness of past mistakes, of sleeping wakefulness?

The chair is turning. The walls are spinning. The floor is pulling me down.

Big strong arms lift me off the floor onto the sofa. I try to pull away. I don't want to be touched, don't want the feel of someone else's skin against mine after what had been done to me.

Something strong is under my nose. Ammonia. Why do the Guides have him touching me? What are they preparing me for? Why is Tim gone? Why isn't he here to protect me? What is this lesson? Graduation from this place must be very far away.

I still haven't mastered the hole in my heart that was Tim. It won't close off the terrible feeling when I realize he's no longer with me, that I'm alone. I forget I can re-create him, draw a visual picture of such intensity that he can be made whole once again.

Then I step over the threshold of reality and enter the world beyond, the world where Tim still exists, where once again we can hold each other for what feels like lifetimes. We come together more intensely at those times than before he "died".

I tend to forget that quite often now, falling instead into the despair of emptiness labeled, Tim.

A fat black Mont Blanc pen moves across a yellow legal pad, grating into the paper, etching into my nerves. I've become very sensitive to outside stimuli, experiencing things super physically like the simple action of pen against paper which sets my nerves on edge.

Scanlon looks at me, assessing me. I let our eyes meet. He's relieved, and then upset to see I'm not cringing. I'm exhibiting power. His intuition says I am reading his mind. But he doesn't trust it, deciding instead to put on his veil of professionalism.

" If I can't come to see you in the morning, I'll call. I told you, I leave for London tomorrow." He shifts, straightened, and weighs his words. "This talk about being in two places at the same time and higher powers is not good. You lose credibility."

"That's what the detectives said," I whisper.
He's thrilled I talked, yet shocked by my words. "What?"

"The detectives said it doesn't make sense."

"What detectives?"

"The ones in my apartment."

"When?"

"While I've been here with you."

He leaned forward, intense. I shrink away. His energy is too strong, it's upsetting.

"How do you know that?" His tone is grim.

"One of them almost caught me when I bumped into the night table."

He stared at me "What?" he asked again.

"The water glass fell to the floor." A smile fights to enter my lips.

"I don't believe this." He pulls his face into shadow. His secretary had called just a short time before he landed to tell him a search warrant had been issued for Jenny's apartment. No one else knew about it. Certainly not Jenny.

"Who told you they were there? Did I mention anything to you about a search warrant?

"For detectives Boyle and Parker?"

He froze, scrolling through his mind how she could possibly have this information. He was uncomfortable with this strange feeling of confusion. He was used to dealing with more clarity than this.

"Did you read my mind?" he tried joking.

If I had, it would have had to be in his unconscious. He had not given the warrant a thought once it was out of his hands.

"You're imagining these things." It almost was a question.

I met Detective Parker when Mannie was killed. He's a kind man.

Scanlon writes something on his legal pad then peers over his glasses. "You were not in your apartment this afternoon," he declared, acting as judge and jury. "Your apartment is in Los Angeles." He was patronizing, treating me like a child or an alien.

"You've been in this room for the last two hours. Maybe you've been daydreaming, you certainly haven't been communicating, but your body has been here."

The smile once again plays at my lips. The Guides decided to answer him. "That's right. My flesh, I do leave physical shapes around."

"Jenny," he slams his hands on the desk, making me jump. He doesn't seem to notice. "How can I believe what you've just said? How can I? I've been with you for over two hours and you tell me you weren't here. How could you be elsewhere? I see you. I'm not hallucinating. Should I videotape future meetings to prove you don't go anywhere? It's your imagination, and if you continue to talk like this you'll be committed."

I brush stray hair away from my eyes.

"One day you'll find yourself with your fantasies gone and locked behind bars with a bunch of crazy people and with no way of getting out." He stands up, his head shaking from side to side as if he's blocking the reality out.

"May I go back to my garden now? The flowers miss me. I haven't spent any time with them this afternoon and I'd like to tuck them in for the night."

"You can be with your flowers when we're through." He takes a deep breath. It sounds shaky. "You're making this difficult. You have to trust me."

Sidelight came through the window touching off the gray in his hair and outlining him in white. It's a sign from the Guides, I can trust. Settling back into the hard, upright chair, I start to cross my legs, then decide I need the power to have both feet on the ground.

He sat down, breaking the light halo. "The D.A. has put one of his best detectives on the case, Sergeant Boyle. If they build a case the Grand Jury will indict you." He takes out his handkerchief and wipes his damp brow. "Nobody believes or understands what you're saying. They think you masterminded Tim's death." His lips are turning even paler. "We have to prove your innocence. That's how it works."

I don't respond.

"Have a good time with your flowers," he sighs and waves his hand dismissively. "Give them my love."

I smile at him and leave.

I know he's watching me walk into the garden though he can't see my face with my hair blowing around it. I bend toward a bed of white daisies. A soft breeze moves them toward me as if they're saying hello.

A chill runs up Scanlon's spine as he watches the girl and the flowers bend toward each other in what looks like a greeting.

He had tried reading up on some of the things Jenny talked about when he took her case. It was true that a high Lama or Yogi in India and Tibet had been reported doing some of the things she had said. But the reality of that with a young woman in Twenty First century America is highly unlikely. In all probability the high-strung demanding life she has led simply catapulted her into a nervous collapse. She's sensitive, intelligent and motivated. If he had to work day and night, he was going to make sure Jenny Webster is not indicted for murder or committed for insanity.

He sat back in the chair and closed his eyes. Suddenly a small light starts to glow in the middle of his forehead. He catches his breath and opens his eyes.

Standing in the midst of the white daisies, I smile at him and gently stroke the petal of a flower. I wink and smooth tendrils of hair from my face, then turn and walk away.

I look back again, smile and wave.

He doesn't wave back but watches as I walk up the path. Shaking his head, he packs up his briefcase to leave.

CHAPTER THREE

On my way to the tree shaded path leading to the cottage where I've recently been moved, I pass the women's wing of the Central Hospital's main building and turn my head to avoid the shrieks and screams escaping through its bars.

"*You should leave, you should leave...*" patters a singsong in my head hurrying along with me.

Slowing with relief I see my new lodging, the institution's version of a halfway house. Here, twelve female patients live. We have our own hours and permission to walk the grounds unattended during daylight hours. Some even have small pets like cats and birds. Penelope, a former housemate had kept Mortimer, a large rat she found outside the kitchen that she was trying to train to sit up and beg. She was starting to have a little success. But when she left Mortimer alone for a moment to get him a treat, an attendant not knowing Mortimer was a pet, saw him as a rodent and chased him down the corridor, unmindful of Penelope's screams to stop. He cornered the rat in a broom closet and quickly ended his life. Traumatized, Penelope was returned to the main house to be injected with tranquilizers and wrapped in icy wet sheets. I never saw her again.

I don't have a pet though I once had an argument with Carolyn, another housemate, over Ra, the large yellow Tabby, now lying on top of the balustrade, sunning himself as I climb the stairs. He yawns as I stop to scratch his head.

I had recognized Ra the moment I saw him curled up on a rug in the dayroom at Carolyn's feet. Ra was an old friend from a past life in Egypt. Picking him up I knew he recognized me too as he started to purr and rub his head against my cheek. When I started to take him to my room, Carolyn, who called him Ernie, told me to put him down.

I tried to explain that Ra had appeared at the halfway house so we could be together again.

But Carolyn said that wasn't true and tried to take him away. Shielding Ra I tried to get away from her but Carolyn lunged for both of us. Ra settled the disagreement by scratching both of us and running away, staying away for two days and nights. During that time the voices instructed me to give up attachment to possessions. Ra had been put in the house to show me nothing could be owned, the universe was to be shared by all, ownership was a concept that caused division. Accepting the voices' explanation I gave Ra up. The next morning, the cat pranced into the day room and leaped into my lap as if nothing had happened. When Carolyn walked into the room, he jumped down from me and went over to Carolyn and wound around her legs, purring.

"Lesson time," Carolyn grinned. "It's always nice to meet another new-age nun."

"What do you mean?" I asked.

"I just figured we both understand the reason for Ernie's disappearance - to give up the concept of possession."

I smile with surprise. "Yes."

"Therefore," Carolyn continued, "I assume we're treading a similar path."

I was afraid to ask but knew I must. "Do you hear voices?"

"Shh," Carolyn whispered and glanced around. "If anyone hears you say that they'll do a report and bottom line you'll be tagged "crazy". Then you'll lose the possibility of getting out the front door. Anything that gives them the excuse to keep you here is used for that purpose. Never forget you're in a research hospital, and though it's plush and they charge a lot, with the kind of diagnosis you've got, anything and everything will be used against you. Just mirror everything they want you to do. Don't give them flack, don't stand up to them. Behind these walls, on this side of the door, without a key, you have no resource other than yourself. It's a lesson in discipline. Don't talk about anything interesting because the staff will report you as delusional. Most of all, never mention the voices. They'll take them away with electrodes and medication. I know. They tried to do that to me. But the voices helped me to shut them out. So now, for the most part, they are my means of emotional strength and support.

We both exhaled at exactly the same time and broke out simultaneously in giggles, which made us laugh even more.

"Do we have the same voices? " I ask.

"I don't know. I haven't been trained in reading minds yet. I've got to get all the groundwork done first, like selflessness and love. You know, the basic elements." She waved and walked away. Ernie/Ra started to follow, then changed his mind and jumped up on the windowsill for his morning sunbath.

I thought about the time I started listening to the voices. It had been shortly after the rape. I thought I had been pushed so far that I made them up, or I was having a hysterical reaction. But when they continued to come unsummoned and sounded so rationally clear about emotional things, I began to listen to them with more objectivity.

Actually the voices first came when my father died. Never questioning their validity I found encouragement in their words. In fact I felt blessed by their caring and understanding. But as I grew older and stronger they disappeared and I had forgotten about them till that rape.

Now I understand the voices are never to be taken lightly. They come when I need them. I call them my *Guides* for good reason.

With uplifted feelings I walk toward my newly decorated room, when suddenly a shadow of anxiety makes me stop. I don't want to leave here. I value the friends I've made here. There is a handful of people who understand me and with whom I can share these perceptions. And because I have the voices to advise me, I'm safe and protected as long as I'm here.

Pausing in the doorway of my room I think how different it is from my home in Los Angeles. It's sparsely furnished, Spartan almost, and has only the bare essentials. Yet it's soft, personal and feminine. The iron bed is covered with a pink silk Japanese quilt a friend had given me when he left the hospital. There's a picture of stars and comets painted by Billie a patient who speaks only through her art, and little rows of seedlings that I had started after the voices told me that plants were important for survival. Little things, yet so precious.

Drifting to the window I gaze across the lawn toward the setting sun. A soft white mist covers the grass and has begun to climb the trunks of the massive oaks bordering the edge of the gardens. Pressing my forehead on the cool glass of the window as the fine white mist rises from the ground like a translucent curtain, I think how different this clean white mist is from the gray smog that covers Los Angeles. Al Rudnik, my boss at the news has an office that's dirtier than the inside of a chimney. He smokes enough cigarettes during the fourteen to sixteen hours he spends in his office, despite the no smoking signs posted on the walls, that it could permanently coat every square inch of wall, furniture, and floor with residue, the smell won't be gone till the building is razed.

I'm having trouble breathing. Perhaps the shortness of breath is from anger instead of smoke.

Rudnik wants to kill one of the best and most controversial stories I've ever investigated. Perhaps he's right. My life would have been very different if I had listened to him. But would it have been for better or worse? Would I give up what I've learned if I was given a second chance?

Leaning on the windowsill of my room, it's no longer a window but Rudnik's desk. I stretch to see his computer screen with the proposal I had written as he rotates it toward me. "What is this?" he shouts, a lit cigarette dangling from his lips. Not waiting for an answer, he spits out, "Baby Factories? Bullshit! Yellow journalism! You're not producing for Fox News." A flush of red spreads from his neck to his chin, racing across his nose to his forehead. I know his danger signals and I keep silent.

"**Electro Magnetic Energy Chips**?" Al is practically choking on his words, "**Implanted transponders to monitor minds**! What the hell are you proposing here – a sequel to BRAVE NEW WORLD?" He spins the computer back to face him. "You're supposed to be developing a series on bio- genetic engineering, not crap about mind control."

"Bio genetic engineering is mind control. If you'd just read it all the way through..."

"If I could read it all the way through," he interrupted, "I'd be the only person in LA to get beyond the first paragraph. It's secondhand science fiction. If you were a rookie, I'd fire you."

Trying to suppress the anger rising in my throat I take a deep breath. "Al, I have a friend who is working in the genetics division of Anson Industries. She's been giving me a lot of information about this."

"Like what?"

"Like what you just labeled *bullshit*. She can produce documents proving there's technology available to measure the output of electronic activity in a person's brain and break it down into graphs to interpret into words. Techno mind reading."

"What do they do with it?"

I'm incredulous. "Are you kidding? Everything!"

"Why?" He looks amused.

My friend is afraid she'll be in danger if someone finds out she talked to me.

"Industry theft is a fact of life." His tone   is unsympathetic."

"Al, it's not as if she's working for the KGB! Anson Industries is an international public company based in the U.S."

"Corporate secrecy is cutthroat."

"Cutthroat. Exactly. She's not worried about losing her job. She's worried about losing her life."

"Not likely."

Taking a deep breath I decide to compromise my friend's confidence. "She's working on something that has to do with artificial blood and sperm."

Rudnik shrugged. "I'm surprised it hasn't been done already."

I'm not sure if he's joking, so I continue. "Do you realize how advanced they are and nobody knows it? In addition to Mannie's work combined with the technology to read brain waves, Anson can make a component small enough to implant a device to send and receive signals."

Rudnik leaned in a bit closer across his desk with interest. "Keep going."

"When they can read minds, they can reverse the process and replace the thoughts with different ones sent by electronic impulses. Do you realize how mind boggling this is?"

He doesn't react to my attempt at humor. A professional skeptic who disbelieves most things until every option is exhausted, I can see he is starting to turn off.

Trying again. "Al, this gives them total power over the world! When thoughts can be read and then manipulated, populations will be monitored and controlled. This technology makes it possible."

He shakes his head. "Too bizarre. These are old theories that hold no reality."

I look at him steadily. "When one can control another's mind, one controls everything."

Rudnik shakes his head no, his chin in his hands, his mouth in a frown.

"Look." I move in closer as I point to it in the text. Rudnick's tension is contagious. I have to force myself to stay calm.

"That's Schizophrenia." He draws away like I'm contagious.

"It's reality." I lower my voice." Our world has become what we used to call science fiction. Think about the atom smasher, television, astronaut stations in space. How about flying around the Earth in a few days in a single engine airplane, or circling Earth in a spaceship in less than 90 minutes moving at 17,500 miles per hour.

Satellite transmission? That was a science fiction concept not so long ago. How about heart transplants or even the internet? Anson has been developing artificial conception and gestation."

Rudnik pushes away from his desk and lights another cigarette off the tip of his old one. "Who is this friend?"

"Someone who got very angry with me when I wrote the article on animal sacrifices in the temples of science. Remember that?"

"Ha! How can I forget? Thanks to you my grandchildren still lecture me when I use certain products or eat meat. You certainly had an impact!"

"I'm glad."

"That wasn't meant as a compliment.," he growled.

"I'm glad it had an impact." We were starting to get off track. "This topic is very important."

"Visions of Emmy dancing in your head?"

"No. You know I don't think like that."

"O.K. Mother Theresa, go on." Sighing he leans back in his chair, his eyes closed.

"With this kind of technological advance we can all be thrust into an adolescent state. The futurist Isaac Assimov once warned if we all become adolescent which means thinking alike, acting alike, and feeling alike, then one catastrophe affects us all. A powerful weapon."

Rudnik sits up. The concept of a single source of control on a world wide basis sobered him. I've broken through to him, so I went on.

"Who are these people trying to play God? How do they think? What do they want to do? The News has to find out." Tapping his computer as if to wake him up.

"This is important Al, it can't be dumped. We're talking about domination - complete world control."

He pushes his chair back. "And you sound like an episode out of "X- FILES."

"Al, science fiction has become reality."

He starts to interrupt but I don't let him. "What this means is some day you or your heirs could be sitting here totally manipulated, your minds being used like a keyboard for some other person's thoughts and beliefs."

"Impossible!" His face grows redder, his lips pursed in a tight pout that meant major anger. Taking off his glasses he pinches the bridge of his nose so tightly it leaves two red marks. "Who's your source?" he asks wearily. "I need a name."

I hesitate.

His face puffs up like an adder's. Another bad sign.

"Give me the name of your man or forget it. The story is killed."

Before he explodes I quickly answered, "**Her** name is, Dr. Manuela Cristal de Sebastiane. We call her Mannie. She's a scientist working with biogenetic engineering at Anson labs. She was my roommate at Radcliffe, and her credentials are platinum."

Rudnik starts to interrupt, but I go on. "She's a dedicated scientist and she's concerned about what is happening at Anson without any kind of monitoring."

"Great, another whistle blowing conspiracy monger," he growls.

I continue quietly. "Mannie's concerned her program will contribute to incalculable danger if it gets out of control." I look at Rudnik sharply. "Someone has to stop it before it happens."

Rudnik turns away. "Nothing's happened."

"Yet. Look, Mannie and I have been good friends for a long time. I know she can be trusted. She's more like family to me than the one I had."

"Well that's a great reason to give you the go ahead for a story that will bring lawsuits against this network. You're talking innuendo, not facts."

Ignoring him I continue. "There is solid evidence. In the mid 1970's a woman in Nebraska claimed she was going blind because of microwave beams being sent across her farm from one Army base to another. She sued the Army and they gave her a huge settlement with a do not disclose. Her story is still under wraps."

"What does that have to do with anything?" He rubbed his eyes and they began to water.

"Microwave beams cause behavior modification." I pause, unsure whether to go ahead, then decide to go for it. "You're getting headaches aren't you? I noticed you were pressing the bridge of your nose like you had one."

He started to protest.

I kept going. "Do you remember what the Russians did to our embassy in Moscow? Since the late Sixties they've been beaming microwave transmissions at the Ambassador's office and so far three Ambassadors have died of Leukemia. As we speak the fourth is in a naval hospital in Bethseda, getting chemotherapy treatment. And it's not for gallstones."

Rudnik looks at me, his hand over his mouth.

I'm on a roll so I continue. "At first our government thought the Russians were transmitting microwaves to jam transmissions, but it was later proven the microwaves caused changes in behavior. That is public information."

"I remember reading about it," he concedes.

"Now a microscopic chip has been developed capable of receiving and sending information like a transponder. Used in the various zones of the brain the simple stimulation or lack of stimulation could alter and control behavior. They no longer have to use microwave. This is easier. They've been doing it with monkeys in the labs. Remember my animal abuse story?"

"Yeah" he rubbed his chin, thoughtful.

"Think of what Stalin or Hitler or any of the other tyrants could have done with this technology. The person or group that develops this first will have control of the world in days."

Rudnik shakes his head, allowing a smile to pierce his red-veined cheeks. "Conspiracy theories. Who are THEY? I hired a novelist instead of a reporter. You better check with our medical editor. You'll find your theories are classic schizophrenia. It's impossible."

"This information has to be exposed. It can't be kept secret!" I pull my chair closer to his desk. "Our minds will become open books."

"On line or hard copy?" he asks.

"Hard." I answer back. Suddenly I see clear silver streaks starting to cut through the room with a charged electrical sound. Squinting the beams grow clearer. All sounds from the newsroom stop. The charged sounds grow louder as the grid of silver streaks becomes dense and encapsulates us both inside ."This room is filled with electricity!"

"Of course it is!" He flicks the desk light on and off a few times. "It's called technology." He pulls the cigarette out of his mouth, incredulous. It's burned down to the filter. His hand trembling, he stubs it out in an ashtray filled with dirty filters and burns a finger. "God damn it."

The stench of stale cigarette smoke fills my nostrils. The room is getting close and hot. I try to dismiss the unpleasant sensations, but my skin is getting prickly.

"Mannie has further information for me."

Rudnik pushes his chair around and looks out the window at the smog- covered city below. "I don't want this discussed with anyone. We need lots of clearances if this can be aired. Understand? Half of me thinks you may have gone totally out of your mind." He looks past me at the wall and a shiver goes through him. Passing a hand over his face he becomes aware I'm watching him.

A jolt goes through my body. I jump up and start toward the door.

"Jenny!"

Pausing I keep my hand on the knob.

"Do you want me to put Siegel on this with you?" he asked. "He's available."

"Is he ever! No thanks. If I run into trouble, I'll let you know. It's best I work with Mannie alone."

"All right." He swivels his computer around and starts to read, totally cutting me off. Dismissed without a word, I leave.

Stopping for a moment, I squint, looking for the lines of energy I had just seen but don't see them anymore. Walking past rows of cluttered desks to my own, I pause to look back at Rudnik through the glass wall. His head is bent in deep concentration, the light on his desk turned off. Had I really seen those streaks a few moments before? I keep squinting as I walk to my desk where the phone is ringing. "Jenny Webster".

"Am I interrupting?" It's Tim. I feel better now. My cheeks burn and a little excited. I always do when I first see or hear him.

"You never interrupt me." I ignore the writer at the next desk trying to get my attention. I turn my back, feeling my cheeks grow hot.

"Listen," his voice is gruff and throaty. "I've got to be in Washington first thing in the morning, so I'm taking the 4:00 p.m. flight this afternoon. Let's have lunch before I leave."

"I'd love to."

"I haven't much time."

"It's ok." I look at the bank of clocks lining the wall, the time of day for each major city in the world. "Do you want me to take you to the airport?"

"No. Roxanne hired a car so we can go over some last minute details."

I stiffen, a wave of discomfort falling over me. "Is she going with you?"

"Yes". His answer is matter of fact. If only I could feel that way about Tim's young, beautiful and supposedly "brilliant" assistant. Unwilling waves of jealousy sweep over me. I try to make the feeling stop, but I can't do anything about the unease I feel about this woman. Roxanne is efficient, ambitious and doing everything she can to get Tim away from me.

"How long will you be gone?" My voice is tight.

"Let's talk at the restaurant. There isn't much time."

Looking at the clocks in front of me I see it's already tomorrow in Tokyo. It's too late for lunch there and much too early in Hawaii. Why did one always measure time? It's so relative.

"Right now?" He sounds annoyed.

My heart clutches. "Of course. I have one call to make. Tim, I must tell you. I just had a really tough talk with Rudnik. I want to..."

"Please Jenny," he interrupted. "Wait till we see each other."

"All right." Rejection sank in. He was always cutting me off lately. He didn't seem to care about what I was doing or thinking or god forbid, feeling. I find myself doing monologues to unheeding ears. And as far as our sex life, we could be brother and sister. There is no longer the touching, the little stolen moments in public where he would put his hands in places I hoped no one could see. I inhaled deeply, "La Scala? It's still early."

"Roxanne called and got Simone to reserve a table." My jaw clenched tighter. Reservations were never taken at the trendy boutique restaurant. It was first come, first serve. Even famous Hollywood faces had to stand around and wait in the tiny entranceway. Jenny didn't know how Roxanne managed to reserve a table. Pushy and tenacious she seemed capable of doing anything.

Tim hung up the phone before either of us said good-by. I held the phone close, swallowing bitterness, feeling distanced and heavy, lonelier than ever. Something has happened and I don't know what it is.

The second hand of the clock labeled London clicks away another minute of precious time as I pick up the phone to call Mannie. I'd almost forgotten. That was happening a lot lately. I get so carried away with the way Tim is behaving, or usually not behaving, I forget to do things. Emotion is overtaking my focus and time.

The phone rings nine times before the Anson operator finally answers. I hear my voice sounding angry when I ask for Mannie. I'm so tempted to tell the snippy operator she could easily be replaced by a computer, but I'm disturbed more by my thought then the operator's rude behavior.

"Yes." Mannie's soft weary voice sounds pre-occupied and thousands of miles away.

"Mannie, it's Jenny. Are you all right?"

"Jenny! I want to talk to you."

"I've got to talk to you too. Tim's going out of town, how about dinner tomorrow night?"

"What time?"

"Seven."

"Fine. Do you mind if we go to my favorite place? I'm on a junk food binge. I'll tell you why when I see you."

"Whatever you want. But I get to make the next choice after this one."

"Done."

The long-haired reporter at the next desk starts to come over. Quickly I bury my head to search through my purse, pull out a mirror and freshen my lipstick. I don't want him to start talking. He could talk for hours unless he's on deadline. Then he'd scream at anyone who coughed or closed a drawer too loudly.

"Got to go." I jump up as he approaches me. He backs away bowing. Behind him I see one of the clocks — it's growing later in every part of the world. Guiltily I put the mirror back and snap the lock on the purse, and head for the stairs next to the elevator before Rudnik or anyone can call me back.

CHAPTER FOUR

People spill out the door of La Scala Ristorante jostling others in the entrance who wait for a coveted table inside. I manage to weave my way through the throng, slipping past two less than thrilled Chanel-clad matrons as I walk directly to the welcoming arms of Simone the hostess who guards the tables beyond.

"He's waiting for you. I gave you the quiet booth in the corner," she smiles, always the romantic.

"See," whispered one matron to the other. "He *is* somebody - sitting there alone! I see her on the television news but not enough to get her own table. No one gets a table till their whole party has arrived. He must be famous." I feel their eyes following me to Tim's table.

Tim s handsome face is set in a frown, his head turning nervously from side to side. Moving quickly to him, I kiss his cheek and slip in beside him. He is my picture of perfection, the aquiline nose, angular cheek bones, even the few strands of gray in his dark blond hair and the tiny lines that are beginning to crease the corners of his eyes make him a portrait of wholesome distinction. I take his hand and squeeze it. "Are you all right?"

He shrugs. his face a mixture of emotions which have a strange quality teeming beneath its poster-like perfection. A chill flutters through me. These past few weeks I've been trying to discuss the barrier I feel rising between us, but communication is growing difficult with the love of my life. A few days ago when I brought it up Tim shrugged and said I was imagining it and insecure for no good reason. He offered me a "lift" at a spa or a shopping spree.

I had tried to explain it wasn't *things* I want, it was to keep our spiritual and emotional connection.

He had smiled and pulled out his credit card and dangled it. "You have me. And this connection too."

I walked away, but as usual, the anger melted and I went back to him. It was always that way. No matter how angry he made me, I always forgave him. That single focused love blurred out any shards of reality that I should have seen in those difficult moments. And if I had to do it again, I'd probably do the same thing again.

Tim was my dream come true. My Prince Charming, a Knight in Shining Armor. Even now, with the problems we've been having, my heart still skips with excitement when I see him. Can it be my imagination that his heart had closed and his eyes were cold? Or am I hanging on to my own perceptions and insecurity because of my first marriage and it's unhappy consequences. Maybe I'm creating problems where there are none because I don't trust love.

Tim is getting ready for his first big election and he's under a lot of pressure. Groomed to run for public office since he was a child, his first major political goal is near and I know he doesn't want to disappoint his father or even the group of professional handlers who have laid out a plan of action for him when he graduated Harvard Law. They started by putting him in the old-line law firm of Laramie, Rogers and Fowler, a powerful company with international, political and financial connections where in his first year he was made a junior partner. Plans were made for the two of us to be married after Tim's nomination to run for Congress. It would be an ideal time to garner publicity and build Tim an image of stability and romance patterned upon the image of the Kennedy/ Camelot era.

But at this moment all I wanted to ask this promising young politician how he would feel if I got up and left the restaurant and walked out on him? Would he be more responsive? Would he follow? There will be cell phone pictures of our silent mini drama.

No, he probably won't care and it's too risky from a public relations point of view. So I stay frozen in the booth, trapped by my own assumptions and passive beneath this uncomfortable blanket of silence.

Seemingly oblivious to the silence or my feelings, Tim takes a piece of paper from his jacket pocket and studies it carefully.

"What's that?"

"My itinerary for Washington."

"Let me see? " I hold out my hand and he reluctantly gives it to me. I take a lighter from my purse and set the itinerary on fire, dropping it into a water glass.

People at the next table turn to stare. "There, now you don't have to go to Washington. Your schedule just went up in smoke!"

Tim didn't laugh. "It's on my phone." With annoyance he signaled the waitress.

Beverly Hills' perfect flesh and blood version of a Barbie Doll slithered to the table. "Hi Tim," she purred seductively, "Are you going to cook your lunch?"

She ignored me, holding her pad and posing with an assurance that every man in the restaurant was watching her.

"Just sending smoke signals to get you over here," I interjected.

The waitress tossed a silky head of hair cut and colored to give her plain face the illusion of glamour and inhaled deeply to recite the lunch- time specials. The silicone mounds she called her breasts were stationery despite her well-choreographed breaths to rub her nipples against her flimsy jersey blouse. Sucking in her cheeks she widened her eyes, her green contact lenses glistening under the lights. But despite her concerted choreography, Tim's head stays bent in deep concentration over the simple menu we both know by heart.

We had dinner at La Scala two or three nights a week, sometimes more since neither of us have the time or inclination to shop for groceries and cook.

The waitress caught my eye and together we waited for Tim to say something. Sensing our attention he put the menu down. "Bring me Jean Leon red."

"Bottle or glass?"

"Jenny, would you like to have wine?" he asked.

I nodded.

"A bottle."

The waitress shifted her weight against the table, her crotch practically resting against Tim's arm. "Do you want to order lunch now? I know you have a plane to catch."

"Has it made the afternoon news already?" I ask, wide eyed with innocence.

"Roxanne called and told Simone he had a plane to catch and asked if she would make an exception."

"Of course she did." Bitterness rose in my throat as I thought of Tim's Executive Assistant. Dressed for success and spouting canned philosophies, the woman appeared to entrance Tim with her pulp level intelligence. Roxanne had a sponge-like mind and laser sharp ambition. Combined with a lack of scruples she is a prototype for a fame hungry woman. Why couldn't Tim see that? Or am I being suspicious and maybe jealous?

"You know we never hold a table for anyone," the Barbie Doll dug in, "but Roxanne has a way of getting what she wants."

"Veal Piccata", Tim interrupted.

Betrayal hit me. Ever since I investigated the beef slaughterhouses and wrote a series of exposes on their atrocities and what they do to the babies, let alone their mothers, I couldn't think of eating meat – especially veal. Tim had respected my wishes and never ordered it. Now he had. Why?

"I'd like the chopped salad, with basil and no salami," I ordered, leaning away from the love of my life.

The waitress left the table with a hole between us. I turned to Tim and tried to fill it. "Are you all right?" I touch his arm but it was stiff and unyielding, like a mannequin in a shop window.

"I have a thousand things on my mind," he said, adjusting his body so we would not touch.

Words flew out of my mouth. "Obviously I'm not one of them. Why did you want to meet me for lunch?"

"Because I'm hungry and wanted to see you before I left."

"See me? You haven't looked at me since I sat down."

His face grew tense. "Do you want to start a fight? I was hoping there wouldn't be any more problems before

I left, but if a fight will make you feel better, I'll be happy to oblige."

"More problems? Really?" I took his bait. "It doesn't matter if you leave, you're not with me anyway. You're like a silhouette."

"I don't know what you're talking about."

"Of course you don't." Bitterness threatened. *Change the subject* raced through my mind. "Al read my proposal and he may let me go ahead with the Anson story."

"He can't."

"I think he will."

Tim's voice was low and impatient, "I don't want you to waste your time or destroy your reputation. Your friend Mannie has had too many experimental drugs. She's paranoid and is leading you down a blind alley. You're going to hit a wall."

"That isn't true. How can you say that?"

"Can you prove her story that Anson is using her program to control minds? When she couldn't find her work she probably deleted it from her computer herself and forgot about it. Now she's paranoid. No one has to use devious technological means to control people. Madison Avenue is the Mount Olympus of Mind Control. What do you think marketing research is all about? No one's going to bother with complicated technology. Mind control is built with pictures and words. The technology is called marketing and advertising."

I leaned closer to him. "Advertising does not control minds." I kept my voice low, "it persuades. This technology replaces normal thoughts with implanted, manufactured ones. There is no chance for personal choice or individual thinking or feeling. This is a weapon and it's an extremely dangerous one."

"I wish I had one right now."

"That's not funny."

"It wasn't meant to be. But you must admit the delivery was cute." He grinned at me in his most adorable way. It usually worked but his disposable charm wasn't working right now. Like a good warrior, he saw his failure and gently took my hand. This time he looked deep into my eyes. "Your thoughts my dear, are not rational. I think you should talk to a doctor."

Tingling uncomfortably like poison was poured through my body, I search for the waitress. I need a drink.

"Why don't you re-focus?" Tim was saying. "Work on something positive. Richard Laurence is going to create a big political upset in the coming election. I know him. He's good - a winner. You could become one of his speechwriters or even his press secretary. But you've got to start working for him now. It can be arranged. Just give me the word."

"Tim, Washington and power is your game, not mine. Been there, done it and it was disastrous. Why are you so concerned about my doing the story on Anson's genetic engineering if I'm wrong?"

"Because I love you and I don't want to see you ruin your career or our life. My God Jenny, it's not as if I'm trying to keep you from your work. I'm suggesting you focus on real issues, join with the sources of genuine power, be a success."

"You want me to turn my back on what I know is the right thing to do. On most levels I hope this information is wrong and I have wasted time. But it requires investigation. If this technology exists, then it will change the world as we know it. A Presidential campaign will mean nothing. I know you don't believe it, but it's possible. Can't you appreciate what I'm saying?"

"It's insane." he shook his head sadly.

The tone with which he said that sent a chill through me. My jaw clenched and my stomach tightened. I was seething. Taking a deep breath I close my eyes to release the anger.

"You're walking in a field of land mines," Tim was saying, but I'm not really listening. My head is spinning.

Tim bumped my arm as he reached for the bottle of wine. I had been unaware the waitress had brought it. He was starting on his second glass, I hadn't touched the first. Picking up my wine glass to toast Tim, he lifted his and drained it before I could say anything. A sharp pain hit the side of my head. Recently, every time I want a sip of wine a headache hits me. Putting the glass down I pick up Tim's water glass because mine had burnt paper in it and sipped from it. My eyes blink shut. A red light appears. I blink again, it turns white.

"Are you all right?" Tim asks.

"Yes,"

"You look like you have a headache."

"One is starting. I can't drink anymore."

"Nonsense. You should have your eyes checked. You're getting too many headaches. Maybe that's why you're acting so strange. Why don't you call Dr. Friedman?"

"That's the second doctor you suggested I see since I've joined you for lunch."

My eyes have started giving me trouble. Sometimes, when I'm doing an interview, the person who I'm talking to will start to look fuzzy and I think I can see different colors coming from them. Then I would forget what they were talking about and focus on their colors. Afterward when I played the recording of the interview back I seem to be fully engaged, but I know I wasn't.

In Eastern philosophies they say the colors surrounding people are auras, each color delineating a person's essence. But I'm not sure I can accept that, though it's good to have as a reference when I'm dealing with different types of people.

Tim watches me. I smile but he doesn't smile back. "Where are you going this afternoon?" he asks abruptly. "Back to the News?"

"No, UCLA bio med library to read up on genetic engineering."

"I wish you'd find another story."

"Are you starting?"

In response Tim looks over me and rises to greet a small square shaped man who had suddenly appeared at our table. He wore a three-piece suit with padded shoulders and a nipped in waist, his sunglasses were tinted so his eyes were hidden. His smile appears frozen and his voice comes uncomfortably from his throat. Tim introduces him as Melvin Phillips and invites him to join us.

"Only for a quick drink," he says sitting down a little too close to me.

Strange feelings run through me as the man introduced as Melvin Phillips orders a Bloody Mary with a voice so deep and smooth it sounds like it's been artificially calibrated to sound like an announcer's, a technique to cover what he's thinking or feeling.

"Synchronicity," Tim said a bit too loudly. "We were just talking about Anson." He turned to me, a friendly smile on his face, a smile I know he isn't feeling.

I mirror him with the same kind of smile.

"Melvin is Senior Vice President of Human Resources at Anson."

I keep my smile. "Yes, I know. I recognized Mr. Phillips from pictures and of course the name. As you know I've done a bit of research on Anson."

"So we've noticed. We read your articles. "

"Thank you." I give him a dazzling smile.

Pulling his thin lips into the guise of a smile, he returns mine. "How do you feel about fraternizing with the enemy, " he asks, punctuating the question with a sharp staccato laugh. Tim chuckles in harmony.

I look at one then the other, mirroring each other, playing a duet with my head.

The waitress brings the Bloody Mary and Phillips grabs the glass so tight, I fear it could break in his hand. He raises it in a toast.

I ignore the offer to toast. "We're not enemies, Mr. Phillips. The series I'm developing about company influences over employees by no means targets Anson in a negative way. Anson is used as an example because of the vast extent of your social services for employees. As far as the questions that are raised, public companies should be held up to public scrutiny, don't you agree?"

Phillip's tight smile spreads wider. "Anson is an honest company."

I cock my head a bit. "Then you must be pleased."

He matches my smile. "We prefer positive publicity."

My smile fades. "Mr. Phillips..."

"Melvin," his lips stay upturned like an ancient Toltec mask.

I nod acceptance. "Melvin. That depends on the inference you take."

The man adopts a pose of sincerity. "Our commitment to excellence stands up to your kind of scrutiny."

I'll ignore that. "I'd like to do an in-depth story on what Anson is about -- the day care centers, nurseries, rental communities for workers, your health services that include pre and post natal care and of course, your advances in genetic engineering." This last was slipped in quickly. I noticed a tiny twinge cross his face.

Composed he answers, "Anson's employee benefits are quite wonderful."

"Then you should be happy to have this story. A visit to the labs should be included," I add.

He doesn't react but adds, "I want to impress upon you the fact that Anson's housing and benefit packages are strong incentives for our workers."

"I'm sure they are." I smile brightly at Tim who shakes his head behind Phillips' back. He wants this conversation to end.

"Your gated compounds where thousands of people depend on Anson can be compared to a modern feudal system," I continue. Phillips doesn't return my smile. I go on. "Your employees depend on you for almost every necessity."

Phillip's head stretches up to ease the tension in his neck.

"They don't have to take advantage of our services," Phillips answers.

I study him carefully. "Families who have a good part of their income deducted for their special mortgage packages, whose children go to your company schools and day care centers, depend on your health care plans and insurance are essentially invested in Anson. If they leave, they lose their pension plans, their tenure, and maybe even the deed to their homes. After researching this thoroughly it appears to be factual."

Tim pours himself another glass of wine and frowns at me. I smile back and turn my attention fully on Phillips. "I think it's interesting that every six months your employees receive training videos in the Anson philosophy," tilting my head I wait for his answer.

A wall starts to build and secure itself around Phillips, chill surrounding his words. "Those are incentive builders for workers to move them forward. We don't like the status quo. We want every worker to move up to the next level. We want the lowest paid worker to believe that with hard work he or she can eventually become CEO of the company."

"Has it ever happened at Anson, or any other large company?" I ask. "Has a janitor or someone from an assembly line or even a secretary made a Vice President or even a top level executive or Board of Directors?"

Phillips was unflappable. "That takes time."

"How many generations? I'm questioning the reality of your company promises."

"The drive to succeed is what this country as well as Anson is founded on."

"Education and lucky genes have much to do with executive appointments," I counter. "What I question is the exploitation of dreams without the hope of tangibles."

Tim closes his eyes and leans his head back on the banquette.

I continue. "Your workers have to sign pledges to conform to Anson guide lines. They can't even smoke in the privacy of their own homes. They can be fired if their child or someone who doesn't like them, snitches. Are not those edicts Fascist, like Nazi Germany?"

"That policy has been instituted for health insurance reasons."

Tim starts to say something, but Phillips waves him off. "It's fine Tim, Jenny is trying to justify her unjustifiable distrust of our company. Perhaps we can make a believer of her."

Responding to Tim's growing impatience, I go for the jugular. "Let's cut through the sound bites. I'm asking if there is a danger you're creating a despotic situation cloaked in the guise of corporate America?"

"Your articles have that tone, but you're mistaken. We're talking about corporate standards - every company has them. No one is forced to work for us. We get hundreds of applications daily. Our salary scale is higher than most. Our workers follow company policies because it gives them security and pride, as well as perks. For the most part the Anson group is one large, happy family."

"As long as they don't behave like black sheep, then they join the ranks of the homeless." I purposefully avoid Tim's piercing glare. I better change the subject. "Why won't Robert Jordan give interviews? He used to be terribly good at them."

"Perhaps you'd like to ask him that yourself?"

"I certainly would."

"I'll arrange it."

"That would be wonderful." I stay cool though inwardly I'm brimming with astonishment. Robert Jordan, President and CEO of Anson Industries had stopped giving interviews three and a half years ago. The last time he appeared on a program he had been assaulted with questions about Anson's ties to organized crime. He never allowed another personal interview.

An attractive man in his mid fifties Jordan is a Patrician ; graying hair, strong, sharp features and a trim athlete's build. He is a Yale man who sailed in the America's Cup, but beyond that he concentrates only on Anson Industries.

I've known men like him all my life. I grew up in a community where many of the men were top executives in Fortune Five Hundred companies. When I was young I attended some of the grownups' parties and listened to policies being discussed that would benefit the companies and individuals who were guests there. The grownups assumed I was too young to understand what was going on. They were wrong. Their power astounded me but it never felt right.

Years later I had the opportunity to question those who took the public trust and then compromised the very people who put them there. Was it greed or power that motivated them? Betrayal without remorse just to feed their expensive overhead?

Once I came out of a long self imposed exile trying to decide what to do with the rest of my life, I chose whatever skills I could use and became an investigative reporter. I interviewed executives from large corporations, but rarely got a straight answer about simple responsibility. Perhaps at times my questions step over the line of tact, but I feel these multibillionaires who live in sublime security and comfort should be in touch with the people who do the real work for their companies as well as supplying the consumer base for their products and profits.

A few times I asked Tim to help with political connections but he refused. But now, the man I most wanted to interview is being made available. I have little time to wonder why.

"How soon would you like to meet Robert Jordan?" Phillips is asking me.

"Yesterday!" I smile, not trying to conceal my excitement.

"I'll see what I can arrange." Phillips slid out of his chair and went to a private place to make the call.

I give Tim a quick kiss, "Thank you, thank you," I hug his arm happily.

"Don't thank me," he took his arm away. "You shouldn't be going on the offensive with these people. You should use these contacts positively. This can backfire. You're throwing away an incredible opportunity."

"Life brings opportunity, not Anson industries."

"Will you stop? You should be their partner, not their opponent. It could be beneficial to both of us."

"I'll keep it under advisement, counselor."

"Do that." He patted my hand. "When I get back from Washington, we'll go to the mountains to Winrock. We need a vacation."

Parker returned to the table. "Tomorrow, 11:00. Is that good for you?"

"Perfect." I thanked him.

Phillips turned to Tim and gave him a little nod.

"Thanks for the drink Tim, good luck in Washington." He turned back to Jenny, a cold smile on his lips. "Come a few minutes early to get your credentials. I'll be there."

"I will, thank you."

Tim signaled for the check. I put my hand on his arm. He gently removed it. "Sorry darling, I have to go, I have lots to do before I leave. Finish your lunch." He seemed upset.

I look at his half eaten lunch, resenting the slaughter of the unappreciated baby calf that suffered and died only to be left on the plate as table scraps. I start to get up to kiss him but stop as I see him stiffen. Rejection punches me in the heart. "Have a good trip. Call me when you get there."

"Jenny," he stops and takes my hand and looks at me closely. "Take good care of yourself." He kisses my cheek. "I love you."

"I love you too." A warm flush fills me. I wish I could ask him to sit back down, forget the appointment and Washington, exclude everything but our love. I reach up to kiss him, but he had drawn back any emotion he had been feeling. The good-by was over.

Picking up the wine glass I hold it in front of my face to block the feelings I'm having in case there is a camera recording my face.

CHAPTER FIVE

Cameras are mounted everywhere. I assume the photo on my i.d. tag was taken the moment I walked through the door. Reluctant to pin the plastic sealed likeness of my face onto my expensive Row suit, a gust of immediacy impels the decision to push the pin through the buttery soft cashmere as Melvin Phillips walks quickly across the polished lobby floor toward me. I lock the pin in place and rise to greet him.

After the briefest of pleasantries he takes me to an area where two burly, uniformed security guards, a Caucasian and an Asian who look like lethal weapons, accompany us in a private elevator to a reception area on the penthouse level. Melvin Phillips confirmed my suspicions that the bronze pillars at the elevator door contain x- ray equipment. "For weapons," he explained. I hope it hadn't erased anything on my phone or tablet.

The penthouse is vast and monastic in its severity. Two-story marble pillars reach up toward vaulted ceilings that look like they had grown out of the polished marble floors. The only sounds were from elevator bells and the soft hum of skyscraper technology. Anson Industries headquarters is a contemporary cathedral of commerce.

Perhaps I'll title the article " Temple of Trade". I hope I'll remember that because I have no time to write it down. The guards are walking too fast as they lead us through a labyrinth of stark white hallways with recessed lighting that make the ceilings glow. Turning and twisting like a maze it appears the design intention was to cause disorientation. It worked. Without an escort, I'd never be able to find my way back to the elevator.

Everyone, including Phillips, the elevator operator, the receptionist, and the guards, wear I.D. tags with photographs that had been taken that day.

Robert Jordan didn't need a tag or even a picture to identify who he is. There can be no mistaking him. Surrounded by an intense energy Jorden is like a jet-propelled engine gearing to take off. I imagine it's a power he has used to weaken others on his climb to success.

Though I'm accustomed to powerful men I still have to take a deep breath as I meet him. Jordan's presence is overwhelming --a soul crusher. And better looking in person than I had expected.

I've been struggling to control my judgmental emotions from the moment I entered the towering glass atrium outside Jordan's private office. Inspired by a rainforest the two-story atrium had a waterfall, tropical plants, and a sprinkling of exotic birds that occasionally fly through the foliage. The effect is breathtaking till I thought about the genuine rain forests Anson Industries must have destroyed in order to afford this simulation on the top of their high-rise.

All impressively disturbing., like Robert Jordan's appearance - beautiful -- but only on the surface. Perhaps such a mundane thing as love has never touched him. His face seems to contain no sensitivity, no compassion but rather a touch of cynicism etched in his eyes and across his sulky lips – a breathing, walking portrait.

I had wanted to use my phone to record the conversation, but it wasn't allowed. I had to leave my all-purpose Balenciaga bag at the secretary's desk and was told not to take notes. "Mr. Jordan believes it would break the flow of the interview," his private secretary said.

Jordan's office looks out over Century City the way one would see it if they were a bird. Streets and buildings are laid out in perfect precision, thought and planning. Even the tiny dark specks on the sidewalk I identified as people from that height appear to be strategically placed as a reminder to Jordan that ordinary humans did, after all, inhabit his empire.

Jordan rose from his chair but did not come out from behind his desk to greet me. Instead, he motioned toward a large cushioned sofa on the other side of the room. The distance made me feel vulnerable which is exactly what it was intended to do.

Before I could speak, an impeccably dressed butler in a three-piece suit brought in a silver tray with a tea service that could have been on display in a museum.

"Lemon?" the butler asked, his tones dripping with elegance.

"Cream," I answered, trying to match his tone.

Formal and methodical, the butler served the tea and offered biscuits, which we both refused. We didn't speak a word till he left the room.

When Jordan took a sip from his cup and looked up, I grabbed the initiative. "Mr. Jordan, is there any connection with the quarterly retreats you host at your Adirondack estate for executives, all male, with the similarity of your advertising campaigns?"

"Really?" His eyes narrow. "Why would you think that?" He sipped his tea.

I try to ignore my quivering nerves. "The advertising campaigns focus on the ways ANSON seems to focus on the way workers live and feel, rather than the products these workers are producing. A subtle advertisement for a way of life rather than a consumer product."

"I have no idea what you're talking about. Our advertising has always been focused on product."

"Mr. Jordan, we only have to look at your media campaigns to see that *The Anson Family*, as you call it, are being featured rather than the company's specific products. That's a departure from your previous advertising strategy."

"Ms. Webster, it wouldn't be in our best interest to ignore our own products. It would do no good to sell only the corporate name as you suggest."

"But in your recent commercials you've been doing just that. You go into employees' homes and schools and personalize the products with them."

That's right. What better advertising than our workers using the products they produce." he interrupted. "This is a silly line of questioning."

I take a deep breath. "I've studied Anson's new advertising approach as well as several others, and all seem to be pushing the same message - we take care of your lives better than the government or anyone else."

"We're giving customers background on who makes the products they buy," Jordan said. "I like it, it's a new approach, peer oriented. Different. Surely you can't find fault with that. We don't sell our name like Apple."

"Oh, but you do. That's why I'm asking you about this change of direction."

"This is ridiculous," he snapped. "You're wasting my time."

He's shutting down. I have to keep the meeting going, change the tone. Shifting my weight I take a sip of tea. "Mr. Jordan, You appear to be focusing on achieving a certain kind of public confidence and support."

"Ms. Webster, you're naïve.," he snarled. "Of course we want public support and confidence."

"Is it political confidence you're seeking?" I suggest quietly.

His eyes turn cold, almost lethal. "If I wanted political power, I would run for President, wouldn't I?"

Pushing ahead I ignore the lines of anger forming between his eyes. "In your last series of television commercials, you compare the superior quality of your planned communities to government projects.

"They are."

"The impression is that your workers have better working and living conditions than the government can give them."

"We do. Especially with the present administration. Successful business people are geared to run things more efficiently and profitably than government parasites. A community is no different than a well made product. But I think you're reading more into this than necessary."

"Good to know."

He sat back, his eyes gleaming with a cobra-like stare.

I try to hide a shiver, but he had seen it.

"You have a very imaginative mind, Ms. Webster," Jordan said softly. "If you'd like a position with this company, I'll arrange it."

I try to look flattered and smile. "Thank you, I'm happy with my present work. But if anything changes, I'll take you up on it." I pause a quick beat. "With that in mind, what are Anson's future plans?" I ask casually.

"To continue creating products and systems that benefit mankind," came the stock reply. He starts to rise, indicating that the interview is at an end. A bland smile now masks his face, shutting me off like a faucet.

I hesitate, it's now or never. I must ask the most important question of all, before he calls his secretary to show me out. His hand is reaching for the buzzer on his desk.

"Tell me about Anson's work on genetics." My voice sounds calm, but my heart is pounding

His hand stiffens and he straightens and stares at me. The stare is ice cold.

"We're very diversified, anything is possible. I'd like a copy of this interview before it's aired."

I keep my face impassive, but my body is tingling. My question struck like a diamond bullet. Robert Jordan was shaken. The one word "genetics" had breached his defenses. By asking for a copy of this interview before it's produced reveals vulnerability. He's afraid of what I might produce. Robert Jordan has been shaken.

Managing a polite smile as I rise from the sofa. "Mr. Jordan," I cleared my throat. "I'm sorry. It isn't possible. It's against the news policy. But you know I'm always fair."

"Thank you for your interest in Anson, Ms. Webster," he said distantly. A secretary was coming into the room. "Please show Ms. Webster out."

My mind is racing. I have to be careful. I have to keep this interview as objective as possible. I can't indict this man in print.

Turning to say good-bye, Jordan is involved with papers on his desk. "Thank you, Mr. Jordan".

Robert Jordan did not look up. I had been dismissed.

The click of my heels make a marching sound as I hurry across the marble lobby to the candy stand to buy a power bar. Without missing a beat, I head for the large glass doors leading out to the park -like entrance of the building where I settle on a small bench perched next to a pond with bubbling water spilling over marble and granite slabs.

Taking out my cell phone I call Rudnick's private line and wait as it keeps ringing.

Checking the time on the phone its 11:45. He should be there. He never takes a break.

Ending the call I then resend it. It continues to ring. Absentmindedly eating the power bar, I try to recreate the essential parts of the meeting I missed and put that into my phone. I hadn't asked him about the surveillance in his employees' housing complexes, or more about the meetings at his Adirondack compound.

Rudnick's phone continued to ring. Uneasy I hang up and finish the Power bar. A humming in my ears starts to fill my head. Swallowing hard I try to clear it, but the hum gets louder. Trying to ignore it I re-dial the number and this time Rudnik answers, out of breath and curt, signs of a bad mood. I brace myself.

"Al, it's Jenny."

"I see that. Where are you?"

Glad he can't see my big smile, "I just left Robert Jordan's office."

"Was he there?" Rudnik snapped right back.

"Of course. Why?"

"He uses doubles. Been using them since he stopped giving interviews."

Churchill and Hitler had used doubles. But Icould not believe that the man I had just met was anyone but Robert Jordan. His presence was exceptionally powerful.

"It was Jordan," I insisted.

"Well I just had a meeting with Eriksen." Eriksen was Vice President in charge of personnel, the Publisher's hatchet man.

"What did he want?" I'm concerned for Rudnik. He's 'old generation' and this new publisher is from the disposable generation that tends to see more value in whatever is young and new with little concern for the old school. His reality is instant information with the touch of a key with little regard for the layers human experience can offer. I hope Rudnik didn't lose his job.

"Management says you're too opinionated. They want you to tone down. They don't want lawsuits."

"I've never caused one!" I'm shocked.

"Not yet, but you're close," he sighed deeply. "Listen, there is pressure coming in about you from high levels."

"Advertising," I groaned.

"No, Board of Directors. I have no choice. I'm going along with them, Jenny."

That stopped me. "I totally understand." And I did. Mad at myself for eating the candy, I throw it on the well-swept ground then pick it up and put it in my pocket.

Al filled the silence. "What about Jordan? Did he give you the blueprints for his plan to take over the world?" Rudnik was not trying to coat his sarcasm.

I carefully focused. "Not yet, but I think parts of the meeting were revealing." It's an effort to stay calm.

"Which parts?"

"The subject of genetics threw him and he ended the interview and asked to read the hard copy and see the interview before its aired. I told him that was impossible. He didn't like hearing that."

"Great header. Let me hear the interview."

"Uh, I didn't record it. It wasn't allowed!"

"Perfect." His words dripped through the phone like acid. "You're going to be in the unemployment line if you keep up like this," he growled. You haven't given us anything we can broadcast and you're making enemies. You better ease up. I'm not able to cover for you. If you're getting paid to research stories, and they're not aired you know what happens. I've been letting your last few news clips slip by because I wanted to see what would happen. But we have to pull back. Understand?"

"No, wait a minute," I try to keep my temper down. "I'm an investigative reporter. This is the kind of reporting you should have."

"Find another story," said Rudnik.

"Al, this is important. That's why we're running into flak. If it can be proven it has to be told."

"I have our science editor looking into it."

"You weren't going to tell anyone!"

"I gave him your research," he continued, "If he thinks there is any credibility, you're going to work with him."

Shit! Pulling rank. I hate that. It's at the core of everything. Some entitled to powers that others can't have. It maddens me.

I hadn't thought about rights or injustices and the way people are treated till I was a young teen-ager and my mother became ill and was hospitalized. Suddenly I saw my pampered, protected mother become vulnerable and lose her rights and a little bit of her mind. Without her husband to protect her she was forced to let others take over her decisions and tell her what to do. And even though my mother was in a luxurious private room in the exclusive pavilion section of the hospital, the fear engendered by my mother's vulnerability made a lasting impression.

That hospital experience was the first time I experienced my emotions being controlled by strangers. I merged with the many patients and families in their common helplessness; hostages snared in a medical net of chemicals and foreign terminology, Scrubbed surfaces hid the chaos of the hospital's disease and pain, yet it was always there, bubbling along the halls and filling the rooms with threats on so many levels.

The medical staff dressed in uniforms setting them apart has the power to use painkillers and tranquilizers to mask their patients' symptoms. When the inevitable happens and a patient dies, they pile pillows on the corpse to keep death discreet as they move it out of the place it took that final breath to the hospital morgue.

No one seemed to tell the truth. No one seemed to deal in a direct way. The time I spent in the hospital with my mother showed me how fear and reality was covered with layers of boxed and pre-recorded responses.

Now my eyes are opening to another kind of fear, management's fear of losing their 3 P.S., paychecks, pensions and power. Clearly, Al Rudnik feared more for his job then he cared for the truth. Up to this moment he had been my role model; the selfless, dedicated newsperson.

"Al," I heard myself saying, " We have to deal with this." I sensed his anger before his voice reached me.

"You're a journalist, for god's sakes. I need NEWS stories. If you want to produce fiction, do a novel or get a crystal ball and set up shop elsewhere

"Oh, come on Al," I pleaded. "You can't take me off this - not now. Give me some time. Please, I'm begging. I'll bring information you HAVE to air - it will wipe everything else off, it's Emmy time, I promise."

There is a long silence. When Rudnik finally speaks, his voice is hoarse. "I doubt it, but you have a week. Not a day more. If it doesn't knock my socks off you're going to become a statistic and join the unemployment line."

"Al," I almost giggled with relief, "did I ever tell you I love you?"

"One week," he repeated, "then you're going to start on something else. The primaries, that's your next assignment." The line went dead.

I pushed the *end* button and leaned my head on my hands. I needed time to think. Everything was falling into a pattern. First there is Tim wanting me to work the primaries, and now Al. Is there a connection? Can they be working together? No, that's paranoid. I must stop thinking like that.

CHAPTER SIX

I put the phone away and start toward the escalator to the parking garage.

"Jenny, hello!" A good looking man in his mid thirties, close-cropped beard and mirrored glasses walks over to me. He looks familiar but I'm not sure. No recognition is coming to me. The sport jacket is Hermes as is the cashmere sweater and the perfectly pressed jeans. The man is a poster for affluent L.A. cool, one of hundreds I've met through the various incarnations of my life.

He laughs. "You remember me but you're trying to figure out who I am. I'm Larry Martin, Tim's friend. We met at a party some time ago."

"It must have been. I'm sorry I don't think I know you."

He was growing less and less familiar the more he talked.

"It was at least a year or so, I dunno. But I do remember meeting you with Tim and thinking how lucky he is."

His handsome face with its patina of expensive grooming glows perfectly. He could have just stepped off the cover of L'Uomo Vogue. And his words are as thin as the paper magazines are sometimes printed on

But giving him the benefit of the doubt, I run his appearance through my mind again but nothing comes up. His overt friendliness isn't coming off sincere either. It's making me nervous.

"Well, I guess I'm forgettable." He waits for my denial but I don't comply and start to walk away.

The man lifts his sunglasses for an instant, his piercing eyes unsettling me then quickly puts them back on. "Probably a fund raiser."

"Safe guess."

He doesn't blanch. "I know, Councilwoman Gail Major's party at the Marina."

"I don't think so." The man was fishing. He had never met me. If he had an inkling of who I am he would know that supporting a person like Gail Major for City Council was not remotely possible. "To quote Raymond Chandler, that would have been like taking a tour through a sewer in a glass bottom boat."

He doesn't react. The guy has no humor.

"It must have been somewhere else."

The man who calls himself Martin is digging himself into a hole.

"Whatever. Well, bye, I've got to run." I begin to walk away.

"Would you like to have lunch?" he asks, practically skipping next to me. "Maybe we can figure out how we know each other over food.

"Sorry, I don't have time."

"Coffee?" He walks with me. "Ten minutes?"

"Ten minutes too long. I have to get to another appointment. Give Tim a call and we'll all get together."

"Tim is going to be away for awhile."

"Oh?" I stop, a chill passing through me.

He smiles confidently. "He said he was going to Washington last night and not sure when he's coming back."

I studied him closer. I thought I knew most of Tim's friends. Every once in awhile someone would pretend to know one of us because of our high visibility, which is what I thought this man was doing. But his nonchalant knowledge of Tim's whereabouts grabs my attention. I'm not sure if its curiosity or the focused energy one is capable of directing when there is danger. Keeping my tone light I ask, "How do you know that?"

Martin laughed. "He told me you had burned his notes in the restaurant."

I don't like what I'm feeling. He talks too much, tries too hard to prove himself. Why? What does he want? My experience says he has an agenda and I'm not sure I want to know what it is.

"We're wasting precious time. One more chance at coffee? Seven and a half minutes top?"

I don't smile at his humor and start to walk away. "Not possible, thanks anyway, " and start toward the escalator to the underground parking garage.

"Struck out!" He smiles boyishly as he takes a long graceful stride and easily catches up to walk beside me. Heat seems to be radiating from his body, or is it my nerves?

"Are you parked in the garage?" He asks the obvious. I give him a quizzical look. Maybe I should turn around and not go down yet.

"We can go together." His closeness makes me step on to the escalator. When I reach the bottom I'll go back up. Say I forgot something. He's too close behind me.

For some strange reason I make a point of registering the blue sky before we descend into the cement recesses underneath the former Twentieth Century Fox Studio lot.

"Still have your BMW" he asks the back of my head.

Another chill goes through my spine. "Yes." The words are nearly choked out in an attempt to remain casual. "How did you know that?"

"We discussed cars when we met." "Tim wanted you to buy a Tesla."

I stared straight ahead as I reached the bottom of the escalator then turned toward the next set to continue down even further into the catacombs of Century City.

The man was too close. My heart is beating faster, my breathing is getting short, fear is taking over. At one point some time ago Tim wanted me to trade in my car and get a Tesla or a Range Rover. I will not acknowledge this to this obtrusive man whose private information about Tim is making me nervous. How does he know all this? Am I wrong and forgot I had met him with Tim? We've been on a social whirlwind for some time. So I ., forget my plan to go back up and follow only some part of me that said to keep going down the escalator deep into the depths of Century City, He's still behind me as I step off four levels below the ground in the direction of a silver arrow on an orange background pointing toward a gray cavern marked Red.

"Nice to meet you," I toss off trying to make it sound light as I walk away. My nerves are tingling and I feel scared but if I run will that set off something I can't handle. I'll just keep acting natural till I get in my car.

"My car's over there as well."

I pause. I don't like that and I don't like how he sounds. I'm really getting scared.

A young couple emerge from around the corner holding each other around the waist. I want to call to them, but what should I say? Call the Police ! Help? Because he lied about knowing me and wants to have coffee? The couple continue up the escalator.

He puts his hand on my arm, startling me.

"Thanks but I can make it to my car alone" I try to walk away.

His hand tightens. "I have to make sure nothing happens to you while Tim is gone and you're all alone."

"It won't." I try to pull away but he won't let go. Dread starts to swirl. "Let me go."

"Relax. We'll walk to your car." His fingers close tighter.

He's bruising me. I wish I could see a guard. "Please," my voice just below screaming. "Let go of me. You're hurting me."

"Not yet." His hand tightened even more, painfully digging into my arm. "Keep quiet, or this will hurt a lot worse." His grip tightened till I thought his fingers would touch.

Faintness threatened from fear and pain. How could this be happening? Where are the people who belong to these cars? No one is here. Its empty. Empty. "Please let go," I try yanking away but he holds on tighter. The garage stays deserted.

"Don't fight, I've already won."

He starts to drag me towards the silver blue BMW in the far corner. How did he know that's my car? Terror is overtaking me. This man is not kidding, he has control. He's kidnapping me. What does he want from me?

Strangled with fear I begin to shake uncontrollably. He grabs my chin with one hand and the back of my head with the other and in a quick, whiplash kind of movement, twists my head and pain screams through me. I slump and he scoops me up and carries me the rest of the way.

Everything is hazy. This can't be happening. It happens to other people. I write about them as pieces for stories, not for real. My invincibility fails me. There is no one to see or hear me, no one to help, I'm totally alone.

The pain is excruciating. Sweat is ruining my good silk blouse. My heart is pounding so loud it seems to reverberate outside myself.

Squealing tires negotiating the ramps overhead mix with a slightly familiar sound. Am I screaming, or is it the cars?

He shoves me into the passenger side of my car, my beautiful car and straps me in, pulling the seat belt as tight as he can, then moving the seat up so my knees are against the dash. He grabs my head again and twists it. The pain is intense. All I can do is cry. He gets behind the wheel. I want to ask why , but the pain is so intense the *why* is not important. I want the pain to stop.

As he drives up the winding ramp I try to steady myself with my hand on the door, but he grabs it and twists it till I can't feel it.

His white teeth glow eerily as he turns and smiles. He is enjoying my pain.

"You're going to take pleasure from this."

"No," I'm whimpering, pleading.

"You'll have your chance. Don't blow it, in a little while you'll be blowing me."

"Please,"

"Right. You catch on fast. Always ask permission. Now don't say anything else because I'll kill you."

I look at the black leather gloves gripping the steering wheel and believe him.

He glances at me. "You need a good fuck. Tim hasn't touched you in awhile."

His words explode in me. How did he know? Bleak foreboding crashes through me. I'm not sure I can survive.

The car stops at the cashier booth blocking the exit. He hands the parking attendant a ticket and money and pulls away just as the barrier is raised. He closes the window, trapping the exhaust fumes inside with me.

Arriving in daylight, the man reaches over and pushes an artery in my neck that sends the people in the other cars into a fog of haziness as darkness closes in. So I jump on to the tip of a comet for safety and hold on till the comet tilts backward and I fall head first into space.

CHAPTER SEVEN

My eyes start to focus when the car screeches to a stop. The man is saying something but I can't make out the words. My heart is pounding. I feel sick. He's shaking me, telling me to wake up.

I look out the window and see my apartment building. The sidewalk is still damp from an afternoon shower so none of the old regulars are sitting in front. But it is definitely the building where I live.

He drove me home. My head is spinning and I have to get out of here. But as I reach for the handle he pulls me back. A finger catches between the handle and the front passenger seat and my nail brakes as he yanks me across the front seat, over the gearshift to the driver's side and pulls me out of the car then props me up like a rag doll or most likely, like someone drugged or drunk.

A gang of children play across the street - cosmic cowboys in yellow goggles firing toy laser guns don't notice us. Before I can shout to them the man leans in close and presses his lips against my ear, whispering, "One sound and you're history." He grips my sore bruised arm and propels me across the sidewalk to the front door.

At the foot of the steps I try to grab the handrail but he shoves me through the big swing doors.

Music is coming from one of the apartments inside. I try to call out but he clamps his hand over my mouth and frog-marches me down the long corridor to my own front door. My neighbor's cat scurries away as we arrive. He's smarter than I am. He knows when to run.

Holding me against the wall he jabs the doorbell with his thumb - two long rings. "Please," I beg, "If it's money you want..." I got no further. The door is opened from the inside and the man hurtles me headlong into the apartment.

The living room is dark. Someone has closed the oriental window screens. I barely have time to register this before another shove sends me crashing to the floor. I try to get up but a stinging slap hits the side of my head. I reel into the coffee table, knocking a silver framed picture of Tim onto the floor.

"Not her face," says a deep but feminine voice. "No marks."

A shadowy form closes the front door. I scramble to my knees but the man puts his foot on my hip and pushes me back down.

"Anybody see you?" asks the voice.

"Er, no," the man grunts. He sounds strangely muted, deferential. There is a click of heels on the polished floor as a pair of pointed toe high-heeled snake skin stilettoes come to rest inches from my face.

"Pick her up," orders the voice.

The man grabs my arms and yanks me to my feet. Heart pounding, gasping for breath, I find myself looking into the pale face of a woman with angry eyes framed by a no nonsense straight hair cut blunt around a slash of red lipstick. Fortyish and expensively dressed, she has a definite air of authority around her.

"Hold her still," orders the red lips and the man locks an arm around my neck, lifting me onto my toes. I can feel his hot breath on my cheek. In the same instant, the woman reaches out and tears my blouse open down the front.

My blouse! My beautiful silk Armani blouse! How can I care about a blouse at a time like this? But it means a lot.

I'm not going to let her do anything else to me as I feel a burst of new energy and struggle against the man's grip. My heart is pounding so hard I hope it won't burst as I try to kick the woman away with my feet. The man jerks me backward by the neck till I almost black out.

My skirt is being unbuttoned. I twist and turn but the man's grip is like a vise that makes me choke. I feel my panties rip as the woman pulls them down past my knees.

"Put her on the sofa," said the woman, "it'll be easier there." The man relaxes his grip for a moment and sensing my chance, I push him away with all my strength and run for the door. Flying when he trips me I land face down on the oak floor. Something is pinning my right hand. It's the woman's silver snake stiletto standing with enough force that a little more pressure can cause damage. I cry out in confusion and pain. "Why is this happening?"

"Get the rest off her," says the woman. "If she moves, I'll break her hand."

The man kneels down beside me and starts to yank off my bra. The woman's full weight on my hand is unbearable.

I'm sobbing out of control. "Oh God, please let me go!" Please. Why are you doing this?

Stripped naked the woman slowly removes her heel. I roll into a fetal shape, cradling my hand, sobbing and whimpering. I'm naked and vulnerable with no way to get out of this.

The woman's eyes roam over me like she's appraising an object in a display case. "Good body," she says to the man, then walks calmly into the kitchen and reappears with a cup of coffee in her hand. She steps over me like some impediment and goes to my favorite Eames chair and sits, elegantly crossing her legs and examines me, a scientist examining a moth in a jar as she slowly sips her coffee.

I'm trying not to cry but I'm losing. Tears stream down my face. After a few moments the woman carefully brushes a piece of lint off her sleeve, then places her cup on the low table beside the chair and produces a Dunhill lighter with which she lights a cigarette or something that looks like one. "Calm down, Jenny," she says evenly, speaking in a sympathetic professional tone, a doctor delivering life changing news.

"Nothing's broken."

I look up at the woman through tears. A wounded bird in front of a cat. The pain in my hand is starting to go away, supplanted with a horrible fear of what's going to happen next. The woman had called me Jenny. She knows my name. Who are these people? What do they want from me?

"Go sit on the sofa," she says. "We need to talk."

I can't move. I'm totally naked and my hand still hurts and I'm afraid.

With a sigh the woman stubs out her cigarette and gets up. Her movements are slow, deliberate. Suddenly she jabs my ribs with her snakeskin wrapped toe. "On the sofa. Now."

I look up at the man., a sentinel, daring me to defy the order.

Hesitantly, I begin to move. Then realize I'm totally naked and try to cover myself somehow. The woman snaps her fingers and the man takes a pace forward.

Without warning his hand flashes down and grabs my hair. Tearing hot pain sears through my scalp as he drags me like a caveman, backwards onto the sofa and shoves me down.

Instinctively, I grab a pillow to cover myself and cringe, waiting for a blow.

None came. There is silence in the room. I can hear children still playing in the street outside - so near and yet so far. Had one of them seen me being pulled out of the car? Would they tell someone? Will somebody come soon and end this nightmare?

The woman is speaking again. "Let's get something straight," she is saying, "I don't repeat things. Ever. Understand?"

I nod quickly but I don't understand. I don't understand anything. Who are these people and why are they doing this to me? Why?

The woman moves away and opens a large, black Alligator handbag on the coffee table. I hadn't noticed the bag till now. It's a rare Chanel and I can trace the woman through that bag if I ever get out of here. I also hadn't noticed the black leather Tom Ford coat thrown casually over my desk. There a half- filled glass on the mantelpiece, together with an open bottle of scotch. My crystal ice bucket was on the table. How long had this woman been in my home? How did she get in?

This building is like a small community. Everyone knows the other's business. I'm a bit of an enigma because I don't join the gossip, but they would definitely notice a woman like this when she entered the building and had a key to my apartment.

The woman was pulling a small, shiny object out of the Alligator purse and tossed it to the man who caught it in the air and put it in his pocket. What was it? A pen, a knife? I watch with terror as the woman takes a small can out of her purse and walks over to the window. She pauses there and looks out. I don't dare move. I feel so vulnerable I hardly dare to breathe.

After a moment, the woman turns to me. "Now listen carefully," she says. "We can make this unpleasant, or we can make it rewarding. The choice is yours."

I draw my knees up, trying to cover myself. My mind is racing with the obvious thoughts - she was in my apartment with a key. She had made herself at home here, poured herself a drink, even made coffee for god's sake. What is she doing here? What did she want?

"I believe you ride horses," the woman was saying, "so you'll know why they have to be trained." I'm not listening. I wonder how I can get the phone. If only I could reach it.

"I use the word trained because it's much nicer than broken," the woman continues, "but the purpose is the same - helping the animal to reach it's potential. Well, that's what we do too," she added, "only we do it with people."

She stares at me a long moment then steps over to the couch. "You haven't understood a word, have you?" She sighed, "Forget trying to escape." She indicated the man with a wave of her hand, "He's very well trained."

She stops in front of the couch and shakes the small can in her hand. I can read the label. It says Quick Foam.

"Open your legs," orders the woman.

I try to shrink away along the couch, but the man moves like lightning, suddenly gripping my knees, bruising my flesh with his thumbs, and forcing my legs apart. Almost simultaneously, the woman squirts the can between my thighs. The foam is cool, with a faint aroma of mint. Its shaving cream

"If you don't want him to cut you, keep still," the woman cautioned. The man held a slim straight razor in his hand.

My heart is pounding. What is he going to do? I know the answer and I pray I'm wrong, Closing my eyes tight, trying to blot out the nightmare, as the blade touches my skin I hear *"Mustn't move..."* whispers a voice in my head. *"Don't give him any excuse..."* Hot tears of shame and anger well up behind my eyelids as the man begins to shave me.

"Total nakedness leads to total openness," says the woman, "and thence to complete acceptance."

With swift and easy strokes, the razor did its job. From time to time the man rubbed the foam in with his fingers, touching me like a lover. There were other voices in my head now. One of them kept saying, "*You're going to survive...*" And another said, "*Stay calm...*"

I tried to imagine my mother standing over me, sprinkling talcum powder on my soft baby legs. But it doesn't help. This reality is too powerful. Openness? Acceptance? I just want this to end!

"Finished?" Asked the woman.

I squinted through my lashes and saw the man nod as the woman hands him my torn silk blouse that he uses like a rag to wipe the foam from my thighs. Some of it had run onto the sofa and he wipes that up too. One of the voices in my head starts to giggle. I know why. This man had slapped and choked me as if a human life didn't matter, yet here he is wiping flecks of shaving cream off the sofa. Moving I close my legs.

"Wait till you're told," snaps the woman. Then she leans in and feels the newly shaved skin with her fingers. "Good," she nods to the man. "The water's in the tub." Then she turns and opens her phone.

The man grabs one of my ankles and pulls me to the floor. The woman is starting to talk, but I can't hear what she's saying. The man is dragging me across the floor by my foot. I claw for a chair that I pass but the man is moving too fast. My head hits the doorframe as we enter the bathroom. My cry of pain doesn't seem to enter the man's consciousness at all.

But my cries are stifled by shock as my body hits the water. The bath water is ice cold.

The moment he threw me in, the man plunged my head under the surface and held me down. I kicked and tried to grab his arm with my hands above the surface. But it's no use - my fingers keep slipping and my lungs are bursting. I'm panicked. I'm going to die. This is it.

He lets me up for a moment and I gulp in air. Then he pushes me back down again. I can see the undulating image of the woman behind him. The man lets go once more and I come up violently, coughing and splashing water everywhere. The woman steps back with a look of irritation on her face. A few stray drops had landed on her suede leather skirt. Fastidiously she takes a towel and carefully blots them off.

"Enough," said the woman, "Take her out."

Coughing desperately as the man pulls me out of the water, throws a towel over his shoulder and slings me over it like a sack and carries me into the living room. With surprising gentleness, he lays me on the floor. I roll to my side, helplessly coughing and gasping for air, but the woman nudges me with her toe. "On your back," she demands. "You were placed that way for a purpose."

I try to obey but my body isn't listening. I feel the man's hands on my shoulders as he rolls me onto my back.

"This is your test of acceptance," says the woman, "you'll offer no resistance. No resistance at all. Is that clear?" She stands, waiting for a reply. When none comes, she shouts "Answer!"

I manage a nod. I have no fight left. I'm cold and shivering and coughing as the woman ties my wrists with the belt from my bathrobe.

The man is walking toward me with the crystal ice bucket.

"Acceptance is a very great virtue," the woman says quietly, "so just let this happen."

The man switches on the TV set. A game show fills the room with raucous laughter, then without warning, the woman's fingers push an ice cube into my vagina.

Screaming and writhing in pain as a contestant on the television show hops up and down like a chicken, the studio audience roars with appreciation, covering my pain.

Gasping with shock as the woman pushes another cube into me I can't believe this is happening. I can't fight back. My hands are tied and I have no strength. All I can do is lie on the ground, trying to handle the rape as the woman fills me with ice.

Picking up my torn pantyhose the man hands it to the woman who uses it to bind my thighs together above the knees. "This takes ten minutes," she says to the man, "Go pour yourself a drink."

My legs tightly bound, the woman casually smoothes her skirt and walks away.

Trying so hard to handle the pain of the freezing ice slowly melting inside me, I hear the voices calling "*You're not alone ... we're with you ... we're here to help you through...*"

Let me join you, I call soundlessly to them.

The woman calmly flicks through a magazine as if this were her home. After a few seconds, she picks up the remote and zaps through the channels then begins to watch the news. The man pours himself a scotch. "That's my glass," said the woman. "Get one from the kitchen. Top shelf on the left."

As the man wanders into the kitchen, he pauses and looks down at me, my knees drawn up, breathing deeply against the pain.

He opens his mouth as if to speak then notices the woman watching him, and sticks two fingers in the sugar bowl, puts a sugar cube in his mouth and quickly moves away.

By the time the man returns with his scotch, the ice has nearly melted. The woman checks her watch, then switches off the TV and kneels beside me and sweeps some hair out of my eyes before gently untying my legs.

I don't move. My breathing is shallow, my body heavy and limp with exhaustion.

"You bore this bravely," the woman says approvingly, "I'll make sure it goes in your report." Then, with a silken touch, she begins to caress my breasts. "We must all learn acceptance, Jenny," she murmurs softly, "then we can be accepted. Imagine a world where everyone serves the same ideal - some in mind and others in body. Isn't that a beautiful thought?"

The woman's fingers are coaxing my legs apart, and I stiffen.

But the voices whisper softly, "*Don't tense up ... we'll help you ... we're here to guide you through...*"

The woman's red nailed fingers are opening my shaved vagina like a flower, gently stimulating me as I lay there, my eyes lightly closed but open enough to see the man step over to watch as the woman leans in to use her tongue. I shudder. "*Don't fight it...*" call the voices "*let her have you ... give her what she wants...*" The woman's tongue begins to probe. I bite my lip and taste blood.

For a moment, I think I'm on the ceiling looking down at myself, watching this all from above. But only for a moment. Then I'm back in the real world, feeling the woman's tongue. Opening my eyes I look straight at the man looking down at me, studying me. But when our eyes meet, he looks away and puts another sugar cube in his mouth.

How strange, he's embarrassed, I hear in my thoughts, "*Yes...*" answers the voices. "*That's your strength ... he's starting to feel your power.*

The woman is sliding her lips up my ribs, softly kissing my breasts and fluttering her tongue on a nipple, encouraging it to harden. It complies.

She whispers in my ear, "you're wetter now than in the bath. You're going to be easy."

Is that true? Is my body responding? How could it? I hate this woman, loath her. She's brutal and disgusting. She has hurt and tortured me, how can my body respond?

Or did the siren voices betray me? Telling me to relax and go along with this. Oh god, am I going crazy? This is a horrible dream, a nightmare and I'll wake up soon. Please let it be a dream. Please ...

"*You can't...*" the voices answer, "*it's real and you have to survive.*" My mind is reeling now and tears are starting to come. Who are these voices and why are they telling me these things? Are they trying to drive me insane?

"*No ...!*" they all babble, "*You're starting to win just give her what she wants ...*

I move my hips a little, and the voices shout, "*Yes...!*" Hot tears roll down my cheeks as I force my body to move, pulsing in rhythm with her fingers - slowly at first, then faster and faster. My skin grows warm and starts to tingle. I catch a glimpse of the man smiling down at me and as I wrench with anger my body arches upwards.

"*Now!*" choruses the voices as my cries mingle with theirs.

Quite suddenly the woman is on her feet. "I said she'd be easy," she smiles to the man, "Put her on the door." Her voice is detached, professional. She is wiping her fingers on my blouse.

Very slowly I curl my body into a ball. I'm devastated. The woman humiliated me and used me, mocked me, and I didn't resist. I hadn't been able to. "God how I hate you," I whisper. I don't care if she hears me. I don't care what happens now. My own body has betrayed me. What greater betrayal can there be?

The man's strong hands are lifting me to my feet. My head swims as he carries me to the bathroom door. With surprising gentleness, he sets my feet on the ground and lifts my bound wrists above my head, throws the long end of the cord over the top of the door and pulls my arms up high. Then he ties the cord to the inside handle, and pulls the door firmly shut, jamming the cord tightly in the top of the door.

Like some medieval sacrifice, I stand there on tiptoe. With my back to the door and my hands held high by the cord, I'm utterly helpless. The woman stands in front of me.

"Sex is the greatest control mechanism in the world," she says in a clinical tone, "Things you hate, you can be taught to love. And things you enjoy, we can make you hate."

I watch the man undressing near the sofa. He has the tone and muscled body of someone who works out. There is not an ounce of fat.

"After this, you'll be a different person," the woman is saying, "Our kind of person. You'll be grateful to me."

The man is naked now. Slowly he comes to stand next to the woman. He doesn't look at me.

"Nice isn't he?" she chuckles. "He's one of my favorite toys." She says it with the sort of throwaway pride that a rich person might use to describe an expensive car or a work of art. "He understands acceptance perfectly," she adds, "which is why we use him so much." She lifts the man's penis and starts to stroke it, taking care that I can see every move. I watch it rising in the woman's hand, smoothly, almost elegantly, I wonder if they're lovers. Searching the man's face for a clue his eyes never flicker. He just stands and lets her work him up, avoiding my gaze.

"I've often wondered what it would be like to be him," the woman muses. "He's just an animal really," she smiles, "all libido and little brain. Still, he satisfies me when I need it. Let's see what he can do for you."

She's treating him like she treated me, just an object, something to be used.

By now the man is as hard as a rock and the woman tests his readiness by flicking his penis with her long red nails. It makes him wince and he takes an involuntary step backwards. "Stand still," she orders and flicks it again. This time he doesn't flinch. "That's better," she says. "Well don't just stand there, go and fuck her. And make sure she breaks."

As the man comes toward me the voices start to gabble "*Use your body ... use your power ... use it now, and win...*"

But I don't know what the voices mean. Panic has gripped my heart. The man puts his arms around me and guides each of my legs around one of his own. Then supporting my buttocks with his hands he enters me smoothly and starts to thrust.

"He won't stop till I give him permission," the woman says, "so this could take a while." Opening the large Chanel bag she takes out a miniature video camera, Aiming the lens at my face she taps the man on the shoulder, "Break her," she orders. "Do it right. They need to see this."

The man grunts and thrusts into me like a bull, pounding me into the door, as the woman points the camera at me.

"*Use your power...*" Jabber the voices, "*use it now ... use it before it's too late...*" My mind flies in all directions, trying to grasp their meaning. What power? How? Then, suddenly I understand.

Slowly, very slowly, I lifted my legs higher and wrap them around his waist.

"*Yes...!*" cheered the voices, "*Take him from her...*"

I thought I saw a glimmer of puzzlement on the woman's face as I tighten my legs and clasp the man to me. Maybe it's my imagination. Everything is moving so fast. The woman is stepping around us now, squinting through the lens and giving the man instructions. "Good, that's good. Now slap her. They'll need to see her cry."

But the man doesn't slap me and I don't cry. I'm whispering softly, "Ignore her. Do it your way. Have me how you want."

The man moves his head and looks at me with puzzled eyes. I knew the voices have saved me. He isn't a robot, just a man. He wants me for himself. I can feel his excitement mounting as I whisper, "Enjoy me. Fuck me your way. Fuck me for yourself," and gradually his body relaxes, his rhythm changes, he holds me tight and presses his cheek to mine.

"What are you doing?" the woman snaps, "Use her!"

I laugh inside and bury my head in the man's shoulder. "Really use me. Come in me. Come in me now."

The man cries out. He can't hold back. He explodes inside me and throws his head back and gasps then buries his face in my breasts.

The voices shriek, "*You've won...!*" Sweat is pouring down his chest, trickling on to my stomach. Slowly I unclasp my legs and the man subsides completely.

The woman lowers the camera, her face contorting with rage. "You Cretan," she hissed, "get away from her." The man let go of me and leaned heavily on the doorframe, breathing hard. Then the woman slaps his face. My heart leaps. I had used my body to conquer the man and now I would deal with the woman.

"You were right," I smiled at the woman. "He's great. Shall we do it all again?"

The woman's eyes were slits. "You don't amuse me Ms. Webster," she growls, turning on her heel and striding into the bedroom. I can hear her opening the closet door. The man is still leaning on the doorframe, breathing hard and looking down at the floor. Despite myself, I can't help feel a twinge of pity for him. What had they done to him - whomever "they" were - to make him like this? Perhaps he wasn't a brute after all. Perhaps he'd been beaten and tortured like me. Maybe he could help me escape.

My thoughts went no further. The woman stands in the bedroom door holding something in her hand. Through narrow slits of her eyes she glares at both of us, then goes to the man and hands the object to him. It's a long thin whip, my dressage whip. My mind goes numb as I realize what is about to happen to me.

The woman steps back with her chin high, a ringmaster about to control the ring. Her voice is shrill. "You use this on horses." She points to the whip. It was a statement, not a question. "Well let's turn the tables, shall we? Let's see how it works on you." Then she snarles at the man "if you can't control your body, do it with this. Break her."

The man swishes the whip downwards, testing it in the air and its apparent by the way he handles it that it is the first time he has ever held a whip in his hands. He's hesitant, undecided.

"What the hell's wrong with you?" The woman's voice is dry with anger and she keeps licking her lips nervously. "Do it," she grated, "or I'll have you killed. Now thrash her."

I tensed, preparing for pain. The man raised his arm, then WHACK! The whip slashes across my thighs. It was a glancing blow and it seared my skin like a hot wire. "Not her legs," the woman jeered, "her breasts. And I want to see blood."

WHACK! The whip stings my arms, narrowly missing my face. He's agitated and uncoordinated. "Oh for god's sake, get out of here!" she snarls. snatching the whip out of his hands. As he turns away the woman suddenly brings the whip up sharply between my legs. I scream and the woman does it again. Then she takes a half pace backward and hits me across the midriff, leaving a thin pink welt almost a foot long.

"I'll break you if it's the last thing I do," she promises and raises the whip once again. This time, she finds the target. There is an explosion of pain in my right breast, then an agonizing blow to my left. I can't stop screaming. Tiny traces of blood are trickling from two thin stripes across my breasts and the voices are calling again. "*Use it, Jenny ... use the pain ... use the pain to fly...!*"

SLASH! My breasts are bleeding freely now. And the voices shout, "*Fly...!*"

"Oh god!" I sob, but I can feel myself rising. A force rising inside me. I hear the whip hit me again but I don't feel the pain. I'm leaving that all behind. With each new blow the force takes me higher, and the voices chant, "*Fly...!*"

It's thrilling, it's ecstasy. I'm lighter than air. I laugh out loud as the whip cracks down and I close my eyes and feel myself fly.

Then suddenly the voices fade. They just die away and stop. I open my eyes. The woman is standing with the whip in her hand, confusion on her face. Far from breaking me, the whipping made me laugh. I had actually laughed.

I gaze at my tormentor and in that moment, the battle is won. I whisper softly, "hurt me again, as much as you like. You're never going to break me."

The woman stands her ground for a heartbeat, holding my gaze, then she blinks. Its the smallest flicker, the tiniest movement, but it's meaning is louder than thunder. She turns away.

"*YOU'VE WON!*" screamed the voices, and I laugh again. I laugh at the woman who can't control me. I laugh at the fear and the pain. And the voices chant "*yes-yes-yes.*" and I'm flying again.

Up and up I soar. Up through the ceiling and into the clouds, away to a secret place, leaving my body behind. I don't need it anymore. The man and the woman are mere flesh and blood, but I'm different. I can leave my body- the voices have taught me to fly. I can see the world spread out below me, and even see my room, but I'm not there anymore. I'm free.

I can fly like the angels.

CHAPTER EIGHT

I hear tapping and turn my head and catch my breath in alarm at the sight of a man's face looking at me through a car window. A car? I look around. Its mine, but why am I in it? I start to move, I'm panicked. Tied down. No, it's a seat belt. Panic stops.

The man is wearing a hat - some kind of uniform.

Who is he? Why am I in my car?

"You okay Miss?" the man shouts through the glass.

I sit up straighter, my head pounds, I feel groggy, I desperately need some air and start to open the window but stop. What if he grabs me? He taps the window again, "You all right?"

I'm not. My head is spinning and I feel dizzy, my eyes are grainy so I can't see well. I need some water. Why am I here? My memory is foggy. I don't know what happened to me.

The man's face shows concern. He has a badge pinned to his jacket. Can he be a policeman? He looks too old. Hammers are pounding behind my eyes and over my forehead. I can't think clearly. "*Take a breath...*" says a voice.

I did what I was told and the pounding subsided. SECURITY is printed on the man's jacket, and "ANSON" stamped on the badge. OH GOD! I'm in Anson's parking garage. What am I doing here? Did I pass out?

The man frowns, "Do you need help?" he yells and taps again. He unsnaps a leather pouch attached to his belt and takes out a phone.

On the floor of the passenger side of my car I see the tip of a fingernail. My hand on the door handle flashes through my head. I remember the sensation of someone pulling at me, but I can't remember what happened then.

I shake my head no and yell to the man, "I'm fine," then start to search for the keys to the car. I have to get out of here, I'm going to smother. The keys aren't in my handbag, I pull everything out. "I can't find my keys..." I call to the guard. He taps the window and points. The keys are in the ignition.

"Are you sure you're all right?" the guard shouts through the window. "Can you drive?"

His words set me on edge, I have to get out.

"Yes, I'm fine."

The smile is not from my heart as I turn the key in the ignition and sigh with relief when the car starts up. Giving the guard a small wave I quickly back out of the parking space and make my way toward the exit signs. In the rear view mirror I can see the guard writing down my license plate.

I just miss hitting the barrier as I skid to a stop in front of the exit booth. The garage attendant's eyebrows raise with annoyance as she watches me sift through everything, searching for the parking ticket. Opening the window, taking a quick gulp of the relatively fresh air, "Uh, excuse me," I asked the attendant, "but what does the ticket look like?"

"Like a parking ticket honey," said the attendant, "Try your glove compartment or the sun visor," she advised.

"Oh." I feel stupid. Just the other day I had bought a large plastic clip to hold things like parking tickets. I remembered using it when I entered the garage. I paused, trying to grab a fleeting thought about the garage, but it flew past. BLAM! I jumped. The driver in the car behind blew his horn, losing patience. I took the parking ticket stamped ANSON INDUSTRIES out of the clip and handed it to the parking attendant who handed it back. "It's purple," announced the woman, "that's yesterday."

"What? It can't be. I just got it from the machine, uh - today," I'm stammering.

"Nope, it's yesterday's," the attendant repeated. Today's tickets are white." She held one up for display.

"But, I - I got this today," I keep protesting, foreboding creeping into my thoughts. I couldn't have been here overnight. Wouldn't a security guard have noticed me? "It has to be a mistake," I say as I watch the walls of the garage begin to undulate and come close.

"Never mind," I say to the attendant as the wall behind her starts to move up, "I have to get out of here, how much do I owe?"

"That's sixty-eight dollars, forty eight for yesterday, and twenty for today," the woman gloats, obviously relishing this aspect of her job.

I fumbled till I find my wallet and pulled out three twenty-dollar bills. "Do you take credit cards?"

BLAM! The man in the car behind used his horn again, BLAM! Then another one. My heart pounds as I stick my fingers deep into the secret pocket of the Gucci wallet where I hid extra money for emergencies of this kind. BLAM, BLAM, BLAM - other cars are joining the dissonant band.

I'm shaken, embarrassed, and then relieved as my fingers find a hidden folded bill. I pull it out and it's a fifty. Shaking with relief I hand the woman the fifty and a twenty. "Keep the change. Just let me out."

"Don't you want a receipt?" asks the woman, "it's a lot of money," she opens the cash drawer and extracts her tip then begins to write a cash receipt for my seventy dollars.

"No, please." I try not to sound desperate "Just lift the barrier, I don't want the receipt"

"Oh don't let them bother you," the woman lifts her chin to indicate the other drivers, "it's good to make them wait. Makes you more desirable." She winks. "I read that in NEW WOMEN." She hands me the receipt, which I threw on top of the other articles strewn on the passenger seat. "Hey" she said as recognition hit her face. Didn't you use to be Jenny Webster?

"I still am."

As the barriers lift I press the gas pedal to the floor and drive unsteadily up the dark twisting ramp, brakes squealing, nearly bumping into the wall a few times as I search for a radio station to give me the time and the day.

Like a spot light hitting my eyes bright daylight hits my eyes and I have to blink a lot to bring Pico Boulevard into focus. Cars are whizzing by at breakneck speed. Behind me impatient drivers blow their horns and inch forward to make me go faster into the oncoming lane. I won't take the chance. My nerves are too shattered to drive aggressively, and I can't see clearly because everything is blurry. There were other times toa be macho with my car, but for now, I have to stay at my own pace.

A break in the traffic gives me a chance to turn, but as soon as I start, I feel a terrible pain in my arms. The pain spreads to my shoulders as well as my right hand. Whenever I take a deep breath, a slight pull and burning crosses my midriff. My whole body aches as if I was beaten. What's happening? The panic is returning, with the physical pain. Why are the cars going so fast? Is there an emergency exodus?

Holding the wheel tightly for dear life, I feel like I'm choking. I have to loosen my collar. Tentatively I take one hand off the wheel and reach for the top button of my blouse. Something is wrong - I adjust the rear view mirror so I can see myself. The blouse I'm wearing is not the one I had on before. The buttons on the Armani had been pearl, these are plastic, in fact, the blouse is pink instead of off-white and made of cotton instead of silk.

The car swerves. Someone has changed my clothes! What is happening? I find myself in my car in the Anson garage with a parking ticket from the day before and wearing different clothes! Had I blacked out? Lost a day? What is happening? I have to pull over, my head is swimming so badly I can barely see. I have to stop somewhere because my skin is burning.

The car swerves, moving almost independently, the directional signal blinking wildly, as I pull over and get to a yellow line. Turning off the ignition, my fingers shaking I unbutton the bottom part of the blouse and lift both the blouse and the silk camisole up to my breasts.

The welts are frightening. I can hear the snap of the whip as the slashes pulsate angrily. Once again I see the ripping blouse, the bra, the man, my surrender and the woman's empowerment, the terrible dread and utter helplessness. Oh God I sobbed as I traced the crisscrosses of congealed blood across my midriff and breasts. They were warm and very sore, bringing back that nightmare of a few hours before. A nightmare I wish I'd been dreaming, but which the physical evidence made painfully real. I want to go home. I need to take care of myself.

It took twenty minutes longer than usual till I pulled in front of my building. The tires bump into the curb, the hubcaps make a loud scraping sound. This time the gaggle of old people are sitting out on the lawn and turn as a single unit to make judgement on how I park my car. Where were they yesterday when I needed them? They're here to annoy and disappear when they could help. Despair and resentment is starting to grow with anger. I fight to keep all the negative feelings away. I don't want anger to control me. I need positive strength, positive energy.

I nod a quick hello to the ancient gaggle and walk quickly to the front door, pretending not to hear the raspy voice of a neighbor, Carol, calling to me. Out of the corner of my eye I see the hefty woman dragging a loaded shopping cart up the sidewalk with one hand and her squirming four year old son with the other. They're the last people I want to see right now.

My legs are stiff as I climb the stairs. All I want to do is soak in a warm bath but, oh my god. How can I even think of getting into a bath after what happened. Now

I'm not sure I want to go into my apartment. Full of dread I put the key in the lock.

I hadn't considered those two people could still be here. I want the security and familiarity of my own home. I had forgotten what had happened there. How could I forget even for one moment!

I can't go in alone. I hear footsteps coming to the door and the lock turning.

Just as the door starts to open I turn and run. OH MY GOD! They haven't left! Will they shoot me? Am I going to feel hot lead go through my back?

"Meez Jeennie," a voice cried out. "Meez Jeennie."

Clarita, my Guatemalan maid! The dark haired woman, once a beauty but marred by hard work and angst is calling to me.

"You not come in?"

"Clarita," I motion to her frantically. "Come here Clarita. Venga! Are you alone? Estas sola?"

Clarita looks confused and takes a few steps towards me. "Si," she hugs herself, "No anyone, solo me."

"No otra personas en la casa?" I ask.

Clarita shakes her head.

Walking cautiously toward her I peer in the door. The apartment looks sparkling and shinning, and different, like a stage set.

"Did somebody help you?" I ask the woman waiting nervously by my side. "It's muy bueno, very clean. You did a good job."

Clarita shook her head, uncomfortable and embarrassed. "I no able to work today," she apologizes. "My little boy, he sick. We go to hospital. He okay now, but I have no time."

"Oh." My heart drops. Someone cleaned the apartment. It was immaculate. Had they gotten to Clarita? Paid her to stay away? Was that why she was so nervous?

"Que pasa?" I ask the woman wringing her hands.

Clarita looks at the floor. "Mi hijo," she began, and suddenly I realize the woman's problems have nothing to do with me. "Do you need money?" I ask.

"Si," Her eyes are very sad. She's uncomfortable saying this.

I motion her to come with me into the apartment. I would have paid anything to have someone with me at this time. The house feels alien, sinister. Are the deeds still alive in the walls? Since energy cannot be destroyed but only transmuted into another form. will the memories come to haunt me if I'm alone? A shiver goes through me. My home isn't mine anymore.

Gingerly I touch the drawer of my desk and take out the checkbook. I quickly check the numbers and everything seems intact. It wasn't money or goods those people were after, it was my soul.

I make out a check for a month's wages, and hand it to Clarita who hadn't expected that much. I case the living room and try to see into the bedroom as Clarita starts toward the door.

"Clarita," I stop her. "Would you come with me as I go through the house?"

"Ees problem?" Clarita asks, her eyes no stranger to dangerous times.

"No, no problem," I try to soothe this refugee of revolutions and killer earthquakes, "I'm sola, no Tim," I shrug a little shaky to assure her nothing is wrong. But the Guatemalan shakes her head with understanding and together we tour the house.

There's a strange new scent, a medicinal disinfectant that loosely covers the environment with a cheap floral. It's the kind they use in hospitals and other public buildings.

That's a mistake. If they use professional cleaners there is a possibility they can be traced.

A chill goes through me. They have to know that. They just don't care.

My bathrobe is hanging on the back of the door, the cord through the belt loops, all clean and ironed and freshly done. The bottle of Scotch has been removed from the living room and when I look in the liquor cabinet it has been replaced. The crystal ice bucket is back on the shelf. The ice – Can I ever touch ice or look at that bucket again?

Clarita is getting antsy. She wants to leave. "Los muchachos, my boys," she explains. "They home from school now."

"Go ahead, Clarita."

I wish someone I loved would be home for me. Wish I could call somebody and tell them what happened. But who? I don't want to call Tim. I don't know why but I just feel I can't. I don't trust him anymore.

There are no messages recorded in the answering machine - or at least, none remained if there had been any. Was it possible Tim hadn't called? The announcement I had made is still on - at least they hadn't erased that. But what had they erased in me? What damage has been done? How soon will I know?

I'm still in shock, but why had they taken me back to the garage?

Sitting on the sofa I run my fingers through my hair. My scalp is sore where my hair had been pulled. Leaning back I put my fingers inside my blouse and nudge my silk camisole up till I feel the tender welts on my body still warm.

I survey the room, the bathroom door where less than 24 hours ago I had hung like a primitive sacrifice. It could not have been a random act. I'm not a victim of being in the wrong place at the wrong time. No, the man knew too much about me and the woman had been in my house. They had done a lot of research, it was well planned.

The woman referred to the "others." Who are those others, who did the woman call? These people are professionals and would leave no clues behind that they didn't want left.

I have to talk to a friendly voice, definitely not the police or any other authorities. I need a friend, not a probe.

Mannie! I rush to the phone. By providence I don't have to wait long for the operator to answer and then Mannie picks up on the first ring. "Mannie," my voice catches in my throat. I can't contain the tears covering my voice, "I need help."

"What's wrong? You sound awful. What's happened?"

"We can't talk on the phone, can we meet earlier?"

"Sure. My God. Are you all right? Do you want me to pick you up?"

"No, that's all right. I can drive." I took a breath.

"Your favorite place? In about an hour?" Everything has to be kept vague because of Mannie's tapped phone. My home is probably bugged now as well.

"All right, but take care of yourself, all right?"

"I will, I promise. And Mannie, drive carefully."

"I always do. You know I'm the best driver around."

I laugh, surprised I'm still able to do that. Mannie is one of the world's worst drivers though she believes she is the best. It always makes me laugh - even now.

God how I love my friend. I can hardly wait to see her. Mannie is good medicine for me.

CHAPTER NINE

The car phone isn't working. Every time I pick it up, static makes it impossible to hear. Although it's early, construction on Wilshire Boulevard is causing a major traffic jam so it will probably take another fifteen minutes just to go a few blocks. My hands are clutching the wheel. I don't want to wait. I need to be with Mannie.

Checking my watch with the one on the dash, they show the same time. At this rate it might be twenty minutes or more till I get to the restaurant.

I try Anson Labs again. The operator can't hear me, too much static.

There are so many cellular phones in Los Angeles the circuits overload. Trapped in gridlock on the street and in the air, movement and communication stopped, I feel very alone.

What if someone tries getting into my car? Can I defend myself even with all these people around? I hadn't before. I grip the steering wheel tighter.

I should have called Tim or did he already know? Anger creeps into swirling despair as I make myself suffer with my imagination. Why am I so ready to indict Tim, to cast him in the role of a villain? Had he hurt me so badly and made me so angry I only have negative thoughts? What if I'm wrong?

Thank God I'm meeting Mannie. She's the kind of friend I can talk short hand with. She knows about rape. Her older brother molested her when she was ten, then an uncle attacked her six years later. When Mannie left Brazil to go to school in the States, she changed her name from Manuela to Mannie and never wore dresses, high heels or make-up again. She cut her hair short and wore men's style clothing. But with her long legs, chiseled cheekbones, shiny black hair and blue eyes, she was a standout beauty despite her attempts to annihilate her looks.

I had roomed with Mannie for four years at Radcliff and despite what the other coeds and even Tim used to say, I know Mannie isn't gay. She's just not interested in sex or dating. Her sexual energy goes into her work. Science is her passion, Research her love. Her desires are only that she be allowed to use her brilliant brain in pursuit of scientific discoveries. After receiving her MD, Magna Cum Laude, from Harvard Medical School, Anson Industries offered Mannie a research position in their state of the art laboratories along with an experienced support staff and a salary three times larger than she ever imagined she could earn. Personally, I was relieved Mannie would be in Los Angeles when I moved here with Tim.

A space was available near the front of the restaurant as I pull up, the first good sign in what has been the worst twenty-four hours of my life. Checking myself in the rearview mirror I put on dark glasses. There is a slight chance I'll hold up and pass through civilization.

Grease fills the long narrow room of Mannie's favorite restaurant, Kaplan's Deli. I can't understand how an elegant cosmopolitan person could love this place as much as she does. An edible smog seems to be the only decoration in a room filled with tables so close to each other they practically touch.

Next time I'll choose the restaurant.

I search the room for Mannie but she isn't here yet. She's always late.

A short heavy- set man wipes his greasy hands on a bloodstained apron and comes over to me.

I back away.

"One?" he asks, a heavy scent of tobacco seeping through the gap in his teeth when he opens his mouth to talk.

"I'm expecting someone. I'll wait here, thank you."

"You can have a table," he said, reaching out a hand to lead me.

My body involuntarily shrinks away before his bloody fingers can touch me. "No thanks, I'd rather wait here,

He shrugs "Whatever you want," over his shoulder as he goes back behind the counter.

I examine the contents of the deli case. Orderly rows of red fish lay on their side, mouths opened in silent screams. Sensing someone behind me I turn, my throat closing before I scream.

A sinister looking man stands too close to me. He wears dark black glasses and a threadbare felt hat with strands of greasy gray hair sticking out from the bottom of it. I back against the deli counter, afraid, wanting him to move, but he stays his ground. The counterman comes out and takes the man by the elbow and leads him down the row of tables. It's then I notice his red-tipped white cane.

I wish Mannie would hurry. I don't think I can keep myself together much longer.

Pacing I try to think about the last time Mannie and I were together.

It had been a three-day weekend and we went to the mountains to get fresh air and clean snow. We had just come back to the lodge after a long hike and were warming ourselves with the help of steaming hot toddies in front of a large roaring fire when the conversation got rough.

Mannie was justifying the ethics of sacrificing laboratory animals in medical research, but I wasn't accepting the word "*sacrifice*".

"It's murder. They're tortured then you take their life. Cruel. All because science believes one species is more entitled to their needs than the other ."

Careful, we teetered between genuine anger and restraint for the sake of our friendship. Mannie knows I belong to animal rights activist groups but still insists the use of animal sacrifice in laboratories is necessary for the good of the world.

I shake my head again as I think about Mannie confiding in me she's thinking about having a baby, but is unwilling to conceive with a man. She had added that she also disliked the idea of carrying a fetus in her body for nine months so she was working on a way to create artificial gestation and have it functional within the year.

I had accused her of using an incredible amount of research money and animal life only to fulfill a personal need to circumvent her genetic impulses, all because she didn't want to carry a child. "Adopt." I had suggested. "As long as there are children in this world who need homes and protection, it's incumbent upon anyone of passable intelligence to ignore their throbbing biology and adopt a needy orphan,"

But Mannie insisted she was working in the interests of emerging generations. "A developing fetus surrounded by an artificial placenta in an artificial womb under optimum conditions fares a much better chance of having a fuller and healthier life once it's born," she tried in justification to me.

"No drugs, no accidents, no tension, no pollution, and the female genetic contributor you call *Mother*, is not faced with nine months of physical and emotional discomfort. Because the conception will be a conscious act it will cut down the burgeoning world population and also, why must a woman suffer? If I got pregnant, I couldn't function as I do. It would affect my work. Being pregnant doesn't seem like a necessary enrichment to my life, and it doesn't mean I would be a better mother. Being a good parent is what is important, not how you become one."

I didn't know how to answer that, but I find the concept of artificial gestation sounds inhumane and frightening. "It's Mary Shelley's Frankenstein."

"An actual pregnancy costs a woman a minimum of six months," Mannie went on. "What if she has no one to support her and she can't work because of complications? It happens."

"I agree. People shouldn't have children when they're in difficult financial circumstances, especially single women. I think children should be brought into this world with every advantage possible."

"Great, but unrealistic. Tell that to the testosterone carriers whose fun is to send their sperm into women mostly with little regard as to what can happen to the recipient and fetus from that sperm," Mannie said bitterly. "But that's another argument. My financial circumstances are good and I have a lot to offer a child. So I'm bowing to my genetic nesting urges and bending my scientific knowledge to create a newer generation for myself and others."

"Wouldn't it be better for you to adopt or even find a surrogate?" I said again.

"Well," the scientist answered, "I had planned to use one but all these law suits from surrogate mothers changing their minds, scared me. So I put my ovum in cryo storage until the artificial womb is ready, then I'll combine my ovum with the sperm of the best genetic type and use the artificial womb to gestate her."

"Her?" Then quickly. "forget what I said. I don't want to know.

Shivering a little I pull my jacket closer and look for Manny through the streaked windows of the deli but there is still no sign of my friend.

Taking a deep breath I think about the excitement Mannie had shown when she thought of a way to market the concept.

"Once the development of the artificial womb is successful, we can go into business and have baby factory franchises."

"Terrific," I lied. "You can call them *Manny's Stork-Inns*. But before that happens, how about letting me produce a story about this? At least a pod cast."

"I'm not sure. Let me think about it. I'm not comfortable with the idea. Jenny, I want you to understand - I'm afraid of being intimate, having intercourse with a man. And as far as artificial insemination, I don't want to walk around for nine months in that hormonal and physical condition. Would you?"

"Well yes, I do. Isn't this way of thinking what the Nazis tried to do? Sorry but I have to ask you."

Mannie stiffened. "I'm not a Nazi... I'm trying to be practical and think objectively."

"Oh Mannie," I interrupted. Don't get upset. Nothing's happened yet."

"No, you don't understand." Mannie looked anxious. "The creation of these artificial wombs isn't just for me, it will give great freedom of choice for so many women. The project has great financial potential for Anson and they have been very generous with research and development money."

I smiled. "I bet."

"They have given me a small point participation on each unit. It could make me very rich."

"You already are."

She ignored that and pulled a magazine cover from a stack near the fireplace and started to draw on it. Excitedly she sketched the general outlines of a transparent artificial womb. "We're trying to clone amniotic fluid so we're experimenting with lots of different chemicals. So far it kind of looks like chicken soup. But I know it's one of those things waiting to be discovered. I'm making the artificial womb look like one. It will be soft and expandable as the baby grows. It's hooked up to a simulation of a human mother's body processes; breathing, heartbeat, blood flow. Nutrients and other life supporting needs will be carried through the fetus' umbilical cord just like any ordinary womb for any ordinary fetus. But much healthier."

Strange surges were going through my body as my dear friend expounded on her creation. Do I really know who and what she is? "I would hardly call these circumstances ordinary," I told her. "And I suppose more animals will have to die for their intestines or artery material."

Mannie ignored that. "The body processes and systems will be connected to a main computer terminal that monitors everything for the nine month gestation. When abnormalities occur that can't be immediately corrected, the gestation will be terminated. Back up eggs and sperm are going to be kept in case this happens and will immediately be combined in a Petri dish to start another life. Parents will not be notified till it is time for their child to be born."

"You mean disconnected," I said.

"Yes, that's accurate. But it could also describe natural childbirth."

"Will the event be catered?" I quipped, remembering how seriously Mannie takes everything.

"As a matter of fact", Mannie had answered with enthusiasm, "the parents and invited guests will come to a viewing room. I want to furnish it tastefully with plush seating and low but pleasant lighting. Afterward there will be a bright and cheery party room so the new family can celebrate their baby's arrival."

I'm blown away. The future is almost here and I'm not ready for it. Science has gone beyond my personal understanding.

Mannie had been so excited as she stood up to emphasize her future plans. "I hope to make the wombs portable so they will eventually be used in private homes hooked up through personal computers to a laboratory's main frame. However, for the immediate future I can see only clinics or call them baby factories, where artificial wombs will be hooked up to computer terminals twenty-four hours a day."

"What about love, nurturing?" I ask. "Isn't it nice to have loving conditions when conceiving a child? Spiritual bonding could impact greatly on a child's psyche. But bonding through a fake womb? What kind of spiritual enhancement is that?"

Mannie anticipated the question. "I intend to find composers and artists to create visual and audio stimuli to sensitize, teach and prepare the fetus for the outside."

"Artificially manipulated feelings." I shook my head. "This is so Orwellian. It's dangerous. You can instill negative feelings with that kind of in-put as well."

"Not with proper guidelines," answered Mannie. "You know, maybe you should produce this. A media story would be good. It certainly would keep everyone honest. Some of the people at Anson have been breathing down my neck. Maybe they need to know the public is watching."

"What do they want from you, besides immediate results?" I ask.

"Just that. They're trying to pressure me to use human subjects instead of animals. I think that's a way off, but they don't want to wait. When life can be created, strong guidelines and regulations should be kept." Her face darkened, as she grew serious. "Only when you produce this you can't use me or my name."

"You want me to try to produce this with my hands tied behind my back," I say.

"Try isn't good enough." Manny said.

"I'll do what I can. You gained some weight and look tired."

"I've been nauseous and feel awful."

"You sound pregnant," I joked.

Mannie laughed and I joined her.

We then picked up our Hot Toddys and toasted each other. "To New Age immaculate conception. No more worries, no more infection. Find the color and type of child you want in a catalogue, shake the contributing father's hand for personal contact - tradition sake - and a signed check will make you a mommy. – No muss, no fuss." We clink our glasses.

Wind and traffic noise signal the deli door opening and Mannie comes propelling through it. Her wrinkled khaki raincoat flies behind her like a cape barely covering a stained lab coat and trousers. Her short dark hair is curled with perspiration and she looks ravishing. Heads turn even though it doesn't look like Mannie has been able to conceal the extra pounds she's gained under her flapping layers.

She hugs me, apologizing, "Sorry about the time, but..."

I flinch from the pain on my wounds "It's all right."

Mannie hugs me again and I almost cry out.

"It's so good to see you," we both say together. Mannie laughs, I manage a smile.

Mannie puts her arm around me and I force myself not to shrink away as we walk toward a large booth in the corner.

Settling in, I notice the blind man sitting opposite us. Something about him makes me angry I'm not sure why. He spoons an inordinate amount of sugar into his cup, and then brings it carefully to his stationery lips. I shudder.

Mannie looks at me soberly, no longer smiling. "I have to tell you something."

"Go first." I waited.

Mannie looked directly at me. "I'm pregnant."

I froze. "What?" The words could barely go through my head. "How?"

Mannie shrugged. "I don't know. I've been trying to figure it out."

"Figure it out? You have no idea?"

"No."

"How about the artificial sperm you've been working on? Could that be operable?"

"No, we're years away from that." Mannie is almost impatient. "That's the creation of life. We joked about it last time, remember?"

"I was thinking about that before you came in and the feature I want to do about your work.

I touch my friend's hand, "Mannie, I have to tell you what happened. Maybe this is connected, maybe not, but I'm scared."

"You scared? That isn't possible. However I'm frantic. Here I am, the Virgin Mary working on ways to create babies without physical contact, and I get pregnant. And without a clue as to how it happened! I'm my own guinea pig, how's that for the greatest irony?"

I can feel my face burning as tears well in her eyes.

"Maybe I've lost perspective," she continued, "but I don't think I got impregnated in the lab. It couldn't happen. We're not that far along yet. But the reality is, I'm pregnant and I don't know how."

I'm angry and frustrated. I wanted to unburden myself to my friend, and she only wants to talk about herself. Any other time I would have jumped in with everything I have to help. The situation is incredible though I think Mannie is in denial. She probably had drinks or something with someone and was either slipped GHB or Rohypnol - Ruffies - a date rape drug. And maybe Mannie just lost control of herself and blocked it out. But I don't have the patience to focus on Mannie now. I need her, not the other way around.

"Do you remember Peter Ballard from M.I.T?" Mannie was saying, "the one who used to follow me around and ask me out?"

I nodded, feeling a flicker of resentment at her continuing insensitivity.

"Well, Ballard is working for some large Japanese pharmaceutical and they give him so much money you wouldn't believe it.

He came over and we started playing with some genetic samples that he had brought from Japan for his artificial blood research."

"Did you have anything to drink with him?" I interrupted.

She nodded. "At dinner. We went to the Four Seasons. His company is very generous. He has a development fund that is richer than most third world treasuries. He also has an unlimited credit card for entertaining. Nice huh?" She smiled, but I didn't smile back. She didn't seem to notice.

"Maybe you had more to drink than you realized and went to bed with him. You did have dinner in a hotel. It's a trick some men use. They get you drunk then take you upstairs."

Mannie shook her head. "Not possible. Peter Ballard is gay. When he came out of the closet he decided to go into research so he wouldn't have to touch female patients."

Mannie slunk down in the booth. "Look at me - I've lived like a celibate nun most of my life, never let a man touch me, though at times I think I'd like to try. And now, I get fucked, and I didn't get to enjoy it or hate it."

I can't laugh. Mannie doesn't care, doesn't remember what I had said, didn't hear anything. Like a baby, Mannie can only think of herself.

"So I'm pregnant," she was saying, "and I don't know how. Some scientist, huh?"

"Are you sure?" I ask. "You've gotten a bit heavy. Could it be a false pregnancy? Women sometimes carry every sign."

"I wish. I checked that out - had an ultra sound. There's a baby in here," she patted her stomach. "I could see it on the screen. Want to see her picture?"

I didn't answer but Mannie pulled out her phone and started scrolling till she handed me the video image of some shape that could be interpreted as a fetus, but it was fuzzy. "I haven't got the wallet size yet," Mannie joked. "Can you tell it's a girl?"

"Mannie, you can't make out anything in this picture." I was losing what little patience I had. A strange feeling hit me, and it gave me the chills. I glanced at the blind man. He was bothering me. He was too quiet, unearthly, like a mannequin. A human shape without a soul.

"I don't know what to say about your information, " I tell her.

Turmoil reigned in my head. Everything that has happened in the past 48 hours is too much, too strange. Mannie must have blacked out. That has to be the answer.

"I'm in my fourth month," Mannie was saying flatly, "and the weird thing about this, is the moment it was confirmed I feel myself liking the concept."

"Concept. Terrific," I don't try to hide the sarcasm. "Now, what are you going to do with this 'concept' that happens to be made of flesh and blood and your genetic parts? What about taking care of it? You don't know how it happened, who the father could be, or even if the father is human for god's sakes! Maybe it's one of your mutants from your laboratory. Look what happened when Albert Hoffman discovered LSD. He was trying to synthesize Ergot for pregnancy and somehow he either inhaled the Lysergic Acid or it went through his skin. A large part of the world was changed from that scientific accident. You have to be more responsible. Contact Peter Ballard. He may be working with other artificial things beside blood."

Mannie was chagrined. "I tried. He's in the Far East somewhere. Dropped out of sight."

"What do you want to do?" I asked, annoyed my friend forgot I had something I wanted to talk to her about.

"How about a baby shower or shopping for a bassinet?" Mannie's lip started to quiver. "She's pretty isn't she?" she holds up her phone and bursts into tears.

I sit back and wait till she stops crying. Normally I would never react this way, but my anger is growing with my friend's insensitivity.

"Manny, I called you for help."

Mannie pulled herself together. "Right. I'm sorry, I totally ignored you. What happened?"

I suddenly don't want to tell her. What if the blind man is listening. Anger toward his intrusion and Mannie's tirade has rattled me. Why should I be feeling anger toward a poor old blind man?

A waitress circles and tries to stop. "Bring us a large bottle of Perrier," I tell her before she can get closer. "And two coffees. We're not ready to order yet."

"Mannie," I take a deep breath. "The worst thing that could have ever happened to me, did. You know how it feels and that's why I have to talk to you."

I choke up.

Mannie looks down, playing with the saltshaker, waiting for me to speak.

"It was so horrible I don't know how it can be true."

"Maybe it wasn't," my friend suggested. "Maybe we're both caught in bad dreams. Maybe one or both of us is dreaming this, or maybe I've just made everything up. Maybe I created this to cover the fact I got fat from overeating or I'm pregnant to prove to the world that I'm straight."

"Are either of those true?" I ask, annoyed Mannie had put the focus back on herself.

Yet she looks a little gray, like her energy is drained.

"No. I wish it were. Jenny, tell me what happened."

I start to speak then stop. If I tell her I'd have to relive it, every moment, each touch. I can't go through with it now, Mannie's problems have drained me and the blind man is upsetting me. How I wish he would leave. What if he can hear everything we 're saying. He's pouring sugar into his coffee cup, like he wants it to turn solid.

"What happened?" Mannie repeats.

The words drop out of my mouth without thinking. "Tim and I are in trouble," I skirt the truth. "He's turned into a real pain. He doesn't want me to do the story about your research, worried I'll step on the wrong toes. That's all he cares about, not stepping on the wrong toes. Since he has decided to go for the White House, he has forgotten about his reason for doing it, the important issues."

"You've lost respect for him." Mannie said.

"I love him," I answered.

"There is no love without respect. You know that," said the sad, beautiful Brazilian.

I don't want to think about that. I motion toward the blind man, "That guy is making my skin crawl."

Mannie leans over to look at him. "That's because you can't see his eyes and he looks like he smells."

I shake my head. "And you, Miss Virgin Mary. Talking about not seeing, you must have been drunk or knocked out with a Ruffie. It's tasteless and men spike women's drinks with it. It's the date rape drug.

"I know what it is," Mannie said.

"It has to be. Think about it. Do some soul searching. Who have you been with besides Peter Ballard?"

"You."

"Can't you do a genetics' test or something?"

"Not without knowing who the father is."

"Right." Knots are growing in my stomach. I want to scream. Then I notice a strange sweetness sweeping over Mannie, looking peaceful and happy, then suddenly fright crosses her face.

"I'm scared," Mannie said.

"Of having a baby?"

Her eyes swam with tears. "Will you be the Godmother? If anything happens to me, will you take care of her?"

"Of course I will," but somehow none of what Mannie said seemed real to me. I wonder if Tim was right - that Mannie lived in a fantasy and much of what she says should not be taken seriously.

Mannie snatched a napkin out of the holder and crumpled it against her mouth. "I know you're angry because I'm acting badly. But something strange is happening - I'm being pressured to use human fetuses, " she pauses, tears streaming. "I haven't been totally honest. I've known that I was pregnant for weeks. You had joked about it, remember? Some of the others in the lab know too. But I honestly don't know how it happened. They're trying to convince me to let them remove the fetus so they can grow her in the artificial womb. I don't want to do that. No one can be sure it's safe yet and I don't want my baby to be the guinea pig. I can feel her. She's alive, connected, and dependent on me. We have a kind of communication already, I know that sounds crazy but it's true. My Supervisor is threatening to transfer me and have someone else take over my work. Of course they won't say it's because they can't use my fetus, they'll say something that will destroy my reputation and then I'll never find first class work. These people are ruthless."

The lights flicker and I jump, but Mannie doesn't seem to notice and keeps talking. "I need you to write and produce the story, keep a public eye on them, do an expose. You're the only one I can trust not to reveal my name."

My breath stops. Guilt rises up. "We have a problem. My producer doesn't want to do the story unless he knows more facts. I had to give him your name, I'm sorry."

Mannie looks shocked. "It could be my death warrant," she mumbles. "But I do think that the story should be done, even if it's dangerous for us." She takes a shaky breath. "I'm so conflicted. Maybe we should wait till the work is finished and I have permission to give interviews. I have a child to think about."

"Mannie, I won't use your name again, I promise. And I think I can trust my boss." A thump of dread hits my chest. "I hope I can. But then." tears block my throat and I turn away. "Look, I'm sorry," I manage to mumble.

"Don't cry, it's all right," croaks Mannie. "Boy, are we messes, sitting here crying." She giggles. At first I stiffen, then start to shake, my tears turning to laughter.

Both of us laugh, prompting the other, escalating into whoops and shrieks of uncontrollable laughter. Tears pour down our cheeks, patrons turn to look, the waitress stops her approach and the blind man continues to stare.

Getting ourselves under control, Mannie pats my hand. "I overreacted. I'm more scared about childbirth. Will you be my partner at Lamaze classes?"

I start to giggle again and nod . Mannie picks up the laughter and we both howl.

Mannie shakes her head, still laughing, "I can't believe this - when I saw that baby on the screen - a real person," her voice catches and she grows quiet. "Don't let them take the baby from me," her face is a portrait of fear. "You're right, they probably drugged me. It had to be. But why?"

The waitress comes over and starts to interrupt. "Please wait," I say, my mind racing. Leaning across the table I look into Mannie's blue eyes. "Don't be scared.

They can take our bodies, but they can't have our minds. Don't lose yourself emotionally. They'll never touch you there. Believe me."

A strength is radiating inside me, the kind of strength I first felt when I left my body the first time. "Don't give yourself away, listen to yourself and you'll survive."

"If I get pregnant unknowingly," said Mannie, very serious now, "then any fertile woman can be impregnated without her knowledge, or consent."

But the big question for now is - why you? We've got to find out who did it and why," I tell her. "I think there is a connection to what happened to me."

"What did happen to you? It's more than problems with Tim, I know that. I'm sorry, I've just been so self-indulgent. Forgive me. What happened Jenny?"

I start to shake. "Not now. Let's finish with your problem. One problem at a time. We have to be very careful what we're saying."

Mannie put the menu down. "I'll get you names, information, everything you need. This breakthrough should be made public. But please, try not to use my name, I don't want to lose my job or be blacklisted. It can happen very easily."

"Don't worry. I'll do everything to help you." I put the menu down on the seat beside me. The last thing I want to do is eat right now. "I'm not thinking very clearly. But I do know that if you give me names and information, the more credibility I have, the more we can accomplish. Your genius may have unleashed a monster that needs to be controlled." I leaned back, pondering. "I wonder if there are researchers doing more than we know?"

"I hope not."

I shake my head. "This isn't about ego. We need to think deeply about the new technology. There is great power in it. Look at us. We're professionals, yet when we question it, we become fearful."

Mannie takes my hand. "Don't get more upset."

I withdraw my hand. "So many people take their lives for granted and put their working brains to sleep in front of their computers and televisions. Then they herd through shopping malls in half wakened states, amassing charges on their credit cards before they drive to chapels to pray for money to pay for those charges. They never give a thought about the deeper lessons of life. There is no seeking for truth, no desire for meaning. Profitable survival is the goal of their existence."

"Jenny, you're on a soap box."

"I can't help it. I have a messianic complex, but I mean it. You do too or you wouldn't have given me this information."

"I'm a scientist, not a savior," She sounds defiant. "I just don't want this getting out of hand, that's all." Drawing herself up she seems to grow stronger. "I'll get names for you. I'll have to do some bribing to get into that area of the computer programs."

"Great." I reach over and squeeze her hand.

"Now," Mannie asked. "What are we going to do about food? She looks around for the now non-existent waitress. "I'm not very hungry. Especially here. Why do we come here?"

"You wanted to come. You like the grease. Let's change right now and leave." I pushmyself out of the booth.

Another waitress with platinum blonde hair piled high and thick mink eyelashes approaches us. The plastic nametag under a flowery handkerchief reads 'Dotty'. "Wanna order?" she asks, her gravely voice deepened with years of cigarettes and booze, her eyes testimony to a hard life.

"We've changed our minds," I said. "Sorry."

The waitress isn't backing off. "There's a minimum charge in these booths. Your Perrier doesn't cover it, and you've been here awhile."

"Is this a time share?" I resent her attitude. "We'll be happy to pay for the water plus the minimum."

"That's all right," said Mannie. "I'll order something."

"Don't be bullied into eating if you don't want to. We're talking principle here. And you shouldn't be drinking coffee. Caffeine is bad for my goddaughter."

I stand up. "I can't stay here anymore. It's claustrophobic. I've got to get air." I throw down a twenty-dollar bill. Mannie picks it up and stuffs it back in my purse.

"Jenny, do you want to come back to my house? Stay with me so we can talk?"

Thoughts of Mannie's small-overcrowded apartment makes me more depressed. Unspent rage is threatening to release. "No thank you, I can't, I really need to be alone. I have to get out of here."

I look over at the blind man staring soundlessly like a George Segal sculpture. I don't know why but there is something about him I hate. My hands are in fists. Why this blind old man? What did he represent to me?

Mannie looks stricken. "I'm worried about you," she says

"I'm sorry. It should be the other way around. It's just personal stuff - I'm feeling sorry for myself. I'll be all right. I feel suffocated. Got to get out. I'll call you when I get home, all right?" I throw her a kiss and leave.

Mannie puts her own twenty on the table and starts to leave. The blind man slides out of his seat.

Mannie leaves the delicatessen and hesitates on the sidewalk. There's no sign of Jenny, she has disappeared. Then she sees Jenny's BMW turn the corner. Troubled by her friend's behavior, she pauses at a newspaper stand and pulls out a late edition of The Times. She scans the headlines then throws the paper into a wastebasket just as the blind man taps his way over to her.

"Can you help me?" he asks, his head tilted to the side and up, as if trying to see around his dark glasses. "I don't hear any traffic noises and I'm not sure whether the light is red or green."

"Which way do you want to go?" she asks.

"South, across Wilshire."

"Sure." Mannie takes his upraised elbow and begins to lead him toward the corner. The man brings his other hand up to steady himself against her arm. The thin needle hidden between the first two fingers of his hand easily penetrates the raincoat and jacket she wears. She doesn't feel the sting when the blind man stumbles and expertly pushes the needle into her forearm, the motion of the fall and his grasping hand diverting her from the pinprick going into her flesh.

The blind man stiffens slightly when they reach the other side as a police car pulls up and stops in front of them. One of the officers gets out and crosses the street to the delicatessen while the other waits in the car. The blind man quickly taps his cane against the sidewalk and walks away. Mannie runs back across the street, stops as she gets to her car and grabs the handle. She's woozy. Trying to shake it off, she opens the door and gets in and starts the engine. Pulling out of her parking space she barely misses the car that is already using that lane. The policeman on the opposite side sees what has happened and puts his red light on, makes a u turn and goes after her, his lights blazing.

Mannie doesn't see the police car. She continues down Wilshire Boulevard toward the ocean, her car swerving as though she is drunk. Ringing fills her ears, her driving glasses are fogged, the windshield steamy. Straining her head to peer through the window, she is captured by the red ball of the setting sun sinking into the ocean. There is a red light in her rear -view mirror as well. Flames dance in her head, a high-pitched sound massages her, as she blinks her eyes and starts to relax. Licks of flame reach through the window, forcing her eyes to stay open and focused on them.

She doesn't blink again as her car crashes through the crossed arms of the statue of Saint Monica that had been guarding the dead end of Wilshire Boulevard.

Hands clutching the wheel tightly Mannie's car continues through the shattered remains. Unblinking, never shifting her focus off the sun, Mannie doesn't see the two elderly people sitting on the park bench enjoying their last sunset. The runaway car crashes through them, separating them in their last moment of life. It glances off the panicked mother and her baby carriage, squashing the white Scottish terrier trapped by its leash. The battered car pauses for a moment at the stone retaining wall lining the grass parkway overlooking the ocean and

Pacific Coast Highway. It's Longfellow's "Children's Hour" or the "Witching Hour" that had brought strollers and joggers to this peaceful place till Mannie's car flips over the wall and floats free in mid-air till the forces of gravity brings it crashing down onto the last vestiges of rush hour traffic, two hundred feet below.

CHAPTER TEN

The tangle of colorful metal and glass mixed with pieces of limbs and blood, appeared less horrific when reproduced electronically on the computer screen on my desk.

As I wait for the answering machine to deliver the recorded messages, the words of the perky blonde newscaster blast out over the picture of Mannie filling the screen. "A friend and co-worker of Dr. Manuela Cristal de SEBASTIANE could not believe she was personally responsible for this tragedy."

I could actually feel the blood drain out of me as I turn the answering machine off and edge closer to the screen. The picture of Mannie makes my head feel like its exploding. I sink to the floor, unable to carry my weight, unable to breathe or see clearly. Another part of my world destroyed.

The newscaster, blue eyes sparkling with well-placed pin lights reports, "Dr. Cristal de Sebastiane's friends and co-workers say she had been nervous recently after learning of a pregnancy." She pauses, the blue eyes sparkling with a hint of tears as the camera pulls back to reveal the roundness of the newscaster's own pregnancy.

The screen now has eyewitnesses to the accident telling their versions to the network minicam. This was their *moment of fame* as predicted decades ago by pop artist Andy Warhol that everyone one day will experience fame.

An excited Latino man wearing a bright blue Adidas jogging suit swayed side to side as he demonstrated for the camera how he saw the car swerving erratically before it crashed into the statue of Santa Monica. He pauses to cross himself, milking his "moment" then declares, "she was drunk, boracha." Someone waved and grinned at the camera from behind him.

The perky blonde newscaster, turns back to the camera announcing her next interview, a spokesperson from Anson Industries, Melvin Phillips.

I don't believe he's on that screen. This has to be some cruel idiot's idea of a joke – live streamed to freak me out, which it's doing.

I look for other news casts but Phillips' interview is on another as well. "It has been suggested," he was stating, "not mandated, that Dr. Cristal de SEBASTIANE, take a leave of absence. She had refused, citing she didn't want to leave her work." Phillips faded off the screen and the camera comes up on another blonde newscaster who wipes her smile off and replaces it with a serious and sad look. She wraps up the segment with Mannie's birthplace and survivors. No mention is made of her genius and her contribution to society. It would take years for any of that to come out, if at all. For now, her work, her contributions, would be overlaid with the stigma of this accident and the lives it took whether she was innocent or not. Her life and accomplishments would forever be stained by these events.

The newscaster is signing off with a huge smile, "We'll have more later." Then the logo comes up for the ten o'clock news. I roll back on my heels and try to breathe, but my emotions are crashing, blurring my thinking. The accident must have happened right after I left the restaurant.

Mannie, my dear friend. I'll never have that kind of trust with anyone else ever again. The flood of tears seems to enhance the overwhelming emptiness I'm feeling inside.

The phone rings. I let it ring. It won't stop. Mind reeling I reach for it to shut it up but Tim's voice is there. I can't speak, tears flood any attempt.

"Are you all right?" Tim asks firmly for the third time. I shake my head and crock out the word "yes".

"Darling," he cooed gently. "I know about Mannie. It's all over the news." His voice grows harder, anger seeping through. "I warned you to stay away from her but you wouldn't listen."

I can't answer. How can he be so cruel?

"I'm coming home."

"No!" I shouted, surprising both of us.

"They'll stop at nothing.," he said softly.

Is he warning me? "I know."

"Where were you tonight?"

"With Mannie."

"After."

"I went to the beach house, then decided to come back to my apartment to write."

"Well, thank God you weren't in that car. Did anyone see you with her tonight?"

"In the restaurant."

"Let's hope they don't put you two together. You don't want to get involved."

"I am."

His voice grew low, sympathetic. "I'll get you out of this, but you have to help me."

"Out of what?"

He didn't answer. "Don't leave the apartment. I'll call a friend, Elaine Jefferson. She's a registered nurse, trained in crisis intervention and, if necessary, has her black belt in karate."

"Why would I need someone like that?"

"To protect you. I want her to stay with you. Do you understand? I want someone with you. You're not to be alone."

I can't talk, my throat had closed.

"Don't be scared. You'll be taken care of." He hung up.

I wiped the tears, turned on the answering machine, put my tape recorder in my jacket pocket and walked out the door.

The Santa Monica Police Station is packed with the aroma of twenty- four-hour use, harsh fluorescent lighting grossly illuminating the kind of seedy, dark aspect of police life most people see only on TV.

I didn't want to be in this dense chaotic place. It had been similar environments that made me switch from being a news reporter to investigative reporting for cable news segments. Because of my early life as a super model, I want to keep my face off the camera as much as possible. Beauty can sometimes be a detriment.

However as a rookie reporter covering the city beat, I would often go home suffering from what I reported; the ragged, nerve-splitting events that refused to leave me once I was inside the relative safety of my own home.

So I switched to cleaner crimes - the white-collar kind - committed in the conference rooms and private clubs of the corporate and political worlds. I focused on abuse of position rather than street crime, though at times I had trouble separating the differences. My past life with its aura of glamour opened many more doors for me than if I had been just a regular reporter from some news agency

And now I'm back where I had started, investigating a multiple homicide. But this one is different. The person accused has been my very best friend and if I want answers its necessary to investigate it without emotion.

Drawing on techniques I had polished as a super model, I assumed a steel coated assurance I didn't feel and headed for the detectives' lounge, walking in without knocking.

Assaulted by the musty odors of stale smoke, body odor and old beer, I almost ran into the chunky middle-aged man who jumped up, reaching for his gun as I came in,.

"Relax." I flash my press pass and muster the toughest attitude I can. "I'm Jenny Webster, THE NEWS. I'm covering that fatal traffic accident in Santa Monica on Pacific Coast Highway.

"Yeah, I've seen you on TV." wheezed a thin detective, his skin bleached by years of fluorescent lights. "That was a mean one. Kamikaze Mama!"

I force myself to stay quiet though my stomach is reeling from those words. I can't expose my feelings.

"Lady," the older detective says, his hand still on his gun, "we've already talked to the NEWS. We had a press conference. Didn't you see Terry O'Malley? He covers your beat. And as far as you coming in here like you just did, this is for police only. We come here to rest and think about things we want to think about. You gotta get permission from one of us to come in. Understand?"

I nodded, "Yes, I'm sorry but..."

He interrupted. "Talk to the Sergeant." He gestured away from himself as he mumbled, "outta here."

I'm so stressed I'm mute and start to leave.

"Wait." A tall thin man, his face scattered with freckles framed by curly red hair comes over to me. His dimpled smile, bright blue eyes, and high-sculpted cheekbones make him comfortably appealing.

I'm Detective Parker. I'm working the case.

His smile is refreshing, his diffident manner disarming. Light, and compassion seem to flow from his eyes, creating a surprised feeling of comfort in me.

"Let's have coffee and talk," he says, ushering me out of the Detective's lounge and choosing a bench near the end of the hallway where it's quiet.

"I am a reporter on THE NEWS," I tell him, "but I'm also a good friend of Mannie Sebastiane. I was with her tonight." This was not what I had planned to say. I was here to get information, not implicate myself.

He listens without reaction.

"Mannie wasn't despondent," I tell him. "She had verification of her pregnancy this morning. I saw a picture of the fetus from the ultrasound. She was very proud of it, joked about making copies." A sob threatened to come out and I dug my nails into my palms. "Mannie had her phone with her. Did you find it?"

"No." He made a note. "I don't think it's possible anything could have survived that crash, but I'll see what we have."

Tears well up, I try to hold them back, but they spill over my lids and down my face.

"I'm sorry. I shouldn't have said that," he awkwardly looks through his pocket for a handkerchief as I wipe the tears with the back of my hands.

I'll check the list of items we have." He moved a few inches down the bench from her. "Go on."

"I left the restaurant, Kaplan's Deli, before she did. I was going through a pity party and wanted to be alone. If only I had stayed or gone home with her..." I stopped. I couldn't tell more. If I did, a whole other can of worms would be opened and I can't deal with that now. "If only I had stayed with her," I continued, "this wouldn't have happened."

"It was her time," he said.

"What?" I look at him closely. I'm not used to hearing a policeman talk like that. Our eyes lock with unspoken understanding and despite everything that has happened, I can feel a strength coming from him. I had someone with whom I could communicate. Someone I can open up with and trust.

"Mannie could not have killed herself," I tell him. "She was filled with new life, excited about her work- besides, pregnant women almost never commit suicide, not with the life force within them. It's a verified statistic." I manage to suppress the next threatening sob.

I look up at him, tears streaming. "Even though Manny said she was tired and stressed I could see a positive difference in her. I think she was seeing herself in a whole new way, as a woman for the first time. There was no way she could have killed herself. It's not possible. Not after the way she was tonight. A new and loving woman had emerged, and now she's gone." I couldn't suppress the sob that came up from me.

He urges me to go on.

"Contrary to what her co-workers say, it wasn't the baby Mannie was upset about, it was the way in which she got pregnant and by whom that concerned her."

He made a note.

"I think when she saw the shapes and outline of that baby inside herself, she was feeling true love for the first time in her life. I didn't see that at the restaurant till now. I wasn't relating to her. I was too concerned about how she wasn't relating to me, listening to my needs, and I was resentful. Oh God!" a huge sob took over and I buried my face in my hands, sobbing.

The detective found some napkins near the vending machine and gave them to me to wipe away the tears.

"I'm dealing in my own feelings and accusing her of doing exactly what I was doing. How could I be so insensitive?"

He patted my hand. "Don't be so hard on yourself. Be grateful you have such a beautiful memory of your friend. That is the woman to remember." He paused delicately, "why was she so concerned about the pregnancy?"

I told him about Mannie's fear of men and her desire to have a child and the work she was doing: the artificial placenta and wombs, the computer programs, everything. He didn't say much but took a lot of notes.

"Didn't Anson tell you any of this?" I asked.

"We just did a preliminary investigation. We're going back there tomorrow."

"Give them enough time to destroy evidence."

"The lab is sealed."

"That doesn't mean anything." I took a deep breath, barely able to get the next question out. "Where is ... where are her remains?"

"The morgue. I don't suggest you go there. It's gruesome. Remember her the way she was. It isn't necessary for you to see what is left."

"No, I guess not. Is there evidence of a fetus?"

"Ms. Webster, I don't have that much experience, but from what I saw of that wreck, I doubt they can find anything except from tissue reports and that takes time."

"But..."

"Impossible," he interrupted.

I don't know why, but he was calming me. Although he was in a position to interrogate and bring things up that would upset me, instead, in the midst of an area associated with fear and violence, he was making me feel better.

"I promise I'll do everything possible to find out what happened. By the way," he blushed a bit, "I know your work. When I was deciding whether to move to L.A. I watched your segments on THE NEWS. You're a fine journalist."

"Thank you." I can feel myself blushing.

He kept talking. "Mannie's accident didn't feel right to me. I don't know much except what physically happened. But I don't think this was a willful act. After what you've told me, she doesn't seem to have the psychological profile. We'll do everything possible to learn what really happened."

"I know you will." I thanked him and left, glad he hadn't offered me a ride home and wondering why he hadn't.

CHAPTER ELEVEN

Bed never looked so inviting. The sheets felt soft as silk, the mattress seemed to reach up and embrace me, cuddling me against the world.

Floating in a world of soft darkness and enveloping comfort the bed starts to shake. I sit up. Is it an earthquake? My heart pounds. Nothing seems to be moving so I take a deep breath and lay back down.

The bed starts to shake again, my body vibrating with an intensity that seems to shut off separation from the bed that becomes a jet pack lifting me into the universe.

Suddenly the jets stop. It must have been a nightmare. Stress.

"JENNY!"

A blast of fear shoots through me. I sit bolt upright. Someone was in the room. The woman who tortured me is back. She's somewhere in the house.

Clutching the blanket to my chest, fighting the impulse to pull it over my head, I scan the room, listening for a telltale sound. I try to calm myself, depress my beating heart. I know I distinctly heard that voice. It was right next to me. It wasn't a dream. Oh my God, someone has to be in the room. It has to be that woman...

Turning on the light I grab the letter opener next to the bed and get out. My heart is pounding, every part of me filled with dread, seconds turn into minutes that drag into eons as I force myself to walk from room to room and look in every potential hiding place – sometimes twice. But the apartment is empty.

Crawling back into bed I prop the pillows against the headboard and lean against them. Closing my eyes, I try to still my racing heart and convince myself this is a dream and I can't fall victim to paranoia, I resist my own advice. My emotions fight with my intellect, turning the struggle into a physical rollercoaster going on in my body. It almost makes me want to vomit. The voice seemed so real. Hearing it in my own room, my own bed, my apartment where everything is so familiar. How could it be an illusion? Or is it a delusion manufactured by an outside force?

If only I had someone to talk to. I don't want to risk another argument with Tim about something that seems unreal.

Reaching for the land phone I punch in the Santa Monica police department number.

"Detective James Parker please,"

"He's not here."

"Can you find him for me?"

"Who is this?"

"Jenny Webster, THE LOS ANGELES NEWS. I talked to him a few hours ago. I have information for him."

I can hear paper rustling in the background. The noise makes me nervous. "Look, never mind. Please leave word I called. I'll speak to him in the morning."

The sergeant's voice changes. "Jenny Webster, right? LOS ANGELES NEWS?"

"Yes."

"All right, he'll get the message."

"Thank you." I put the phone down.

The shrill ring of the phone makes my head snap up. It's light outside. I had fallen asleep and my neck is stiff.

"Hello?" I'm breathless.

"Ms. Webster. Detective Parker here. I hope I'm not calling too early. I received your message and wanted to get to you. The desk sergeant should have called me right away."

"It's okay I told him not to." My voice sounds deep and low. "Something terrible happened to me just before Mannie died and there might be a link. I want to tell you about it."

"Can you tell me now?"

"I'm afraid to use the phone. It might be tapped or there might be hidden cameras – I don't know. I'm afraid and I think I can trust you." My voice cracked. I try to hide my uncontrollable emotion.

Parker scribbled a note to himself. "You can."

"Thank you," I said.

The doorbell rang. "There's someone at the door. I'll get back to you."

"Do you want me to wait?" he asks.

"No, it's probably a neighbor." I hang up and pull myself out of bed. "Who is it?"

"Elaine Jefferson. Tim told you I was coming."

I went to the door and looked out through the peephole. A tall muscular woman, her head elongated by the lens, stood at attention, her hand grasping the strap of a large tan shoulder bag. With trepidation I open the door and let in six feet of bristling authority. Although no more than 125 pounds, she was hard, muscled and ready to fight.

Elaine put her large bag next to the desk, filling the room with her presence. As I watch silently, she slowly unbuttons the jacket of her corduroy pant suit, takes it off and folds it fastidiously over the back of the desk chair. Her dark panther-like eyes hold me spellbound, making me feel fragile in the face of this raw power.

"Tim's worried about you. He thinks I should give you a sedative."

"That's ridiculous. First, I just woke up and you haven't even talked to me for two minutes. And Tim knows I don't take sleeping pills or tranquilizers."

My anger took control. I don't like this woman. Don't want her here.

Elaine found the single hard chair in the living room and drew it up to face me. "Do you feel guilty," she asks.

I stiffen and stare at the woman, shocked at her question. "What? Why would you ask that?"

"Sometimes that happens after a rape. I'll stay with you till you recover from the shock."

How does she know about it? Had I told Tim? My head spins. I can't remember! Shivering I push myself off the sofa. I'm stiff and everything hurts.

Elaine watches me like a hawk as I walk toward my bedroom. "Thank you for coming, but you can leave now. I don't need you. I have to get ready for an appointment."

"Go right ahead - if you can."

My head snaps up. Exhaustion vanished. "What did you say?""

"I thought you might be too tired," soothed Elaine. She looks at me questioningly.

Intuitively my fingers stretch rigidly from my body —a cornered animal in a defensive stance.

Elaine walks over to the mantelpiece and examines the small Rodin bust of Tolstoy.

I don't want to leave this woman in the living room when I go in to dress. "Why are you here," I ask again.

"I told you, Tim thinks you need protection."

"I don't."

She shrugged. "Tim's orders."

"Tim does not give me orders. And I especially don't accept them through you."

Elaine turns from the sculpture and walks toward me. I feel paralyzed as she slinks stealthily toward me. The skin on the back of my neck ripples unpleasantly. This woman reminds me of the blind man in the restaurant. Panic is stirring – they're going to kill me. Tim is involved.

"I want you to know you're safe," Elaine is saying.

I fight for control.

Elaine watches passively, studying me as she formulates an impression. "I'm trying to be sensitive Jenny, believe me. Don't be paranoid. We don't want to hurt you. Rape is insidious. It affects you more than you realize. You won't know who to trust. Like now, you don't trust me."

"That's right."

"There is no reason, correct?"

"Every reason," I answer. But what if the woman is right. There is no specific reason I shouldn't trust her. But something about her is sending warning signals. Is it because Tim sent her, an extension of my paranoia, my distrust of him? When he returns I'll tell him what I'm feeling. If he becomes angry and defensive, then maybe I'm right. But if he shows understanding, maybe it will help to bring us closer again.

"Tim thinks you're in danger." Elaine's face is set hard. "He sent me to protect you," she repeated. "I can and I will."

I tighten with anger. "You say you come to help yet you're doing the opposite. Everything you say feels combative and makes me defensive. I don't want to feel that way now. I want to heal and I can only do that if you leave me alone."

My eyelids are growing heavy, the woman's black leopard eyes drift into pools of infinity. "You're one of them, aren't you?" I think I slurred, but I'm not sure. Everything is drifting.

Elaine comes over and picks up my wrist to take my pulse. I try to pull it away, but can't.

"I want to help you, Jenny," she croons. "You're not thinking clearly. You're refusing help and being self-destructive, punishing yourself for something that is not your fault."

She smoothes my hair. Chills go down my back and I pull away.

"You're creating a situation that will make you entirely alone, distancing yourself with anger and self-pity. I want to save you from that." Elaine's voice is chanting, hypnotic. "Give up your anger and distrust of me."

I feel a surge of energy as I try to deny what Elaine is saying. But the most I can do is shake my head weakly.

"I'll make you tea."

Making it to the chair just inside my bedroom door I slump into it.

Elaine follows me in. "Is something wrong?"

"Headache," I slur. Migraine.

"Nauseous too, I bet." She takes my pulse. "It's shock. You better lie down."

"Can't. Pinwheels of fire are turning in my head. "

"Sit still, flow with it," suggested the nurse. "I'll give you something to help with the pain."

I heard her rummaging through her bag and feel the cold pre-moistened cotton square alcohol rubbed on my arm. I have no strength to protest as the sharp tip of a disposable needle pierces my sanitized skin.

"Flow with it," croons Elaine, withdrawing the needle and patting my shoulders and neck. "Stay cool," she murmured in a singsong way, "You're stressed."

I lowered my burning head to my hands. The rest of my body starts to feel numb and begins to disappear. "Help," I call out as the fiery pinwheels continue to spin crazily, drawing me deeper and deeper into them as I lost contact with the rest of my body.

Elaine rubs my back and neck, working her way down my arms.

"Don't touch me," I slur.

"I'm here to take care of you." Elaine croons.

The sounds of our words fly into space as I become aware of my breathing. Momentum building I fly off to the right. My eyes open. A bright electric light pulsates, daring me to turn it off. I shudder. The light is so real.

The bedroom door is open. I see a form on the couch, Elaine, sleeping. I lean back and stare at the light. It dims as if it is winking.

CHAPTER TWELVE

Light from the electric bulb fades into daylight as the many layers of urban civilization start to wake up. Children crying, laughing, silverware jingling, garbage cans clanging, a telephone rings, an alarm clock goes off. The cacophony of symphonic morning sounds wakes me up.

I don't remember going to bed, but I can definitely hear the blaring resonances of apartment noise: Reports come through the window saying the air people are breathing is *dangerous*. Sensitive people should stay indoors.

"Should sensitive people ever leave their homes?" I ask the announcer.

Traffic and weather reports surround the rings and beeps of microwave ovens offering up vitamin enriched compounds shaped like muffins and bread.

"It isn't a dream," says a voice.

"What?" Half asleep I push myself up from the pillow.

"IT WASN'T A DREAM," says a louder, more grating voice accompanying Elaine who comes into the room and stands looking down at me. "It wasn't a dream," she repeats. "Your friend was killed and you have to deal with it. I helped you into bed yesterday and you slept through the night. You were saying some very strange things. I thought it best to let you sleep. I thought you wouldn't mind if I used some blankets to stay overnight."

"I notice and I mind."

"Come on," Elaine takes my arm. "Time to deal with life."

"Let go of me. I'll get up on my own." I lay back against the pillows, woozy.

"Sorry." Elaine stood stiffly at the foot of the bed. "Guess I can be a bit controlling."

"Please leave me alone." I toss the bedclothes aside and try to get up. A pain strikes me in the lower part of my neck, traveling upward to envelop my head. Elaine watches for a beat then walks away.

Dizziness and pain makes getting up difficult. I'm weak and need a shower. The bathroom door is closed, the shower running. Elaine is in there. The pain in my head intensifies. I go to the living room and sit down.

Elaine appears to be neutral, but she puts me on edge. I know she's not.

Tim had sent her - that suspicion again. I can't help it, it keeps popping up. Chills run through me. I'm not sure if I'm cold from the breeze coming through the open windows or from fear. Maybe both. Elaine affected me the same way the blind man at the deli had. The blind man! Mannie. I go to the phone.

Detective Parker is on the phone taking notes as Boyle returns from the vending machine, unwrapping a Hostess Twinkie. Parker hangs up, his brow furrowed in concentration as he looks at his notes, unable to ignore Boyle standing over him, the end of a Twinkie in his mouth.

"Eating Twinkies can be dangerous, Sergeant. Remember what happened to Mayor Masconi in San Francisco?"

"Huh? " Boyle asked.

"The Twinkie defense - the guy who shot Mayor Masconi said that eating Twinkies made him do it," Parker explained.

Boyle took another bite out of the cake and licked the crumbs off his fingers. He held what was left out to Parker. "Want to live dangerously?"

"No thanks," Parker tried to hide his revulsion. "I don't want to lose control." His brow furrows again. "I just received a call from Jenny Webster, that reporter from the News who came to the station last night. She told me she was with Sebastiane just before the accident.

Said it couldn't have been a suicide. Sebastiane was upbeat and excited about the baby, only confused as to how it happened. She remembers a blind man at the restaurant who seemed to be eaves dropping. She said he made her feel uneasy, as if he was watching them and not blind at all.

Boyle shook his head, "I don't know. Sounds screwy." He opened a can of orange crush and took a sip.

"It's worth checking out.," said Parker. "She also said that she thought the guy could be a regular at the restaurant. What do you think?"

"Be my guest, said Boyle, stuffing the rest of the Twinkie in his mouth. "See if you can buy me a few packages of these over there. Ask them for a discount. We're protection." He chuckles. "I feel like living on the edge."

The pain in my head is so terrible it's making me sick. I dig my fingers into the sides of my temples. It doesn't help. I take an aspirin, something I rarely do, but this headache is going to be a resistant one that won't respond to herbs.

Parker asked me to come to police headquarters and provide details to a police artist for a composite drawing of the blind man in the restaurant. Feeling a comforting glow after I hang up with him, I become aware of Elaine in the doorway, watching me. I wonder how long she's been there.

"Finished?" The large woman seems to have no problem with staring at me without blinking.

"I want to take a shower."

"Not a bath?"

I'm kicked in the gut with shock. " I think you should leave when I do."

"Do you mind if I put some coffee on?" Elaine is saying.

I do mind, but I don't know if I'm wrong about her or not. Again I'm ignoring my instincts because of manners.

"All right, but," I force the words out of my mouth. "How long do you plan on being here?"

"As long as you need me."

"Then, you can leave. I don't need you."

Elaine looks at me steadily. "I'll talk to Tim."

"So will I."

I go into the bathroom and close the door. I'm shaking. She's intimidating me and I can't let that happen. When I emerge from the bathroom Elaine is sitting on the sofa, sipping coffee, looking very much like that horrible woman who had taken over my house, and my psyche. Why is this running through my life?

"Don't wait for me. I'm leaving," I tell her.

I catch Elaine's smile as I close the door, surrendering my home once again from a weakened position.

"Stringy shoulder length gray hair, kind of dirty looking but not really a vagrant." I'm perched on a high stool next to the police artist, my shoulders stiffening as I recreate an approximation of the blind man as it comes up on the monitor. "His glasses are extremely dark and he had on a black hat and overcoat. The kind of look you can't ignore or forget too easily. Like a sinister doomsday cartoon character."

Shivering with dread a crazy thought creeps through me. It's crazy. The blind man and the rapist are probably 25 years apart and have little in common except an unsettling quality. But they seem the same. I want to tell Parker about the rape but the brutal reality of this police station and Detective Boyle's tough attitude is keeping me quiet. Another person to feel fragile around. Especially now.

Parker lightly touches my elbow. I jump from the touch.

"Would you like coffee?"

"I don't think so. I think I better go home."

He seems surprised. "Don't you want to tell me something about a link..."

Yes I do want to tell him about the rape but I shake my head no.

On my way out I put in a call to Rudnik. I can tell he's lighting a cigarette as he talks to me. "You can't do a first person piece. This is a criminal police case."

"But Al, the segments you're putting out about Mannie are not true. I know that woman better than anyone." I keep pacing, looking for a spot to be comfortable while we talk.

Rudnik sounds annoyed. "Jenny, we are getting our material from police reports and eyewitnesses. We don't care about her education and how nice she was. She killed a lot of innocent people in one of the most gruesome accidents I've seen since I've been at this desk."

"That isn't fair. You're condemning her before you know if it was intentional or an accident. Maybe she was dead before she got in the car. Have you ever considered that? You and everyone else are so anxious to point your finger and accuse. She may not have committed suicide. She may have been murdered. Mannie could have been used as a weapon." I lowered my voice as if it were going to make a difference over a telephone that was probably bugged. "Maybe it was because of my investigation."

"Well then, why not you Brenda Starr? Or did your man with the patch and the black orchids come to your rescue?"

"Maybe he did."

"Forget it. You're not going to write her apology. You're not going to plead her case to the public." He hung up.

The nurse Tim had sent to protect me suddenly took on a different perspective. In the light of day maybe I should appreciate Tim's concern and his attempt to help.

I'm just so exhausted. Too much has happened in such a short time. And seeing the construction of that blind man come to life on the screen was more upsetting than I anticipated. His face is haunting me - the way it had when I first saw him that night at the Deli. What was it about him that was so familiar – like I knew him.

My throat is tightening. I can't think clearly. Everything is blurry. Am I in shock?

Elaine was at my apartment when I got back and I think she had probably been going through my things. The thought is creepy, yet nothing seems out of place. I feel a little woozy and appreciate the glass of orange juice she hands me that I gulp down.

"I'm going out for a while," Elaine says. "I'll check in with you later."

"Don't bother. It won't be necessary. You can take your things because I prefer you don't come back."

"You need me. I left a pot of coffee for you and more orange juice on the counter. I'll be back in a little while. Don't let anyone in."

"I don't drink coffee. " The veins in my neck tighten. I can't breathe. My head is heavy.

Parker wrinkles his nose as the smell of grease blasts through the open doorway of Kaplan's Deli. People coming and going, sitting at tables and the counter, moving with the cadence of familiarity, the motion of routine. When the woman behind the counter finally looks at Parker she likes what she sees. "Sit anywhere you like, handsome," she flirts so obviously and openly it's almost a farce.

"Actually, I'd like to talk to you," Parker says politely.

"Can't you see I'm busy?" flirts the Sixty-something platinum blonde whose thick makeup does n't quite fill in the lines and creases mapping her face.

"This will only take a minute," Parker says, flashing his detective's shield.

The woman's face falls with the tone in her voice. "Just what I need. What do you want?" she asks tersely.

"Does this man come here often?" he asks, holding up the computerized rendering of the blind man.

"I've never seen him in my life."

"Take a closer look."

"I did. I've never seen him."

"Do you have the receipts from this week?" he asks, his voice tightening, his resolve growing.

"No. The accountant has everything. It's all on computer. We don't do anything here except push buttons."

She would have continued but Parker interrupted. "Who else was working two nights ago?" he asks

"I wasn't."

"Okay, then who was?"

She points with her chin to an old counterman behind the deli counter. Then, without turning her head she tilted it to the right toward the large open room. "And Stella, she knows everything.

"Which one is she?" Parker asks, looking at two waitresses sauntering through the tables.

The woman swiveled her head. "She's not here. Must have her day off."

Parker stares at her a moment, starts to say something then changes his mind and goes over to the counterman.

"Yeah, I'm here every night," answers the scarred, tattooed man, his tobacco-stained teeth grinning in an unfriendly smile at the detective. "No one's replaced me in over thirty years - birthdays, Christmas, anniversaries, it doesn't matter. I'm always here. And I don't recognize that man's picture. Not at all."

Parker checks with the two waitresses, but neither remembers seeing a blind man. Dotty did however remember Jenny and Mannie. She told him that Jenny "seemed a little too nervous for her own good."

Parker left the restaurant and traced the route Mannie's car had taken. The debris from the statue of Saint Monica had been cleared, though remnants of yellow police tape trapped in branches fluttere in the wind. It was hard to imagine the devastation that had occurred here just a day before. He started to walk toward the edge of the cliff then stopped and turned away. "Such beauty, such horror," he murmured softly to himself as he went back to his car.

A key turns in the lock. Could it be Tim? My heart is pounding as I wait for the door to open. My overweight, frenzied red headed neighbor Carol wobbles in, dragging her four year old son Davis who clings to the rotund calf of her leg like a pilot fish clings to a whale.

"Hi! Hope I didn't scare you. I used my key because I didn't want to disturb you." She talkes loudly, as if I'm three miles away, the large chunk of gray gum in her mouth teetering toward the front of her teeth as she speaks to me. "Could you do me a favor?" she shouts as if her ears were stuffed.

"It depends," I answer softly, hoping to lower the volume of Carol's voice with my own. It doesn't work.

"Would you mind watching Davis just a few minutes? He has a slight fever and I want to go to the drug store and get him Animal Farm aspirins. They're the only ones he'll take. He likes their commercial, he can sing all the words. Sing them for Jenny, Davis."

The little blond boy stared defiantly at his mother, snot running from his nose and over his pursed and pouting red lips.

Carol hiccupps a giggle. "I forgot. He's sick. He won't entertain when he's sick. It's in his contract." She giggles again. The little boy watches his mother silently.

I feel drawn to the person inside this little boy. He seems so bewildered I can almost feel his mind working. He's very mature for a four year old. I wonder how he'll be affected by his environment as time goes by. What kind of women will he be attracted to? How will they treat him? If I had a mother like Carol and I was a little boy, I might end up hating women.

"I'll put the television set on." Carol shouts and turns it on loud. I can understand why her natural volume is a shout.

I correct the sound. "Carol, I have to leave in an hour. Please hurry." Carol propels Davis close to the TV screen and pushes him down in front of it. There is a scene from a war, a real one, going on. Davis is transfixed.

"Don't you think he'd rather watch cartoons then CNN?" I ask Carol.

Ignoring my question she pauses at the door and asks one herself. "Can I get you anything?"

"A newspaper please."

"Why buy one?" she shouted. "Don't you get them free?"

"I'm not going to the office today."

"Okay", she looks at me like I'm crazy. "Okay." She pauses when she opens the door. "It's easier to watch the news on television. That's why I like you. And you have computers." She slammed the door shut.

Happy music came on. Davis had switched the channel. "Cream, Cream, Candy Cream. The Sweetest Thing You'll Ever Need!" Pink pellets dance on the screen. Davis mouthes the jingle silently; his nose tilted two inches from the screen. I try to pull him back, but he wiggles out of my grasp and moves as close as possible. I start to object but decide against it. Davis is prone to tantrums and I don't want him to start one. He looks like a gnome hunched up on the floor, a brown terrycloth towel tied over his shoulders like a cape, brown corduroy pants pushed up and pinned under his knees like knickers, and his long straight blonde hair brushing the shoulders of a brown and red striped shirt. It saddened me to see this child so close to the set. I had done a story on the effects of video rays on humans. Close proximity to a screen can result in eye damage. I told Carol to watch the segment. Guess it didn't connect with her.

Davis looks over his shoulder at me and smiles. I smile back, his infectious personality cutting into the darkness of my deep mourning and making me feel better. He doesn't have to be as demanding and as spoiled as he is. He just needs more conscious care.

Coming over to the desk he leans against it and smiles up at me. He's so cute. I pat his hand. He puts up his arms to hug me and I immediately think of his running nose and all the germs he has and pull away and hand him a tissue. "Wipe your nose." He tears the tissue in half and drops it on the floor. Another loss for my team. He's leading two to zero.

Moving in closer he leans over the arm of my chair.

"What are you doing?" he asks wide-eyed and adorable. I'll tell you if you let me wipe your nose." To my surprise he's docile as I try to clean his nose as much as possible.

"Good boy. You have to learn to do that for yourself."

"What are you doing?" he asks again.

"Going to start writing."

I look at the keyboard, but my fingers refuse to reach for the *on* switch. Tears fill my eyes. Overcome with grief I don't think I can write.

Davis rests his head on my shoulder so I gather him up and put him on my lap. He grunts happily, reaching around and hugging me. Keeping my head averted and holding my breath so I don't inhale his germs, I awkwardly hug him back. His little arms grip me tighter and nestles his lips next to my shoulder. It's making me uncomfortable but I don't want to hurt his feelings as he's being unlike his usual difficult self and I'm happy for the quiet, forgetting for a moment the kid is probably just sick.

He pushes himself up, his knees resting on my lap, and puts his arms around my neck, kissing me wetly on my face. Dodging the avalanche of wet kisses from the child's juicy full lips, he grows more insistent when I try to turn this into a game by dodging his kisses whipping my head quickly from side to side, to keep away from that heavy wet kiss. But as fast as I move the child manages to touch my face. Holding on more tightly he leans up against me and I try to pull away and pry his hands off my neck. But they're locked tightly like handcuffs. I pull and pull but they won't come apart. Davis' face grows bigger and fuller, his shock of blond hair surrounding pink wet lips and a fat pink tongue. His nose is running and saliva drips and bubbles from his large open mouth.

Wet bubbles slip over an open smile, over small perfect white teeth. His mocking smile meets the scream in my ears as it leaves my throat. "Get away. Get away from me," I yell as my head thrashes back and forth. Caught in his grip my neck can't move as the wet pink tongue comes closer and closer. He is no longer Davis, no longer Carol's little boy. He's a monster, a huge crushing force holding me down, wanting to devour me. He eases up for a moment and pulls back, showing me his face. The face of the child has become the face of the rapist. I scream and push him away. The creature falls to the floor. The child's cries join my own and compete with pounding coming from the door.

I stop screaming, the child does not. A key in the lock opens the door before I get to it. Carol crashes through the room, a crazed buffalo barely hesitating to get her bearings as she rushes to the screaming child kicking the floor in a tantrum. Lines of dark smudges cover the surface of my sleek white table as he pounds against it with mud-caked sneakers. Carol picks him up and hugs him.

"Baby, sweetheart, what's the matter? Why are you crying?" She rocks him. "What is wrong with him?" she growls, glaring and ready to blame.

I lean against the doorframe and feel my blood sugar drop as I shiver, my hands clasped as in prayer. "He wouldn't let go so I..."

"She pushed me," Davis screamed. "She hurt me." His small angry red face looking at me, accusingly.

Carol coos to him, her eyes glaring at me

How could you? He's a baby. Are you crazy?"

I withhold reply. My hands cover my mouth. I watch the mother and child, removed from reality as if they are two-dimensional figures on a life size screen. The painted two dimensional living room set appears behind them, bright light flooding the scene coming from the yellow bulb of an artificial sun. Except I can't hear the player's words. The frizzy haired woman called Carol is moving her lips and grimacing her face as she smooths the head of the two dimensional little boy whose mouth is still open, catching bits of the tears streaming down his face. Yet I hear nothing from these cardboard cutouts.

I do feel the cold air however when the two figures — the mother with the child in her arms, rush past me and slam the door shut. The blinds quiver as I watch in slow motion a lithograph of Jean de Ark fall to the floor.

A glint of metal coming from the ceiling behind a heating vent catches my attention. I'll bet it's a camera lens. Someone has been taping me in my own home. I'm being watched. The sound of heavy breathing fills my head. I inch toward the coffee table and pick up a heavy Jade Peruvian head and throw it at the vent. It splinters into pieces of green and white plaster. I don't care it's a fake. Pulling the desk chair over to the wall I climb up and try to reach the vent with a hanger. It isn't long enough. I get down and run to the utility drawer. A game show audience screams as three contestants dressed as babies careen in a fast moving circle and start to slip toward each other. I throw a hammer at the screen as they fall and the screen explodes into thousands of pieces of glass. The laughing stops. I retrieve the hammer from the pile of glass and smash the speakers Tim had just installed. I notice the telephone. That's new and probably bugged too. I send the phone smashing through the remains of the broken television set. An interior pop marks its final demise. Poising in front of the overhead vent, I send an arsenal of household weapons, screwdrivers and awls against the wall, trying to hit the malevolent eye staring down at my travail. Paint cracks and pictures fall as I miss time after time. I finally hit the vent with a wrench but the metal covering doesn't move.

Exhausted and shaken, energy drained, I go to the kitchen where there is a pitcher of juice on the counter next to the sink. I pour a glass and gulp it down. My hands are shaking but I pour another and gulp that too, then another, and still another. I don't stop till the pitcher is finished. I barely make it to my bed before I collapse.

CHAPTER THIRTEEN

Layer upon layer of heavy steel mesh parts as I float from the island of my bed. Furniture and walls disappear as I go through them, their solid reality dissipating into swirls of rotating molecules. I feel no fear as I move free of gravity, free of any of the laws of nature I had known before. I perceive a curtain of white light shielding me from evil. I am protected.

Glancing down I see an elongated body stretched like a grasshopper beside a pool of water, knowing the long green lizard's body had once been mine.

A clear bubble appears behind my left shoulder. I'd never seen anything like it, yet it fills me with such overwhelming peace and happiness I know this is one of the voices that speaks to me.

"Why do you need that body?" it asks me silently.

I look down at the lizard, green as a palm leaf, and know I can't give up the physical, the time isn't right, not enough has been mastered. A warm affectionate connection for the green reptile wells inside. I could never consciously give up my body. The pull of physical experience is too powerful. I need to know more. I start to spin, speeding till I lose awareness.

A split of bright energy tunnels into my brain. My eyes open. A row of bright lights glare directly above me, straps pin my arms to my sides, pressure from a foreign object fills my esophagus. I push against hands that hold my head and see six pairs of eyes, faces hidden by green cloth stare down at me. Directly opposite, between the rows of heads, a plaster statue of Jesus Christ with tortured eyes and splashes of simulated blood on his forehead, hangs suspended on a plastic cross nailed to the wall. Beneath the statue, a round digital clock reads 11, but is it 11 in the morning or 11 at night? I don't know.

The six heads leaning over me obscure any time reference. Day or night in this stark white room there is no difference.

One pair of dark eyes catches my attention. They are panther eyes with an energy their own. Elaine. I acknowledge her. The green head and black eyes nod. A green shirted figure reaches over and puts his fingers down my throat. I gag as the unrelenting rubber coated fingers pull out the tube inside me.

"How you doing Jenny?" the figure asks, preventing any answer. I blink, tears gather. I can see the tube being pulled from my throat, leaving a burning, throbbing sensation behind.

The hard surface I lay on starts to shake. The six heads pull back as the line-up of lights converge behind them. Two aluminum racks holding bottles with plastic tubes running to my arms. They jiggle and sway as we're wheeled down the corridor. The back of my head bouncing from the vibration of rubberized wheels against hard tile floors. Roomless doors whizz past. The green mask I identify as Elaine walks next to me, her strong hand resting heavily on my shoulder to keep me in place. Loud booming voices accompany the journey calling for "Dr. Stone in ER" Red and green lights flash over streaks of colors painted on the sides of the walls. I can't move, tight sheets hold me down. A pulsating ache covers the tops of my hands where needles are inserted and taped to my flesh.

"What happened?" With a hoarse whisper I manage to ask the mask called Elaine as steel walls close us into a rectangular space moving upward.

"You took an overdose."

"I did not." The light hurts my eyes so I turn away. I didn't take an overdose. I wouldn't kill myself. I believe in reincarnation, and for that reason I would never commit suicide. Especially with what I had gone through in my past life. I learned during that totally stressful time that if we can't face up to the problems we have to endure and take our own life, then we have to come back and do it all over again.

Elaine takes off her mask exposing a face etched with disapproval. She turns her gaze away from me and looks ahead as the wall opens before us.

Wheeled into a tiny green room I sense the mustiness of disease and death. Hands reach under me and move me to a bed. Arms outstretched, connected to the bottles, like a virgin sacrifice for the medicine men.

I can't resist, won't even try. I'm too tired. My heavy lids close. Hands reach out and pull my blanket back, startling me.

"Take it easy. I just want to take the needles out."

Drugged sleepiness swells my thick eyelids. I can barely make out the features of the man, only the fine blonde hair covering his arm. I try to push him away, get him away from me.

"Hey!" he calls out, "take it easy. I'm sorry I'm hurting you but you'll feel better with these needles out of your arm."

"Get away. Don't touch me. Get away." I scream, fighting him with all the strength I have. A needle dangles half pulled from my arm.

Footsteps rush into the room, a blur of white uniforms come closer into focus. A pinching burn jabs my arm. Immediately, once again, gray mesh walls close in around me.

I'm confused. I'm in an airport. How did I get here?

Oh my god, Tim is coming out of the gateway of a red eye flight from Washington DC. He looks exhausted and cranky. Nearly all the passengers around him wear campaign buttons of some sort. They must be coming here for a rally. Tim is disheveled and walking quite a distance behind most of the passengers. This means he most likely was not in first class. He wouldn't like that.

A heavy set man clamps a beefy hand on Tim's shoulder. "Nice talking to you. Kept me from getting too bored all night."

Tim mumbles something without directly looking at the man.

I call to him and try to touch his shoulder, but it's as if I'm invisible. He doesn't respond at all.

I follow him into the men's rest room where he goes to the washbasin and turns on the hot water.

He studies his face in the mirror as I register my own face is not mirrored back at all. A metaphor for my time with Tim.

Tim had been flying around the country with his father to campaign stops and political rallies since he was a little boy His father had never been elected to public office but with his financial and corporate acumen he was a prized adjunct to many politicians' entourages. Jenkins Senior was proud that it had been he who had started young Tim on the campaign trail at an early age. From the day he was born, Tim's father had been determined his son would be President of the United States. It was under the umbrella of that obsession Tim's whole life has been directed.

I remember Tim telling me on our first date that before he was five he had been able to put together a puzzle map of America, and recite all the state capitals. Before he entered first grade, he could write the names of all the Presidents of the United States in their correct order and without a single spelling mistake.

Tim's father had shown me pictures of Tim's tenth birthday celebration in which he attended his first White House dinner. And though I loved Tim, I was always saddened by the fact that his father's obsessive ambition for his son had robbed Tim of creating his own life. I accept the fact that by the time Tim was twenty he believed in his destiny and if I wanted to be his wife, I would have to accept that and be a part of it. But down deep it must affect him that it was never his own choice.

In the last semester of my senior year in High School, I visited Tim at Harvard when he returned from the London School of Economics for his PHD dissertation. It was a politically chaotic time in which the old world order had begun to crumble; the Berlin wall had been torn down precipitating a crumbling of Communism over a vast area of the world. The Soviet Union broke up into separate and sometimes acrimonious divisions while the threat of religious wars, dictatorships, and economic collapse loomed through Asia and the Balkans.

Before it could spread to the West, Tim's father acted with characteristic flair and summoned together a group of friends to discuss the disturbing changes, which threatened the peace and prosperity of the United States.

The men who attended the private meeting held at the California home of a former president, represented the full might of America - a chief executive of one of the world's largest multinational corporations, a media giant, a serving member of the Joint Chiefs of Staff, two Nobel Prize winners, four bankers, and no fewer than six ambassadors. Their deliberations lasted three days; at the end of which their conclusions were so startling that even Tim had been shocked by them. For it was he who, one day would be expected to carry them out. They would make him President to do that.

Tim barely noticed the young soldier who had come out of a stall in the bathroom to wash his hands. The harsh fluorescent lighting painted a ghoulish portrait with dark circles on his cadaverously pale face. Tim was staring into the mirror, thinking about what his father had told him. When I realized I could hear his thoughts, I tried not to listen, but I couldn't help it. There was no place to go. I was stuck to him like an invisible Siamese twin.

Tim smiled at his reflection, thinking that with no sleep and feeling exhausted, he still looked pretty good.

I watched my fiancée's conceit as he studied his profile, thinking he was looking more sincere, more Presidential.

"You have the kind of charisma that cameras love to catch," he told his image in the mirror. "You're a media dream like Robert Redford in *The Candidate*, but for real." He gave himself a dazzling smile in the mirror and checked his profile. "You look more sincere and earnest every day," he assured himself.

The first time we met was at the St. Charles Hunt Club. Tim had just come back from school for Thanksgiving and had joined fellow members of the hunt to go out cubing. Cubing was a way to train young hounds for the hunt by dragging the scent of a dead animal from the back of a four -wheel drive vehicle. The dogs learn to follow a scent and horses will be trained to go through rivers and jump fences.

Tim said he had noticed me immediately, far away from the others while schooling an unruly horse. When the horse refused a jump and started to rear, he saw me react in a way opposite most riders who would have made the horse go in circles to get dizzy then be kicked or spurred to go over the jump.

I had discovered it best to lean forward on the horse's neck and whisper to him. It calms them down.

"I don't know what you said to him, but that was one of the most interesting pieces of riding I've ever seen," Tim said as he rode over to me. I could feel my cheeks get hot and was sure they were bright red with blushing.

"I told him he doesn't have to do what he doesn't want to, that's all."

As our two horses trotted back toward the others Tim could not take his eyes off me. "I can't believe how that horses listens to you."

"He trusts me."

"And I'm captivated by you. Can we have dinner tonight? I think I've found my perfect mate."

The door to the men's room opened and a man dressed in madras trousers and a shirt printed with red lips came in, the sweet smell of after-shave lotion unsuccessfully covering his body odor.

I was starting to feel sick but then heard Tim tell himself that he would go straight to the hospital instead of going home. He wanted to see me.

I could feel the beginning of anger and disappointment taking him over. He was angry with me for not listening, and angry with his political team. They had wanted him to stop me from writing articles about Anson Industries, but I wouldn't listen. Tim had been exasperated by my stubbornness, but the group's reaction had shocked him. Even now, he could hardly believe the harshness of their judgment. This was the woman he was going to marry. They should never have said those things. Especially not in his presence.

As the cab pulled out of the airport, it passed the private area where corporate jets take off and land. It had been here that Tim had boarded his father's plane to take him to Maryland for the special training course. It seemed so long ago, but it had been just six months since he walked through the shady groves of Weeping Willows estate and ate buckets of fresh steamed Maryland Crabs. It was at this retreat and training center that he had learned the elements of a new governing order based on intellectual capacity from a group of eminent scientists, politicians, and thinkers. He had learned of a grand design to wipe out poverty, war, and starvation in the world with a breathtakingly radical solution. The plan hinged on a rigid concept of personal worth, and that was to be programmed at the moment of conception - not in a living womb, but on a scientist's bench. In a Petri dish.

Tim was to be groomed and trained to be one of the leaders entrusted with preserving this vision and keeping it in place

I grew cold. The people who were plotting his career had warned him that I was a danger. They assured him that frightening me off was essential, and he had to trust them to do it right. But he had been shocked when I had told him about the rape. *Even these people wouldn't stoop to that* he tried to make himself believe.

Quietly entering the hospital room Tim tiptoed to my bed and took my hand. I hadn't known he left the cab, I had been totally engrossed in the dream and woke with a start when I felt him touching me. His reality is making me cry. No matter what I fear about him, I still love and need his touch, his energy, the way he makes me feel. I don't think I'll ever lose that.

"It's ok darling, I'm here," he was whispering, holding me by the shoulders. "Are you all right?"

"No." I shake my head. How can I tell him I've been ripped apart and holding on by a thread.

"I'll get you out of here."

"Please," I whisper hoarsely. My throat still sore from the tube that had been there.

"I'll talk to the doctor now." He paused and looked at me. "I knew this story you were chasing would lead to disaster."

"Why?" I stare up at him, tears still streaming, feeling broken inside.

Sharply he drew in his breath and held it a moment. "I don't know."

When he left the room, I got out of bed, forcing my rubbery legs to carry me to the bathroom. Bright sunlight poured through the window. The ritual of washing my face made me feel better. I can concentrate now. Tim seemed calm yet disturbed. Was I being paranoid? Nothing was right anymore. What once was solid and "real" now appeared duplicitous and surreal. Only my dreams and visions have the solidity of reality. Fantasy has become reality, and reality is a mere fantasy.

I give my cheeks a pinch to bring back color. I'm alive. I feel better. Tim is here.

Revitalized, I go back into the room and see a contingent of doctors clustered grimly near my bed. Tim stands off to a side, talking to the eldest and most distinguished of the group. The others, identical in green shirts and pants, stand mutely by, their arms crossed, heads lowered as they listen to the two principal's conversation. They snap to attention as I enter the room. All conversation stops. I walk to the opposite end and sit down, weak but smiling. "Do I get to hear the verdict?"

"If you want to leave, you may. You can be discharged," the elder doctor said, "medically, however I would suggest follow a up. You did a very dangerous thing."

I was hurt by his words. "I didn't try to commit suicide. I didn't take anything! I don't know how it happened! If I wanted to die I would have been successful."

The doctor stared back with no expression. He didn't believe me.

Another doctor handed me the release and showed me where to sign. As I started to put my signature on the document the Doctor faced his group while continuing to talk to me. "If you leave the hospital. we are no longer responsible for anything that might happen."

"Thank you doctor, but you never were." I try to hide my hands so he won't see them shaking and hand the clipboard back to him. Tim walks them to the door, assuring him he will take full responsibility for me.

I start to say something to refute that but bite my lips to stay silent. Now is not the time to defend my individuality. Nor is it the time to ask Tim how the attacker had known such intimate things about me, things only Tim could have known.

He came back smiling.

"Tim, it's possible the fetus survived."

"The fetus?" He froze for a moment, shocked. "Darling! I didn't know!"

No, not me." I feel terrible. He had been genuinely excited and now I would disappoint him. "I'm sorry. I meant Mannie's baby."

"Mannie's baby? She couldn't have been pregnant!" he shouted.

"She was near the end of her fourth month," I pause. The pictures of the accident come back to me. I wish I could dissolve them, never see them again. It was beginning to sink in that my friend Mannie was gone; the one person who always cared about me, the one I knew I could trust. If Tim is betraying me, I now have no one. No true friend, no confidant, no checks no balances. "They may have saved her baby."

"Darling, Mannie was a full blown Lesbian. She wasn't pregnant."

"Yes she was. I don't know who the father is, and she claimed not to know either. I have to find out. I owe this to my friend and possibly her baby. If the fetus is saved, I want to know what happened to it."

"Darling, let's get out of here. You're upset and I don't blame you. I'm very tired. I had a miserable flight."

"I know."

He looked at me strangely but I turned my head so he wouldn't see the tears. I had been kidnapped, beaten and raped, my best friend killed and Tim was complaining about a five-hour plane flight.

He hugged me. "I have a surprise." He ushered me out the door and I followed obediently. "Look." Tim pulled out his cell phone and showed me airline tickets. I look at him, questioning.

The hospital doors open and we walk out. "This afternoon we're flying to Puerto Vallarta, Mexico. When we arrive we grab a taxi to the Bay of Tortugo, rent a boat, a "ponga" to be exact, and race the dolphins down the coast to a private cove where my friend has been kind enough to give us his fully equipped hacienda for as long as we like. I know the place well. I used to spend a lot of time there on school holidays. It's heaven."

I throw my arms around his neck and kiss him. For the first time in many months, he doesn't stiffen. "Perfect!

More than perfect. You always know how to make me feel better."

"I love you."

"I hope so."

He was about to question that when his attention is drawn to my focus on a limousine waiting for them.

"Good touch," I say as I settle gratefully into the plush beige seats of the stretch. "I need this. Much better than that hospital bed! I like your reality better. I love you."

He smiles

"I'm glad."

CHAPTER FOURTEEN

The sparkling salty water massages my body and refreshes my mind. I roll on to my back and stretch out lazily. A huge wave comes up and knocks me over just as I'm getting comfortable. Laughing I swallow some salty water. Figures. Pebbles wash into my bathing suit. My focus is changing. Mexico's primitive nudging of my senses is saving me, it's salvation.

The estate on the private cove is primitive in the sense it has no phone, electricity, or transportation. The only way to reach it is by boat and any extended journeys into the jungle are on foot or riding one of the small burros kept in a large enclosure at the far end of the estate's perimeters.

The entire area is saturated with such palpable peace it embraces and comforts me. Here I can almost turn away from the jolting events still too fresh to be mere memories. Yet the soft tropical energy helps to soften the excruciating physical and emotional pain.

Using powerful strokes to catapult myself out a few yards more, I push my body under the next wave, reverse myself and float back to shore. Coming out of the water I feel the hot sun begin to dry me almost immediately.

Tim is wrapped in the cocoon-like netting of a tightly woven *matrimonial* hammock slung between two large Date Palms. He appears to be sleeping soundly, arms crossed over his chest, a sweet smile spread restfully across his face.

My heart lifts. He looks so peaceful. Tim has needed this rest nearly as much as I did. Is it possible I've been wrong? Has he not been the one to change, and I am?

Mulling over the thought I go into the jungle like bathroom and peel off my wet bathing suit. I don't think I'll light the coconut shells doused with kerosene to heat the water. I opt for a cold shower and the decision is wise. The cold water on my warm skin feels good.

Stepping out of the shower I put a towel around myself, hang my bathing suit out to dry and look around, deciding what to do next. It's still morning and I certainly don't feel like taking a rest. Sunbathing is out of the question, my skin is too fair. I'm reluctant to read because it might break the spell.

Feeling compelled I pick up a piece of paper and a pencil and watch as the pencil begins to move in my hand. Putting down words that become thoughts that look like I've written them, but I haven't.

"You can find things to trigger these feeling in yourself, no matter where you are. The words write.

Use them as symbols. Go find a rock. Some time in the future the memory of where you found it will bring you back here where you are soon to receive important messages.

The writing stops. I fold the paper and put it in my diary along with similar notes and decide to go out and find a rock or some such memento to take home with me. Pulling a long-sleeve gauze shirt over my bare torso, I slip into soft linen drawstring trousers but my sandals are nowhere to be found. I'll have to go barefoot.

Stepping through a wall of heat on to the verandah I stop to look at Tim, but my eyes are immediately drawn to a thin black snake slipping silently through the grass, it's tongue flicking in and out -- searching for scent samples in the air. Stopping at the foot of the hammock in which Tim sleeps, the snake appears to have found the source of its scent and coils its forequarters in preparation for a strike.

Afraid to call to Tim, fearful any sound might cause the snake to strike, I search desperately for someone to help us. But once again at a crucial time in my life there is no one around to help me   Inching my way toward Tim and the snake I hunt for something to throw and scare it away. But the movement startles the snake and it rears even higher, spreading its neck into a threatening hood like a Cobra. But are there Cobras in Mexico? I have no time to think about that. I have to help Tim so I call to him without hesitation.

Lurching up at the sound of my stricken voice Tim immediately sees the object of my alarm.

"Don't move," I call to him as I aim a large rock I can barely hold and heave it underhand like a bowling ball toward the snake. The rock barely misses the hypnotically dangerous creature that hesitates a brief yet timeless moment till its instincts make it slither away into the surrounding foliage.

Heedless of the sharp hot stones cutting my bare feet, I race toward Tim who sits with eyes glaring resentfully.

"Great !" Tim croaks, holding on to the sides of the swaying hammock like a rowboat ready to capsize. "Now we don't know where it's gone."

I'm too shocked to say anything. I thought I had saved his life and now he is angry, unmindful of what I've done.

Swinging his legs over the side of the hammock and gingerly putting his feet on the ground Tim doesn't say another word as he walks swiftly away toward the compound.

Holding back tears I plunge through the jungle not stopping till I'm far into the interior and only then to cool my burning feet in a cool mountain stream running alongside the path. Calming down I survey the vegetation and notice three thatched roof huts nearly hidden in the thick foliage.

"Hola," I call in Spanish. No one answers. Curious, I walk to the nearest hut and peak in. On the dirt floor is a large cooking pot resting on a pile of smoking logs. In the shadows are hammocks strung close to the walls. All is tidy, efficient and primitive.

Sensing something behind me I turn and see two Mexican Indian women sitting in the doorway of another hut. A third is on the rocks nearby. Their cloudy gray eyes hooded from inspection, watch me.

I smile and start to walk toward the single woman, but as soon as I take a step a piece of spiked cactus pierces my toe. The pain is instant. Gasping I fall to the ground, grabbing my foot in pain, surprised to hear a giggle coming from one of the women. Startled I forget my agony and stare as one of the three smiles sweetly and offers me a cup of what appears to be tea.

I shake my head no, but the woman gestures again and points to my foot then gestures to drink.

Reluctantly I pull myself into a sitting position and take a sip of the brew. It's bitter. I start to put it down but the Indian woman gestures emphatically for me to finish. I sip a bit more as the bitterness disappears and is replaced with a flowery sweet taste that coats the bitterness on my tongue.

Waves of loving calmness seem to pour from the old woman and everything dissolves into sweetness as the edges of the craggy faced woman softly blend into beauty. I sit dreamily in front of the woman obediently sipping the tea. For a moment the face of the old woman becomes that of my deceased mother. My frail mother who could not wait for me to come out of a coma, died from grief and lonliness.

A ray of light suddenly flashed through the thatched hut and erased the look and thought of my mother. Instead it burnished the Indian woman's wrinkled skin into a mask of copper.

The walls of the reed hut begin to shimmer and become luminescent pillars impelling me to rise and walk through them into what has become a temple of shimmering gold. In the far distance I hear once again the sound of a giggle.

Tempted to look back I ignore the urge and continue forward, impelled by a force I won't question and can't name.

Reaching a vaulted room that contains only a large crystal in the center, I see the crystal is faceted with triangles and flat surfaces which drew me close to examine it.

"*It's a story keeper,*" says the voice that has come to my thoughts so clearly since the terror of the last few days. It has been the energy of that voice and not so much the things it says that catches my attention and makes me listen. It's a separate knowledge that I know without question is apart from my own.

"If you look carefully you will see the past and the future," the voice is saying as I walk through a luminescent passageway that feels like I had known it before. Overwhelming feelings of purity and love make me vow to myself that I'll never leave this place or question those voices. The forces that are leading me are of the good.

"Look ahead," came a soft command in my head. *"If you look back or down you might get scared. Keep this experience. Don't tighten or turn back."*

I obey joyfully, taking the advice with a full heart. Never had I known such peace and happiness.

Little semi-transparent shapes like butterflies appear and flit around me – lilac and gold, scarlet and blue, green and magenta -- a cacophony of pure visual harmony, a ballet of mind lifting proportions.

I know Earth is beneath me - far behind, and that I had entered the inner resources of space that have been hidden and stored in my mind. Clear light surrounds me, the force of "true life". This is where I really live, really belong. This reality is more real than the vague existence I experience with life on Earth.

My natural power has returned, a power I had given up while living in the gravitational confines of the three-dimensional planet. How could I have forgotten this remarkable world inside myself?

"You don't really have to eat anymore," said the voice within me.

"Why?"

"To quickly reach this place you have to train yourself to take the power from plants and the sun and turn it into your own energy. That's what Buddha did. So do many of the great masters."

"But how do I do it?" I ask.

"Be observant about what you eat. See anything you put into your body as a pure unit of energy. Your instincts will lead you there."

"But what if I forget?" I ask.

"What's to forget?" the voice inside me questioned.

"How do I make sure I'll never lose this knowledge again? How do I hold on to it when I return to Earth?"

"Trust and honor your feelings. Truth will never leave you."

"But how do I do that? I want to know."

"Don't worry. You will be reminded, you will be shown," consoled the voice. *"Trust your instincts, those are your guides. You can call them love,"* said the voice, starting to fade.

I can feel myself slipping, back through the atmosphere to a denser space.

"Love will bring you back here even if you're not aware like you are now."

Warmth covered my heart and I stop sliding backward. The dense air dissipates and everything once again is clear.

"Remember what you know," the voice is saying, *"Use symbols if you need them. But don't get caught in them. They are*

only vehicles. Remain a clear thinker -- keep access to the purity that is your freedom.

You've been here before and always have been. Anything else that happens is just a pit stop toward your complete enlightenment. To stay here takes training. It takes time to get it. That's what this voice is for, to guide and teach you."

"But wait a minute – " I call out in the void. "Can I always trust it?"

"Yes but trust your doubts too. Everything is perfect no matter which way you see it. Good or evil are manifestations to reflect each other. Without evil we wouldn't understand good."

"That's hard to accept," I said, tightening and pulling back from the pure joy I had been feeling.

"Following the good is easier and faster," the voice continued. *"Evil will secede to good. When you equate light with goodness and evil with dark, light has power over darkness and can dispel it. With light, illumination, there are no shadows, there is no dark."*

I'm confused I tell myself.

"Sometimes you must be pushed to the limits, taken to the darkest areas of consciousness and tested so these truths of the universe can affect you."

"Please...! No more testing!" But I could feel myself tilting and plummeting back to Earth.

Bells and wind chimes tinkled in the breeze filling the air with brightness and sweet sounds as I rush along the hot jungle path, unaware of the heat or sharp stones beneath my bare feet. I'm worried Tim is waiting for me and I feel a little scared.

He had left me angry and now would be doubly annoyed because I'm probably late. Actually I have no idea how much time has passed --it could have been five minutes, three hours, six days. Time is meaningless in light of the momentous experience I just had.

It's been a rebirth of sorts, a clearing of my cerebral veils. It's most definitely an epiphany in which truths are revealed. Whatever I call it when I tell Tim about it, I'll explain that it's the birth place of my future thoughts and beliefs. My perception of reality will never be the same.

The path curved and the rooftops of the main house come up through the jungle, a man - made oasis in the ancient, lush foliage. Troubled I pause. Had the brew the Indian woman gave me put me into an altered state so I only fantasized what I thought existed? Or am I being tested with doubts to refute what I had seen and experienced?

I would have to deny my own feelings, my happiness and bonding with positive energy. I cringe at the negative thoughts in my head.

I have begun to perceive reality in a new and different way and Tim will be a test, a trigger point because my emotions are so caught up with him. I love him and I've trusted him till now.

But the thought of confiding in him and telling him what I found gives me strong misgivings. This is the second time I decide not to share my experiences with Tim and because I don't trust how he'll react. I don't want to be hurt by him. I don't want to be shaken by him.

If he doesn't believe me and laughs, it will be hurtful and cause an argument. Unease pervades every choice I make.

Turning away from the main house I pace in a circle, my breathing short and labored. Suddenly a gust of wind swirls and envelops me with soft warm energy, reminding me of the new world I have just seen and should be living in now. Tension leaves and positive vitality returns. Mother Nature has taken over and is going to protect me. What I experienced is real and these doubts are the beginning of a whole string of tests. The lesson now is if I stay connected to positive feelings, everything will have an answer, every moment can be an opportunity for a profound life lesson.

I break the circle and quicken my pace toward the house. I can deal with Tim.

Voices are coming from the patio. The few words I make out are English and one of the voices is Tim's, but I don't recognize the others'.

Reaching the clearing I see a man and a woman sitting on the verandah. I can't see who they are because their backs are to me. I hope my hair isn't too messed, I'm suddenly concerned about how I look as I approach them.

In deep conversation Tim continues talking and doesn't acknowledge me as I approach the verandah. The two visitors shift in their chairs and turn toward me.

I nearly sink to my knees. It feels like a bowling ball hit me in the chest. The man is small and thin, almost frail. He has a clean-shaven, bullet-shaped head, small round glasses with tinted lenses clipped on to the frame. He looks like a nerd.

But it's the woman who takes my breath away. I'm not sure they heard me gasp but I did stop dead in my tracks. Her hand with its long red nails posed on the verandah rail is tapping in a taunting way. She meets my eyes with triumph.

Dark hair pulled severely back and tied at the nape of her neck, there no mistaking the pale oval face, nearly luminescent in the fading evening light. Nor is it possible to mistake the reed thin body and those cruel red lips. The long manicured nails are a solid give away as is her arrogant stance, the way she leans slightly back from the hips, the disdain as she twirls the wine glass.

It is the woman who tortured me.

For an endless second my eyes lock with my tormentor. Then she smiles brightly as if she has never seen me before.

"It's a test..." The words chime in my ears, swirl around my head.

Tim's body moves slowly and a little lazily as he rises to greet me, a welcoming smile painted on his handsome face. His eyes are not smiling and his lips are tight.

My breath is caught in my chest. I hear the jungle insects buzzing loudly –like drills, filling my head.

A large white motorboat bobs in the cove off the beach, flying the Mexican flag. I want to run away and almost trip when Tim takes my hand and pulls me gently toward him.

"Darling, we were concerned about you."

He wasn't. She had heard this insincere *sincere* tone hundreds of times before.

"Jenny," he continues with a smooth silicone coated voice. "I'd like you to meet Doctors Jan and Felix White."

Blood rushes to my head and stays there pounding. I can scarcely breathe. Tim's phony voice continues. "The Whites are old family friends."

All I can hear is *family* and *friends*. I don't believe anything he says. He's acting and he's a bad actor.

"They have a lovely vacation home just a few miles beyond that point." He waved his hand in the direction of the North where the shoreline juts out.

The woman called Dr. Jan White watches me steadily, breathing through her mouth. She flicks her tongue to wet her dry lips, her head stationary, scarcely breathing, her back rigid.

"Excuse me," my voice found itself. "Tim, I'd like to talk to you." I turn and walk back toward the jungle.

Tim excuses himself and suggests the guests have another drink.

I try to breathe, praying the lightness in my head will not make me faint. I stop at a large palm tree; its trunk bent and leaning low to the ground so I can sit on it. Tim approaches me.

"What's wrong?" he squats next to me and takes my hand.

I hold the tree firmly as the ground seems to sway. "Are those really your friends?" I try hard to sound in control.

"Yes," His face a portrait of innocence. "Why?"

Tears refuse to stay contained and pour down my face. Everything is tight and burning then I explode. "Do you know who that woman is?"

"Of course I do," he looks impatient, "Jan White. I told you, we're old friends."

"Family doctors?"

Tim chuckles, his look of innocence intact. "Not really darling, Jan and Felix White are psychiatrists." He squeezes my hand.

I pull my hand away from his. It turned oily and repugnant, the stark implication teeming through me.

"M y father would send an employee to the Whites' clinic if they needed psychological help. But our relationship has always been personal and social."

"*Clinic.*" I repeat. The woman's cool, assertive approach suddenly makes sense.

"I knew they were going to be in Mexico the same time we were," Tim continued, "considering what you have just been through I thought it would be good for you to meet them. So I invited them to dinner." He stood up and put out his hand to help me stand.

I stay rooted to the trunk. "Tim," I have to stop, I'm afraid to say it.

"Yes?" Tim's eyes have a cold gleam, chilling, as they anticipate my words will be negative.

I force myself to continue. "She was the one in my apartment."

"That's ridiculous," Tim said coldly.

"It's the truth." My voice sounds very high to my ears.

"Impossible." He searches my face. He appears to be genuinely surprised and concerned or he's a better actor than I thought.

"It's not. I could never forget her. I wish it was a mistake. But I know that's her..." I take a quick breath and turn away. I can't continue. Hot tears are flowing down my cheeks.

Tim reaches down and takes my hand and kisses it. "Darling you've made a mistake," he gently pulls me to my feet and brushes away my tears. "You're in a highly charged emotional state. That's why I was so happy to learn the Whites would be here to meet you. Elaine told me how damaged you've been and I think it would be good for you to talk to them. They could be very helpful."

I stare at Tim in disbelief. How could he be saying this? Is he involved or so completely naïve he's dumb?

"Look, " Tim when on, "I realize that Jan has a classic look and can be mistaken for someone else. In fact, I've seen it happen to her time and time again. It's an easy mistake darling, especially now." He hugged me and patted me on the back like a child. "Don't worry, I'll say something to them to smooth this over. But hurry, we mustn't keep them waiting any longer."

"I'm not going near her." I pull away.

Tim's mouth draws into a thin hard line. "Darling you can't stay in the jungle all night. It's too dangerous. Really, pull yourself together and stop this now."

"Tim?" I'm afraid to go on.

"Yes?" He's brushing leaves and sand off his trousers and palms as he waits for me to speak. Checking in the direction of the compound he seems satisfied his guests are all right. "Please Jenny, pull yourself together. You're embarrassing me as well as yourself."

"Tim, I wonder..."

"Yes, come on darling, out with it, our guests are waiting."

His indifference is crushing. Who is this man I thought I loved? What is he made of? I look in the sky for a moment and think I see a blue butterfly. Instantly all the beings come back to me and I feel a new power.

"Tim," I hear my voice saying, "I don't know if you're involved, but that woman is. She raped me and almost killed me. I don't make mistakes about something like that."

"Now I'm involved! Was I in the apartment as well?" His face is angry, his voice harsh. "Did I rape you too?"

"His words hit me like a physical blow. I hadn't known he could be so cruel. Crushed, in an instant, I realize I'm on my own. Tim will not help me. He's defending my assailant. He'll cut the chord to hang me.

I turn away. "Go ahead, I'll be there in a moment."

Tim walks away.

I lean against the Palm tree. There is no way I can get off this island alone. And even if I had access to a phone, who would I call? How could I direct them to where I am? I have no idea, hadn't paid attention. I'll have to get through this by remaining observant and emotionally still. If I appear weak, they'll tear me apart and destroy me.

Slowly I walk back toward the compound. I've beaten this woman once and I'll do it again.

"Jenny," says the woman with the same polite and professional voice, the same cool sophistication and demeanor as I step on to the verandah. "We understand you've mistaken me for someone else. I'm terribly sorry," she smiles sympathetically. "We know about your recent misfortune. Tim did tell you we're doctors in the psychiatric sciences, didn't he? I don't know if this will allay your fears at all, but we're not villains, quite the opposite, we'd like to help." She smiles sweetly. Her eyes glitter.

Chills run up my back, reach around and choke me. Tim's head is turned away. I do my best to stay calm, but my heart is pounding. There is no escape.

"If I had known you were coming, I would have been better prepared," came forth from my mouth.

"Darling," Tim dripping tones of charm, "would you like a drink?"

My mouth is very dry. "Please. Juice and mineral water."

"Why don't you have something stronger, more hospitable to make amends for this embarrassing mistake?"

"It's not a mistake," I turn to a maid holding a tray with Margaritas. "Una sin tequila."

"Ah," said Jan White. "You're cheating. No tequila."

I nod, my mouth unable to smile.

"Tim has told us quite a bit about you," Jan continues conversationally.

"Really?" I disciplined myself not to say anything more.

The woman maintained her polite smile and adjusted the dark glasses on the bridge of her nose. "We have been hearing about your latest series of articles."

"The ones Tim disapproves of?" I ask sweetly.

Jan ignores the sarcasm. "He's quite proud of you," she turns to Tim who smiles back over his glass.

"I'm glad," I watch Tim with the woman. He never discusses my work with others unless it's already published or broadcast. Especially a work in progress. This was a lie .He's smilingv. He has chosen sides. The dinner bell breaks the tension and everyone gets up quickly.

I don't want to eat. The betrayal and absolute horror of my position is worse than anything I've ever experienced. I've never felt more alone. There's something else going on. I have a fearful sense that nothing I'm seeing or feeling is actually real. It makes me feel empty, all alone in the world. There are no voices to advise me, nothing to help me, only myself. Is this graduation? Am I supposed to survive this completely on my own?

Obediently I follow into the large open space that is the dining room. Its thatched roof sends down crisscross rays of light that creates a mosaic pattern over the table and walls. Or maybe a prison wall. Servants stand stiffly behind assigned chairs blending into the pattern. When everyone is seated, trays bearing platters of tacos, enchiladas, chile rellenos and iced pitchers of Sangria, red wine with fresh fruit, are presented.

"Blood," I mutter.

"I beg your pardon?" Jan politely asks.

"Blood. In the pitchers. Sangria. That's what you're drinking."

"Oh. Well, here's to us Vampires!" Jan announces gaily, picking up the glass of wine and clinking her glass with his.

Vampires – and they don't mind announcing it. Hunger begins to gnaw at me. I don't feel hungry, so why is my stomach growling? I had just been shown profound secrets in the jungle, the process of photosynthesis, and had been told by the voice I have the ability to do that. However, the process requires years of practice and discipline. I have to break my years of conditioned feelings. I close my eyes and send a message to my stomach to remember what I had learned. The grumbling subsides.

I look up and the three are watching me. Deciding to ignore them I look at the food on my plate. The melted cheese and beans are overcooked and fairly dead looking. I look for something else, something fresh to eat, but there is nothing - just some limp pieces of chopped lettuce and over-ripe tomatoes.

"Buen provecho," proposes Tim gaily. They dig hungrily into their food, with soft grunts of satisfaction.

I sit quietly, fork in my hand, watching.

Aren't you going to eat?" asks Tim. "It's delicious."

"Is there anything fresh to eat?"

"The blood." Tim chuckles and they all join in then continue to eat.

I just watch them. Like *a stranger in a strange land…*

Think I better cover my strangeness so dig into the fried chili relleno with a fork. The pleasure of good flavor explodes my senses and makes me want to start eating greedily till I become aware of the speed with whichI've finished most everything on my plate. I look around to see if anyone had been watching.

Dr. White had been, but the other two seemed unaware. I push around the remnants, doing it slowly to ascertain the component of energy in each food source I had eaten. Dr. White puts his fork down and watches me. I don't want him to know what I'm doing, but every time I pick my head up, he's looking at me. After the third time I put my fork down, fold my hands under my chin and stare back. He doesn't flinch, like the blind man in the restaurant.

The thought brings tears again. I haven't been at the TV studio or even thought about Mannie since I left the hospital. I had been in a time capsule of my own making.

Dr. White continues to watch me. "What's happening in the world?" I ask to draw his attention away from me.

"It's still revolving," he smiles.

I don't smile back." "Politically, economically. I've been out of touch."

"Still full of the mistakes and misjudgments of our current administration. Do-gooders trying to protect the masses who don't want to do anything."

"Those are harsh words coming from a man who took the Hippocratic oath to serve humanity."

"That's a totally different argument."

I had touched a nerve and he was growing angry.

Tim intervened. "Jenny, we're here to relax and enjoy ourselves. Must you start an argument?"

"I merely asked how the world was doing. It's called discussion, not provocation. I think you're the one provoking an argument." I pierce a taco with my fork and hold it up. "Why don't we just enjoy this nice dead food and I'll be quiet." My head starts spinning and I put the fork down. "Would you please excuse me," I push the chair back.

Tim restrains me with his hand. "Dr. White, Felix, wants to talk to you. He feels you should discuss some of the paranoia you've been having."

"Paranoia?" My voice was shrill, tension and anger exploding very close to a scream. "Why don't you ask your guest about that. She can give you full details."

"Darling, we understand what you've been through, and see you're not ready to accept your mistake, however the paranoia started before that uh, incident. Your last few articles about technology, the diatribes on mind control, the fear of programmed babies.... We aren't the enemy, Jenny. The Whites were kind enough to come here to talk to you. They can help."

"Help? You don't think I can see what you're doing." I explode. "You think I don't understand your innuendo? I'm trapped here on this island till you figure out what to do with me. Don't you think I can see this?"

"No, I think you're not understanding. All we want to do is communicate with you, and you're setting up barriers," Dr. White said softly.

"As you evaluate your laboratory specimen. Don't think they won't do this to you Tim, as soon as you veer off their party plan."

"That isn't true, Jenny," Jan was using her soothing doctor's voice.

I push my chair back. "None of you want to talk to me. You're here to decide what to do with me. The selection team."

"Jenny," said Dr. White, his face bright red, there is no selection going on. We're here to see if there is anything we can do to help you make this transition easier. That's the extent of any kind of conspiracy you may think we have planned."

"Sure ." I push my chair back further and stand up.

Tim comes up behind me, trapping me in his arms with a hug. "Let's go sit on the verandah and have coffee."

I allow him to lead me to the stone patio overlooking the ocean. A silent servant brings a tray of coffee and cognac and hands each one a separate smaller tray of sugar and cream and a nearly transparent slice of lemon.

White clears his throat when the servant leaves, rubbing his hands together like a praying mantis. "It seems you've been having some difficulties lately."

"Yes, because of the present company. But surmounting difficulties till a comfortable space can be created is called life. Like school, we live to receive problems that will be solved in order to learn. Then we pass the answers and guidelines to help others. I think I may have taught Jan something. Isn't that right?"

Jan smiles without responding.

White lights his pipe. "You've certainly had your share of problems in your work lately."

"Not really." My head is reeling. What was his implied threat now?

"Weren't you given some warnings?"

I wanted to leave, his impertinence was upsetting. "I don't know what you're talking about. But I do know you're making me uncomfortable. If you'll excuse me..." I push myself out of the low slung canvas chair, spilling the coffee, shaking with indignation, and leave with as much dignity as possible.

The reed walls of my room had no real doors or windows. I sit in the middle of the bed and draw the mosquito netting around myself. Tim had not followed me. He cares more about the Whites than me

I lay back, my heart beating. I can feel all the heavy food I had just eaten weighing me down. I focus on a thumping in my chest. It grew louder as it took over my whole body. The thumping vibrations lift me off the bed. I can feel herself flying. I know I better not look down as I might be afraid. I know I'm being taken care of.

White veils flap gently around me as I fly through them. They stretch and I sense they're very much like my bed's mosquito netting. I must be hallucinating, I tell myself. The clouds aren't clouds and I'm not flying. I'm making it all up.

My body comes down with a thump. I start to get up but feel too weak and lay back again.

I sense someone in the room and turn to look. The curtains on the bed are drawn back and Tim and the Whites are talking.

"Because of the rape, her vulnerability has degenerated to the point where she is most highly suggestible," said Jan.

Tim looked sickly but didn't say a word.

Jan continued. "Our next phase is to implant organizational ideals and philosophies in every area of her consciousness and sub-conscious till she is able to use her own sources of creativity to convey what we have put there scientifically."

White films of clouds begin to envelop me as dark clouds roll in from the West. Gray green in color, they tumble over each other obscuring my vision from the clear white light. I try to will them away and bring back the whiteness but the clouds persist.

"What am I doing wrong?" I hear myself ask.

"*You're blocking,*" said the familiar voice.

"What?"

"*Your energy flow. Take a deep breath and let it all go.*"

My body is pulsating tensely so I do what I'm told. My muscles loosen and I'm sure I can feel my blood flowing.

I open my eyes. It's almost completely dark. An owl hoots loudly. I go to the doorway. There is a rustling in the palms - the old Indian woman is beckoning to me. Unmindful of the sharp stickers reaching out to prick me, I follow her to a cliff overlooking the sea. The old lady steps aside and points to a round raised stone in the center of the water. Waves lap at the bottom of the cliff, slapping against huge boulders. I look around. The cliff is bordered by very deep jungle. The old woman has vanished.

The huge bowl of bright stars encircle me and twinkle invitingly. The captivating brilliance of the white slash of the Milky Way is trying to envelop me. Orion's star blinks brightly. Saying hello? The Milky Way gets whiter and closer, sending out a pathway of light. I step on to it without hesitation, knowing the light is the path that supports me.

I walk through a tunnel of that light, powerful energy surging through me, no longer able to tell where my body begins or where the light leaves off. All is merged with feelings of exaltation, a honeycomb of pulsating light opening and growing within me.

Whispered commands in the back of my head tell me to get off the light beam and direct me toward another. I strip off my clothes and stand perfectly still. Legs part, my body arched, I begin to float upward.

Jets of bright lights shoot through me, up through my vagina, up my spinal cord and out through the top of my head. Once, twice the energy shoots through me. I feel cleansed, purified, satisfied like I had never been. Vibrating with good feelings I never want it to end. I spread my legs wider and open my arms. I still float but now I'm shrinking into a corpuscle that surges through my own bloodstream. Everything is red, burgundy, and plush red. I can actually feel it. Its soft and fuzzy, almost makes my palms itch. I turn to the right. A porthole reveals a blue sky outside an orange and red paisley print frame. Clouds are floating by but I'm not a part of them. There is a restraining strap across my lap, the warmth of humans close by and a strong motorized vibration. I look to my right. Tim sits next to me. We're on a plane.

I touch Tim's arm, terror stricken. "What are we doing here? I don't remember. How did we get here?"

He patted my hand gently. "We'll be there in a little while. Don't worry, you'll be well taken care of." He turned his attention back to the book he's reading.

What did he mean? I don't remember getting on the plane. Just the old woman and the sky and the incredible sensation. I try to think harder. Recreate what logically could have happened. But I'm on an airplane and Tim is sitting next to me.

"So soon?" I asked silently. "Why so soon?"

"*Because we have to*," I heard in my mind. I can feel Tim's impatience. I look at him. He doesn't seem impatient now. Maybe the impatience is a memory, a late impression or even a fantasy, a self-delusion. One only I remember. I close my eyes, buzzing taking me deep into dreaming.

CHAPTER FIFTEEN

The back of the seat jerks forward, seatbelts snap into place, passenger noise levels decrease as the plane banks into a turn and starts its descent.

Tim leans over and checks my seat belt then pats my hand. "Have a good nap?"

Looking at his hand on mine I wonder why he has made such an intimate gesture. Does he really care? I have no easy answer.

Watching the approaching landscape outside the window I know for a fact I hadn't been dreaming but rather in a suspended state of flat nothingness. Dreading the need to test Tim but unable to hold back I ask how long we'd been on the plane.

"About six hours."

"How long have I been sleeping?" I ask, trying to calculate the amount of time between the last times I had been with Tim at the house with the Whites.

"Practically since you got on the plane. You've been exhausted darling. And no wonder. After what you've been through..."

He turned back to his book.

"What are you reading?" I asked, fishing for something that would make me understand this man that I still loved, just a little. How I wanted to trust him. How much I had loved him when it had been without stress. The beginnings of our relationship, the attraction then the trusting as we opened ourselves up to the other both mentally and most certainly physically. It had just been so perfect I thought it would last forever. It was so much more real than the time I had barely survived the nightmare of my first marriage. And now, this horrible self-doubt, this constant monitoring has come back just as it had the first time. The feeling that an energy has changed, he no longer looks into me but barely – thinking I'm not worth the time.

TIME! If only I could turn back time and go to the place where we once had been.

Tim smiled brightly and picked up the book. "It's a riveting biography on Roosevelt. The writer shows how Roosevelt was one of the first mass media manipulators and understood the necessity of garnering the masses. He was an expert in understanding group consciousness and knowing how to use it. His fireside radio chats with the population to make those left behind during the war feel cozy and safe with his persona. They were produced with the reality of a sharp and penetrating intellect."

"You love the power of manipulating millions of people, don't you?" I ask.

"I wouldn't call it manipulation. I rather see it as having been privileged in my own right and being able to pass on a consciousness and sensibility to the masses."

"Through restrictions and pre-planned boxed existences?" I ask. "Programmed lifestyles that will not cut into the freedom enjoyed by those who make those rules – the ruling class?"

"I see where you're taking this Jenny and you're wrong. Roosevelt's political decisions, platforms and actions were for the people. But sometimes the public doesn't know what's good for them and the image of an elderly scholar confined to a wheelchair is a comfort that precipitates support. "

"You're talking manipulation – good or bad. I have a problem with that. I also have a problem with knowing where we are and how long we've been here. I'm very disoriented."

He didn't answer but smiled. When I didn't return the smile his smile morphed into a look of concern across his face. "We discussed White's interesting therapy and we thought it would be useful," he said.

"We never discussed anything like that. It didn't happen." I watched him carefully. He was lying. I had been super conscious all the time I had been close to the Whites. Jan White was extremely dangerous and if I had let down for a second that woman would scoop me up and swallow me for eternity.

Tim's concern stayed painted on. "You don't remember our talk?" His words were clothed in the tone of a statement not a question.

I watched him carefully. He was a good actor, but what if he did mean it? I don't remember anything like that. "It didn't happen." I unbuckled the seat belt, to get away, to think clearly, away from Tim.

The loud speaker is advising the flight attendants to go to their seats. Tim holds my arm. "Please darling. We're going to land. You can get hurt."

"I already am." The bottom has dropped out. I want to trust him, keep the tatters of our love intact, but now I have to be duplicitous. I can no longer tell him the truth. I will go to the sanitarium and discover what is going on. It's an undercover assignment from the gods for an intrepid investigative reporter.

The plane bumps down on the landing, the engines rev to stop. Waiting for the other passengers to deplane, with Tim's firm hand on my elbow, we make our way through the customs area. Leading me to a bench he motions me to sit. "Stay here, I'm going to get you some water."

'He was probably going to put something in it," I thought, making a note not to drink anything unless I poured it myself.

I was in an interesting situation and glad I made the decision to stay in charge and use these circumstances purposefully instead of fighting them. This is a big story. The conspiracy I've uncovered is all-encompassing and I would have to play it by their rules to get to the core. to identify those in charge and expose their personal and public ideals. I really don't know what else to do.

Like the others who seem to be players in this mass manipulation, Tim has everything; money, backers with power, a photogenic quality that handsomely oozes a built in prestige.

I wish I could go through immigration now so I can get to a pay phone and call Rudnik. But Tim is holding my passport and phone, even my driver's license. And to be honest, I don't want to leave . Maybe he's still the man I had thought he was and I can trust and love him. Maybe I'm wrong.

I had featured so many aspects of abused women in my TV segments: prisoners invisibly chained in invisible prisons. And now, the Whites and possibly Tim believe I'm that helpless person in a hopeless state, chained by an invisible leash of violence and pain wrapped with the fear it could happen again.

They have no idea how powerful my independent state of mind is. How objectively I can watch and perceive things while seemingly in the throes of complicated emotional factors. I will never be fastened by an invisible collar of fear that will make me close my eyes to my abilities and condition. I know nothing about the place I'm going to other then it's run by a sadistic woman who lost the first round with me. Now I'll be in her private fort with a retinue of biological and emotional aids to control me.

Yet I know in my heart that no matter what this woman tries to do to me, short of murdering me, it won't affect me. I have built an impervious stainless invisible wall from her last attempts to break me. I'm hopefully, a seasoned survivor.

Tim comes back with a paper cup of water and a pill.

"Take this, you'll feel better."

I drink the water but palm the pill and surreptitiously put it in my pocket. It might be useful sometime.

The arrivals area appears to be nearly empty and Tim helps me up. I allow him to take me but feel uneasy. The hospital is waiting. Am I up to the task I set out for myself? I can't help feeling scared.

"There isn't anything to say," came that voice in my head. *"You know what's happening."*

I shook my head to protest.

"What's wrong darling?"

Tim is watching, waiting for a slip up, something, to justify his having me locked away,

"Nothing," I smile, glad I kept my tinted glasses on. He can read whatever he justifies with my words, but I don't want him to see what's going on in my eyes. Eyes don't lie.

The voice continued talking. "*Everything you see and experience, outside yourself, is set up for your learning. It's all a lesson. It's Yoga, being in the present. Your personal world is a reflection of all you've learned. You'll learn from th*is *and get your story.*"

"Thank you," I told my own thoughts.

Our bags were some of the few left in baggage claim. The customs inspector barely looked at us. What would happened to Tim's plan if I told the inspector Tim was kidnapping me and taking me to a mental hospital? But would he believe me? The words "crazy" or "insane" are the most difficult labels to remove. People back away from one who is branded crazy. It's a layer, a stigma, that rarely if ever goes away. I better not say anything.

Tim leads me outside. A long gray limousine waits. Upon seeing Tim, a tall lanky body supporting a faceless driver gets out and puts my bag in the trunk.

"Are you coming with me?" I ask, knowing the answer before he replies.

"Sorry darling, I can't. I've got to get back to work. The election is coming up. I hope you'll be joining me in a few weeks."

"I do too," I answer, impressed with how innocent and sincere he appears to be. Could he not be a part of this conspiracy? Is he being used as a pawn just as they are trying to manipulate me? Can Tim be no higher on the rung then the man Jan White enlisted to rape me? Has he been compromised and forced to aid the devil in her work?

Tim is holding my elbow again as he ushers me into the car. I'm not sure, but I think there is a a glimmer of a tear in his eye. We don't kiss, don't say goodbye. The exit from each other has become a very silent movie.

The interior of the car is dark. The glass was tinted dark gray and there is a solid barrier between the driver and me. I try to open a window. They're locked. An air vent like one on a plane is directly above me and I twist it open. A rush of freshness covers my face.

Flashes of light streak by the window. Red, green, yellow - like the ones in the Indian's hut! Maybe they've come to protect me!

Kurt Vonnegut had written a short story called *READY TO WEAR* in which conscious beings tired of the strife on Earth flee and exist as little blobs of energy in the atmosphere above Earth. Is that what I'm seeing? Did Vonnegut know about the little beings? Had he written about them? Or was he a blob who planted that story so I would unconsciously know and be comforted that we're not alone?

I press my nose tightly against the glass. The outlines of letters are barely visible beyond. I'm seeing neon signs and traffic lights. There are no outer space forces accompanying my journey. I'm picking up things from stories I read and believe them.

Fear starts to take me over. My belief system had been reduced to an inner voice that rationalized everything into passive acceptance. Is it possible to have to live this way in modern society?

I open my carry-on bag and look for my notebook. It's gone. My pens are missing too. Even the book I had taken with me to read. Where is everything?

Betrayal hits like a physical blow. A scream bubbles from the tips of my toes but I manage to hold it back. Did I think I wouldn't be tested? This was just the beginning. I had committed to going through with this and I can't panic and protest with the first sign it's not going to be an easy ride.

Parker slams down the phone.

Boyle saunters over. "Now what's wrong?"

"I can't find Jenny Webster. It's been two weeks since I talked to her. The news office said she's on temporary leave and her boyfriend's office say they're on vacation in Mexico - some place with no phones - no means of communication. I don't know, it doesn't feel right."

"You and your feelings. You need facts, cop. You got to track down leads. Don't worry about that one. Look at the wild goose chase she sent you on to that deli looking for two people who probably don't exist. And no Twinkies on top of it. She's at some spa somewhere getting massaged and pampered to smooth out the edges from having a brush with real life."

Parker flushes, "I don't think she's like that." He's worried about Jenny. Although he had met her only for a short time, there was something about her that is haunting him, keeping her in his mind almost constantly. He accepted some of it was attraction, but there was something else, something more important, a need to protect and shield her from what was happening.

Something felt wrong about this entire Sebastian investigation. When they went to Anson Laboratories to investigate Mannie's employers and co- workers, his partner, Boyle, had been putty in the hands of the company's representatives. Everyone had been polite and helpful - opening Mannie's files and giving them full and complete answers. It was too polite, too polished. When he had mentioned that in the car, Boyle seemed surprised at Parker's "misplaced suspicion". The senior partner said he was satisfied with the investigation and believed that a forensic search warrant for Anson wouldn't be necessary.

"Don't make waves in the wrong places," he advised. Parker wondered why this brusque man was suddenly so accommodating.

"Have we got the chemical results from the autopsy of Mannie Sebastian?"

Boyle shook his head. Not yet. "But we know how she died - hitting cement from a two hundred foot dive."

"What about the preliminary analysis? Was there alcohol or any other substances in her system?"

"No. No alcohol. No cocaine. No sleeping pills. Clean as a whistle."

"What about hallucinogens?"

"Nope."

"You sure?"

Boyle bristled. "I told you already. No coke, grass, heroin, nothing like that. We'll have to wait for the later reports. What was left of her was cremated and packed in a tin and sent back to her family in Brazil. By the way, Detective, this emotional attachment you seem to have for the case is getting a bit hard to handle. You better get your priorities straight. You're a cop. And when you're investigating something like this, there's no room for personal feelings. Get my meaning?"

"No feelings. Yes. What about the fetus?"

"Dead."

I closed my eyes, leaned back and thought about brainwashing. Based on documents supplied by the Freedom of Information Act, I discovered that the CIA had used LSD supplied by the Swiss pharmaceutical company, Sandoz to unsuspecting American pilots after World War II. They were trying to simulate the suicidal mind set of Kamikaze pilots. It hadn't worked. Am I in some way entrapped in some kind of CIA operation? The media is becoming important globally, do they want to use people like me, writers, journalists videographers, filmmakers - all communicators - as they tried with American pilots in the Fifties and early Sixties?

I have to learn if the Technical Services Staff, (TSS), is still intact. T.S.S. was the medical research arm of the CIA. that was founded in 1952, by Allen Dulles, who had been head of the OSS in WWII. After forming the CIA, TSS recruited doctors of all disciplines willing to co-operate in every phase of research, no matter how revolutionary it might seem. This meant human experimentation that could prove to be lethal. One of the experiments was called, "Operation Artichoke". Scientists and doctors found subjects they labeled, "dubious loyalty"; suspected double agents or plants, subjects known for deception - expendables - or otherwise homeless people who ultimately could be terminated. They used electroshock to make the person susceptible to suggestion. Producing amnesia for nonspecific periods of time, they would try to implant ideas into a subject's shocked mind. According to the papers I read, it didn't work. The electroshock caused temporary and sometime permanent brain damage but the implanted ideas didn't stay in place.

I had seen pictures taken during some of the experimentation. There was very little difference from what I had seen in archive Nazi concentration camp films. Had Felix White been in TSS? His age makes it feasible.

According to texts I read, thousands of micrograms of LSD were used by TSS, but no matter how much was used, it wouldn't significantly change human behavior. Contrary to reports they found from Dachau, Mescaline didn't work the way it had been reported either. As far as I had found over fifty years later, there are still scientists and research units funded by government intelligence agencies trying to find a way into peoples' minds. No matter how many experiments they do and how many subjects die from drugs or having their brains burned out with electricity, the answer to how the enemy at the time; North Koreans, Japanese, and Russians, successfully brainwash, has remained elusive.

But now, with EEG expansion and the program Mannie has developed for decoding brain scan impulses, I'm sure that goal is close to being realized. Goose bumps raise on my flesh. I rest my head back on the seat. This reality is getting frightening.

I'll have to find out how many subjects they have with high IQs, extensive education, and independent social skills?

The car turned off the highway and continued through lush green countryside. I feel very vulnerable and scared.

CHAPTER SIXTEEN

Dr. White is in the driveway waiting as the limousine pulls to a stop. His baldhead shining, his eyes glittering in the moonlight. "Hello Jenny, welcome."

"Said the spider to the fly." I don't take his outstretched hand.

"Are you upset?"

My breath caught in surprise at his question. "Of course I am."

"Why should you be?" He feigned astonishment.

"Look where I am."

"Jenny dear," he smiled. "You said you wanted to come. Remember?"

"No. I didn't I'm an unwilling captive here."

"You must be tired. You've been traveling a long time. Come in and rest." He tries to take my arm and I shake it off.

"If you want to leave we'll discuss it in the morning. For the moment just relax and enjoy your time with us."

As we walk across the wide colonial-style verandah, crickets dissolve the pall of silence in the air as a shadow moves from behind a pillar. Jan comes out and takes my arm. A jolt shoots through me and I pull away.

"We're glad you came," Jan said in soft dulcet tones. "How are you feeling?"

"Wouldn't you like to know." I steel my weakening body. I 'm tired, extremely tired. Was it the plane journey or the one in outer space? Could either have happened or have I been dreaming?

Doubts! They're coming back. I hadn't wanted to question anything. I had felt so positive that what I experienced in Mexico really happened. At the time it had not mattered what I should or should not feel. I experienced the power of light energy that exists and I will never forget it.

Yet I must resist fear. It's so insidious and can pop up at any time. The key to my stability will be to keep my objectivity and not react emotionally.

"We have an instruction sheet on your bureau," Jan was saying. We advise our guests to read it."

"Guests?" I let out a sharp involuntary laugh.

Jan unlocks the brown door and steps aside. "Guests," she lilted. "Most people who stay choose because it's best. The life forces of normality as we call *civilization* are suspended here. People are allowed the freedom of discovery, to find themselves and the meaning of their reality. At times we are called upon to enhance that inner freedom."

"Drugs." I cut in. "you dope unsuspecting guinea pigs with drugs that control parts of the brain."

"Inner Freedom Enhancers not drugs. Stop thinking in such a one-dimensional way." Jan says sharply then returns her voice to its melodious crooning. "Our guests return to the urban embattlements we call home or work, or they can stay here indefinitely, for as long as it takes."

"As long as what takes? What is <u>IT</u>?" I see my instincts are right. "And, who pays?" This place is some kind of covert operation. It's not a legitimate hospital or sanitarium. It's a lab, and I'm to be one of the rabbits.

"If you are meant to be here," Jan is saying, "the finances will be found to insure it."

"I'll bet they are." I can't believe Jan expects me to believe that. But she had to be careful. People like her are dangerous as I so well know. I wonder if the covert money used to finance this place is government or private. Government would be easier. If it were the latter it would be more dangerous. Private organizations with this kind of financial power are far more efficient than government sponsored.

"I've done stories on places like this," I lie to throw out a red herring. "How you liquidate assets in return for lifetime care."

"We don't have to operate that way."

"Then who funds you?" I ask with innocence.

Jan ignores the question.

My mouth presses on. it won't stop, It's making me speak. "If it's government, then you're political and therefore lethal. Missionary mentality. Get rid of freedom of thought, individual thinking. Is that what you're doing?"

Jan motioned me toward the bed. "You're excited over nothing. Your finances are taken care of. Tim arranged everything."

"I'll bet he did!" I have to escape from here.

"Don't worry." Jan crooned. "We want the best for you so you can go back into the world and do the work you're meant to do."

"Your work."

"It'll be yours. Your own motivation. We don't implant anything. We give alternatives - alternatives to accept or discard. In the end one person can never control another. You've proven that haven't you? Of course, one can be destroyed, but no one can be completely controlled yet, can they?"

"You don't believe a word you said. You think people can be controlled through physical force and technology. Dissent means death of one kind or another."

"That's your belief." Jan turns away.

"That's what I know. "And what I fear. Shivering I look around. "This homey institutional farce is familiar."

"What is it Jenny?"

"It reminds me of another place. Institutional."

I go to the single bed pushed up against the wall under the mesh- covered windows. With the exception of the mesh, it reminds me of Tim's room at Harvard. I had lost my virginity there. Will I lose another kind of virginity here?

A small carpet of indiscriminate color covers part of the wooden floor. Or is it Tim's floor? I'm so tired. I close my eyes and sit down on the side of the bed. Memories of that first night with Tim begin to take over.

Taking a deep breath I enter the room with Tim, a little nervous when he goes straight to the bed, but the wine from dinner champions a recklessness, convincing me this moment is inevitable.

I'm not sure I would have made the decision to go ahead, but as he kissed me and touched my breast through my soft cashmere sweater my whole body tingled with pleasure. As the kiss grew deeper, he put his hands beneath my sweater, unfastened my bra and touched my newly bared nipples.

I quiver as I remembered the excitement - the churning - a feeling I had never experienced before. It quickly takes over, grinding into me then releasing a dormant energy that fully activates.

I hold my arms up to help him slip my sweater over my head and feel giddy as he unclicks then takes off my bra, letting the palms of his hands slide over my bare breasts, stopping for a moment to squeeze them lightly then follow with his lips to nuzzle and lick the nipples.

My breasts tingle. I run my fingers through his soft blond hair as he bends. Are we going too far?

His lips make me dizzy. They're like an instrument from another new space, playing my body to make my nipples tingle as they grow hard with his touch. I'm crossing a line now and entering a new phase.

His mouth on my bare skin, my body is quivering, I can't control anything, I'm wet between my legs. I can't stop, I'm scared – but I have to - have him. My whole body is opening, ready to receive him.

The door opens. Jan must have left. It's all right, I'm locked into memory, enjoying it as I previously had as I curl up on the bed and close my eyes, remembering how Tim had looked at me as I smiled and waited for his kiss. His eyes were so kind and shining with what I believed was love. I remember our eyes locking, his mouth gently covering mine, kissing my eye lids, my hair, my neck, my cheek softly and gently.

In innocence I strain upward, toward him, his touch creating my need.

Until that moment, no one had ever seen me naked. Even my old family doctor had averted his eyes when he had to move the paper examination gown that covered my body.

Tim was still fully dressed in his tweed jacket and crew neck sweater, as he sucked my nipples, slurping imaginary milk my virgin breasts don't have.

He slid his hand up my skirt toward the wet throbbing place. My hips move higher, thighs part as his hand reaches the place where I'm very wet.

"You act like a professional," he whispers.

"I'm glad," I whisper back throatily, feeling very sophisticated, not considering the implication.

Tim was pulling off his jacket as he caresses and kisses me. The memory is so clear, happening at this instant I arched, driving my hips off the mattress, remembering my wet panties, how embarrassed I'd been. How tingly his bare skin is against mine, the hardness between his legs making me weak. My legs part as he rolls on top of me. How right it feels, how good. I want him inside me. Longing, crushing, anxiously, his hands move to the button of my skirt.

Surprise as his fingers moved beneath my panties. No one's hand had ever been there before. The gentle fingers made me very excited. We had reached the point of no return. I lifted my hips and he peeled off my panties. My heart still pounded with that incredible memory.

I lay on my back, feeling the ripples of the bedspread, eyes closed, rooting from the mental bleachers for my old courageous self.

His tongue had caressed as I moaned with every stroke. I had forgotten my morals, the standards I had lived by and lifted my legs and spread them very wide. He kissed and licked me as my legs formed a necklace around his head. His tongue deep inside, he stroked virgin territory then lifted my legs from his neck and climbed on top, thrusting into me for my very first time.

It was cool and hard as he entered inside me, setting off an immediate chemical change. New awareness surged as the mixture of energies created new chemicals released through my body. Cries of passion and pain, where the burning and semen, the blood, and the loss of innocence come together in so many ways to create a different and new kind of person inside of me. A person willing to sacrifice her physical body and former thoughts for a new totem. A feeling I wanted to keep for a long time.

I open my eyes. Jan is standing, watching. I had thought she left and sat up abruptly, defensive. "This room is upsetting."

"Then brighten it. Use your perception."

"That's ridiculous." Chills run through me. My hands are freezing.

"You know how to create what you need," Jan continued. "Make this place beautiful by seeing it's perfection." She headed for the door.

Anxiety clutched me. I wasn't sure I wanted to be alone.

"Rest well," Jan suggested. She motioned toward the bedside table, then smiled and bowed before closing the door. The latch clicked shut, but it didn't sound as if it was bolted. I assumed it was, but I was afraid to test it, afraid to know if I'm locked in.

On the small bed side table is a tray with milk and cookies. Sitting on the edge of the bed I bite into one, washing it down with the cold milk. Then I lean against the wall and munch the cookie. Somehow or other none of this feels real.

CHAPTER SEVENTEEN

On the top floor of the UCLA Bio-med library, Detective Parker sits huddled behind books in a deserted corner making messy notes on a yellow legal pad.

Near him, a man in a white lab coat, Dr. Edward Verruno searches through a book filled with formulas.

Verruno slams his hand down on the table.

"Ketamine with Epinephrine, that'll do it,"

Parker looks perplexed. "What's that?"

Ketamine is a drug that was used in operating rooms but not much anymore. Veterinarians use it. It separates the conscious mind from the physical body so operations can be performed on patients while they're fully awake. It used to be used on accident victims who had just eaten and couldn't have the usual anesthesia. The problem with Ketamine is that it can cause severe hallucinations. It has been used as a recreation drug but the side effects are dangerous.

Parker is riveted. Maybe this is how Mannie was impregnated. "Can someone drive a car with it?"

"Not unless they want to cause an accident."

Parker held his breath; the implications of what this man was saying shed light on Mannie's case. It looks like multiple murder.

"My guess is they used Ketamine on the victim." Verruno continues, "when it hit her system it divorced her from all physical proceedings while staying in a form of consciousness. She was totally unaware of what she was doing. They mixed it with Epinephrine which makes the fast acting drug last longer. They miscalculated. She never knew what hit her. Ketamine works instantly.

"So, it completely disassociated her from reality."

Verruno nodded. "Reality killed her."

Parker jumped up, excited. "We've got the murder weapon!"

The doctor in the lab coat shook his head. "Try and prove it."

I woke up with a start and reached for a pen to write down what I had just seen. The pen isn't there. Nor is this my bedside table, or my bed. I'm in a strange room. Where am I?

Cookies! I had cookies before I went to sleep. The rest is fuzzy. What had I just dreamed? I know who

Detective Parker is but I don't know the doctor. Maybe it hadn't been a dream. How could I have been there?

The cookies - airplane — hospital - the Whites.

Jan White left the cookies. There was something in them. The tray is gone! Someone took it away. Maybe it hadn't really been there. Maybe... Disorientation is becoming panic. I take a deep breath to fight the panic away.

Mesh covers the windows. I try the door. It's locked. They aren't going to release me. I don't have as much control over myself as I thought I had.

I'm locked in here. Locked! I'm screwed. They're going to brainwash or kill me. Why? Am I thinking too deeply? For having information they don't want me to give out?

A bell rings in the distance. Sounds of doors opening and people walking drift through the walls. I don't know what to do. I pull the blanket closer.

The latch clicks in the lock. A fair young woman, blonde hair cut bluntly around her chin like a Dutch boy, opens the door and peeks around the edge, bright eyes shining, a big smile on her face. "Hi Jenny," Her voice is light. "I'm Elizabeth. I heard you come in late last night. Thought you might like someone to show you the ropes."

"How did you know?" I felt instant comfort. Something about this girl is familiar and appealing.

"I'm reading your thoughts," Elizabeth said teasingly as she steps inside and closes the door. She wears acid washed jeans, a white cotton tee shirt, and a blue cardigan sweater tied around her waist. On top of her head are small round tortoise shell eyeglasses, which she pulls down to stare at Jenny. "You're pretty."

Thanks, so are you. But I feel like hell."

"Well, you don't look it, you look great. Must have had a good rest. Did you eat the cookies?"

"Yes."

Elizabeth nodded wisely. "There's something in them. I don't know what, but there's an ingredient that makes you feel good. I'm sure it's more than carbohydrates. But it doesn't matter, they're good. Don't worry. You'll learn to override them."

I shuddered and hugged myself tightly.

"Why don't you get dressed?" Elizabeth suggested.

When I came out of the bathroom Elizabeth is cross-legged on the bed, her eyes closed in meditation.

As I tiptoe toward the dresser Elizabeth opens her eyes and smiles. "You're fast. Thought I'd get a couple extra minutes in." She grins widely.

Her smile is infectious. She's making me feel good.

Have you had your stabilizers yet?"

"My what?"

"Your centering rods. The inner enhancers, calibers- we have all kinds of names for them. They make everything seem to be better." She hands me two. "There, they'll keep you in balance so you can appreciate the movie."

"What movie?" I'm apprehensive about taking the pills.

"The life movie you're making while you're living on this planet. Once you step over and go into the next stage of transition, the movie gets replayed, so you can see what you've done with your life on this level."

"Step over?"

"Die, drop your body, change reality."

"That's putting it lightly," I'm surprised by her irreverence. "Life as a movie. I like it."

"That's right," said Elizabeth. You're the producer, writer, director and star. And when it ends you get to be the critic.

Planet Earth is the movie studio," she makes a dramatic flourish. "It's a training center for the gods!" Elizabeth literally twinkles like a Christmas tree ornament. I'm spellbound. It makes such good sense.

Elizabeth continues. "The ground rules of the Planet Earth Game are that Earth is, was and always shall be in chaos; it's a testing place for the gods. Those who can rise above it never have to return --unless, of course, they want to come back to help. But there's danger in getting caught here when you come back. Life on Earth is a constant cycle of lessons, which grow more complex and intricate each time one enters. The danger is you tend to forget your past lessons once you're caught in the new ones. It's the big trick in the game."

She draws me closer, drawing diagrams in a notebook that look like Tibetan Mandalas, images that represent an aspect of wisdom or remembrance from which a viewer can allow themself to be reminded or guided.

"Look," Elizabath tapped on the notebook to draw my attention to her. "Once we're on Planet Earth we have to go through this multifaceted experience called *life* with its highs and lows, negatives and positives. The high and low is all in your perspective. Whichever you choose. Be a victim or a student.

"I'm confused."

"No you're not. Let's go get morning refreshments. The hospital movie is just beginning. I'm the narrator. Try to be more of a spectator than a star. Stardom is a vanity trip. Vanity will never keep you happy."

In the hallway people are shuffling in the same direction. Some wear robes, most jeans or sweats. The building and the people have the ambiance of a college dormitory. Many are preoccupied and almost all are young.

Sunlight bounces off the yellow walls of the dining room. Chairs scrape on the wooden floors, dishes clatter, everyone seems to come in at exactly the same time. Few people are talking.

Elizabeth leads me to a table. As we sit a server in a starched white shirt brings a tray with scrambled eggs, bacon and toast. A pot of coffee and a pitcher of orange juice are in the center of the long family- style table. Elizabeth pours a glass of juice for me and one for herself. I start to drink, then stop myself. I had forgotten, I was going to train myself not to eat anymore.

"*Slowly*," said the voice in my head. "*Start slowly. You can drink juices, eat lightly, and start cutting whole things out. But keep your energy. Raw fruit and vegetables are good for that.*"

I lower my eyes and go back to the soft moist green Mexican jungle where I had learned this.

I drain the juice in the glass. It's delicious. Golden energy surges through me. I pour another, ignoring the heavier food on my plate.

When I look up, Elizabeth is gone. I hadn't noticed her leave. Most everyone else is gone as well. The man in the white shirt is picking up plates from the empty tables. He comes over to my table.

"Where is everybody?" I ask him.

"In their rooms."

'Do you know which room the girl I sat next to is in?"

He shrugged. "Looked like you were sitting alone to me. I didn't see anyone."

Her name's Elizabeth. She has straight blonde chin-length hair, smiles a lot. You must know who she is, she's been here awhile."

He shrugs and stacks a few more dishes and starts to walk away.

"Wait!" I call out to him. "Where are Felix and Jan White's offices?"

He shrugged impatiently, his hands filled with dirty plates. "I don't know who you're talking about. You'll have to ask someone else. Go back to your room and wait."

"What shall I wait for? I ask.

The attendant doesn't answer and goes on his lumbering way. Probably an old mental patient I decide to label him as I go out the door. But I don't know which way to go. I hadn't watched when I came here with Elizabeth. Taking a deep breath I put one hand against the wall to steady myself and start walking.

The hall is deserted, stretching endlessly beyond closed doors on either side - a tunnel toward infinity. Slowly I creep against the wall, fearful I'll fall if I step into the center. Activated by instinct alone, I push a door open and see my notebook on the dresser. I found my room. Excited I bounce on to the bed happily till I catch myself in the mirror. I'm acting crazy. Is that why I'm here?

The thought slaps me across the face. Everyone thinks I'm crazy. Are they right? What if the machines and the rape are my imagination? What if it never happened? Even the girl called Elizabeth may not be real. And the automatic writing! Where is that coming from? I could be nuts!

I bang my fist against the wall. They put me away because I'm crazy. Everything I saw, all I believed, were figments of a crazy imagination, a set of visions gone astray. I've gone beyond the boundaries of normal reality.

I pound my fist again. No one believed me! Everything has been unreal! How could it have been unreal when it seemed so real?

I push off the bed and go to the window. People stroll along the garden path or sit on benches in the sun. I go to the door and open it. Tentatively, testing, I step carefully into the center of the deserted hall, heading in the opposite direction of the dining hall till I find a door and open it to the glorious morning sunshine.

The heaviness lifts. I step back inside. The heaviness comes back. I step outside - light. Inside - dark. In- heavy. Out - light. In, out, in, out, - Inside I yearn for the safety and security of my room; outside I just want to be in the light. Inside the energy is gripping. Outside - light.

Choosing light over security I follow a path till I get to a fence running along the edge of the estate. An electrified humming comes from it. I doubt anyone can get over it, it's too high.

Dr. White had said I could leave today, and I had gotten so involved with the external stimuli, I'd forgotten! But what if I am crazy, and I shouldn't be on my own. What should I do?

I begin pacing, emotion taking over. This place is toxic. Its already making me crazy. I'm going to find White right now and get signed out.

As I reach the border of the house a chill drops down on me. The hair on my arms bristles with electricity. There is an electric or static force encircling me, compelling me back inside.

Grids of electronic rays cover the house and spread over the lawns and gardens. When crossing the periphery I get wrapped up in beams. The entire area is covered, horizontally and vertically, a forest of charges vibrating through everything.

The greatest concentration surrounds the building. Stepping closer I squint and put my hand out. A subtle energy draws me toward my room. Trying the other hand it pulls me to the left, squatting on the ground and feeling lighter and happier. They must be using microwaves for behavior modification. That's why I fear going crazy. They weakened me so I'll feel self-doubt. It works!

The people sitting on the benches or walking around the lush grounds look like extras in a movie. Off to the right, a large gray building is hidden between artfully planted trees. I start toward it, but hear screams coming from it so I stop. The building itself seems to be rumbling with intense discomfort and a higher density of beams.

Sitting down and taking a deep breath, I vow to maintain my equilibrium. There is misery here, carried along a maze of electronic beams. Had Mannie been involved with this? Is that why she was killed? What will happen now? How do they plan on using me? Why do they want me? I made a huge mistake. Walked right into their trap.

Fuzziness starts taking over my brain. As hard as I try I can't think straight. Maybe I should have had more than juice this morning.

Feeling hungry I turn toward the central building. Others seemed to be getting the same message; silent automatons in an exodus from the grounds to their respective buildings.

Two more orange tablets are on top of the bureau in my room, a glass of water besides them. Picking them up and weighing them in my hand, I decide to throw them out. But the pills vibrate as if they are alive. Alive like the little pink spots I once found in a field that had been baby mice. I didn't know what to do with them, so I left them in the sun to die. A sinking feeling came over me. I'm guilty of murder! A dozen infant mice are probably dead because I decided upon the meaningless, the non-importance of their lives.

"*They had purpose. So do the pills.*," the voice inside me says.

"Why?" I ask with anguish. Maybe the voice is sending me wrong messages.

"*Dimensions.*"

"Hallucinogens?" I ask.

"*No, brain cleaners, relaxants to open channels to view truth and reason.*"

"All right." I swallow the pills then lay down to rest. I think about Al, the news program, has anyone noticed I'm not there? I try to think of something else, but only anxiety wants my attention.

A hand touches my shoulder. A tall, thin woman, her hair pulled back tightly like Jan's, shakes me again. Her white moon-like face is framed by a black, turtleneck long-sleeve dress, making her pale face and deep-set eyes look haunted. She is one of those people who is such a perfect type they don't seem real. But this woman is real, she either has one part of her head in another stratosphere or she doesn't have another side at all.

"Come," said the woman, "come with me." Her look is mesmerizing. I silently follow her. We pass a large room and I manage to look inside. More than a dozen beds are lined up in the half-light, every patient hooked to intravenous. A few patients in pajamas and robes walk or sit in chairs with helmets covering their heads and faces. A steady murmur of recorded voices covers the room like a sound blanket. No one speaks, no other sound except the recording. It's otherworldly. I pray I won't be put there. It looks like hell.

"What is that" I ask my ghoulish guide. "What are they doing?"

The Moon faced woman doesn't answer and we continue our silent journey through the corridors. By the time we reach the back of the building my heart is pounding. I don't like what I'm seeing and afraid of my feelings.

It's too silent. Is this where they bury the corpses, I wonder? Following blindly is not one of my favorite disciplines. But I'm anxious to learn what this place is doing and following this woman is a good place to learn. However the people in the helmets had unnerved me. I don't want to have any problems or show resistance till I know the punishments.

Entering a small room which has a large black box shaped like an Egyptian sarcophagus with a convex door, I recognize a sense deprivation tank. It had been developed by scientist John Lilly, to explore the psyche when closed off from all stimuli. As I enter there is a stall shower in the corner of the dark room. Somber Moon face hands me two towels. "Wash, including your hair. You will repeat this when you emerge from the chamber. This is a sense deprivation tank."

"Yes. I know." The tank is filled with 800 pounds of salt in 10 inches of water upon which a body floats weightless and without any external stimuli from light or sound.

"What kind of meds did you give me to control my thinking in there," I ask the woman.

"That isn't possible."

"You're trying to control minds with medication." My words are running from me without permission. I wanted to stay silent and register all I'm seeing but my emotions have taken over.

"*Keep quiet,*" said the voice. "*You can transmute any energy that tries to control you. Go beyond it into the power that is yourself. That's the main lesson you want here. Use it.*"

Feeling better after hearing the voice in my head, I remind myself to use everything that happened to me as an experience to enhance my power. To have the ability to inform the world what could happen to them.

"*You can think whatever you want inside or outside the tank. That's a choice you make.*" said the voice. "*Use the energy of your emotions to discipline your perspective and your reason.*"

Keeping my back turned away from the woman, I take off my clothes and step into the shower. The water is freezing. I'm about to get out when it gets warmer. I feel the woman watching me and rush to finish. Rinsing off I rush from the shower to the tank, closing the door behind me. Absolute blackness hits me and sends off throat chocking panic. My eyes open wide, I still can't see anything. Closing them I have the same experience. I can't tell if they're open or shut. Laying back in the water, a cut on my finger stings. I settle back and let my body relax, focusing on stopping the stinging in my finger as my head falls back so perfectly it creates a halo at the waterline.

Breath rushes through my ears like a pump, a great power engine attached to the life force in my body. Watching the rushing sound of air travel through me I feel as if I can jump on and sail along with it. Pressure circulates in the center of my forehead. My jaw is tight and I will it to relax. Breath comes hissing up through my throat, filling the chamber. I no longer feel the water because somehow it has become air on which I gently float. Then energy comes up and takes over and I'm no longer in my body, I'm a speck in the darkness alone.

"*Do you feel it?*" the voice asks.

"Yes."

"*If you use this properly, you'll never have to eat or sleep again. You live off it, you are one with it.*"

"Is there anything else?"

"*When you mastered that, you'll know it all.*"

A shudder goes through me and I become aware of the water. It feels sticky and slimy. With the hiss of my breath, faint lights blinks on and off. I think I can see the stars in the universe. Maybe I'm out there with them. There's music in the distance, like the kind on airplane flights - the kind you're never sure you're hearing till it starts to grow louder like it's doing now. Reaching for the door, I can't find it. I 'm trapped. Blackness! Suffocation grabs hold. I sit up. There is headroom. The door! Reaching up I push outward. The light of the room spills over me. The rush of relief is gorgeous.

The outside door opens and Moon Face looks in. I hurriedly rinse and dry myself, pausing to look in the mirror. I look more at peace.

"I'll take you to your room," Moon Face whispers huskily. "You should rest."

I want that, need it. I'm a bit confused and want to write the experience down so it can be clearer.

Once in the room I go straight to my notebook and try to recreate my feelings into words, to simulate those moments in the tank - but it's not the same, and I can't.

A knock - "Dinner!" It's dark outside. The lights are turned on. I hadn't noticed. Hunger rumbles in my stomach and I join the others in the rush to the dining room. Everyone seems to be hungry. Those who had arrived were already eating, isolated and impervious to the chaos so near them. My stomach rolls with queasiness but subsides when I sit down and smell the sweetness of meatloaf. Putting my fork in I take a bite. Grease spurts and covers the roof of my mouth while the rest of the meatloaf chugs its way to my stomach. The bright canned green beans and mounds of stark white mashed potatoes wait, plastic replicas of the true vegetables they represent.

Elizabeth sits down next to me. I look up, happy and surprised. "Hi" she says.

I feel a flood of relief. "I missed you."

"I did too."

"Where were you?" I ask, but the girl doesn't answer. She's busily eating all the meat loaf on her plate. I watch then look at my own. Grease still coats the roof of my mouth. I can't eat this. All I taste is animal.

Another woman looks my way and smiles. I smile back. A man at the far end catches my eye. I smile. He winks. I wink back. A man sitting at the next table catches my attention. He stares straight ahead, one of the few ignoring the food, watching with disdain the way people are eating.

Someone touches my arm. "Don't get involved." The pressure on my arm keeps me from turning. "Don't worry about anyone. He's doing what you were just instructed to do. He's your mirror."

"You need fuel and energy.," said Elizabeth, pointing to my uneaten food. Her eyes pierce me with brightness.

"I've been instructed on other ways to get it."

"Good. Then I won't have to eat this junk too."

"Are you my mirror?" a tinge of fear grabs me.

"Everything is. We're all a projection of our own thoughts and beliefs. You should learn from everything.

Keep your movie going. You're doing a good job." She winks and pushes her plate away.

CHAPTER EIGHTEEN

Snow! I can't believe it's snowing in May. How is that possible? I rush to my makeshift desk and take out my diary.

"May 22". It's my last entry. That was yesterday, I think. Ripples of dread start to climb into me. I hadn't noticed what the weather was like when I left the Sense Deprivation tank or when I went to dinner. Could I have lost 7 or 8 months? How can I not remember that time?

The room is cold. Winter clothes are hanging in the closet. Wool sweaters have replaced T-shirts in the drawers. Even my washed silk nightgown has been replaced with a flannel nightshirt on the back of the door. How many months have I been here?

I touch the glass in the window. It's cold. This isn't a trick, it's definitely winter. The room starts to spin, frames of reference whirling in my sight and in my mind. I thought I had been in that Sense Depravation tank for only a few minutes. But probably they had taken me out and put me in the "SLEEP ROOM"!

Oh God. I don't remember anything! I was one of those Zombie-like bodies hooked up to intravenous, bombarded with sounds and visuals and who knows what else. I remember shapes now of ghost-like men and women struggling against nurses holding them down as they wheeled them into treatment rooms. I can feel again the visible and almost touchable tension, the uneasiness, the pervasive fear. I remember hearing my own voice saying the same thing over and over, but I can't remember what it had been.

Now I remember the GRID ROOM. Starkly beautiful in a geometric way, lines drawn across a wall, a hard ladder-backed chair placed in front of it. At the opposite end of the room is a concealed hole, large enough for the lens of a camera. The person sitting in the chair is measured to record their energy output as they are thinking.

Somehow the technical aspects of the experiments are clear and although I remember emotions of anger and fear, I managed to stay objective and apart from them. I had mastered an important aspect of myself, my emotions.

Now I'm remembering the ISOLATION CHAMBER. The onion of memory is being peeled and a twinge of the terror at this moment serves to remind me that I can't control my feelings. Just thinking about that isolation chamber affects them now. Essentially a prison cell it had heavy double thick doors and padded walls. In there I was isolated and disoriented. It could have been weeks, months, maybe even years till they thought I was ready to say what they wanted. They had used PSYCHIC DRIVERS, ceiling microphones with disembodied voices booming from nowhere. They did the same thing with speakers inside the helmets as well as disembodied voices coming through pillow speakers and virtual reality contact lenses. I hadn't been allowed to think or see anything other than what had been programmed.

I don't remember wearing a helmet, but for some reason I know that patients had worn them for up to twenty-four hours. I had focused on screening out recorded voices, by knowing the difference in my feelings when they were not technically altered. The purity of truth came through with my feelings. My head listened to my heart.

The door opens and Tim walks in. He wears a bathing suit, his bare chest tanned and glistening. I'm astonished, breathless. He approaches, smiling.

"Good morning." He sounds tentative.

"Hello." I try to sound normal but I'm visibly trembling.

"Did you rest well?" He looks tan and fit. He doesn't seem to notice my terror. Or is ignoring it.

"Aren't you cold?" I was hugging myself to get warm.

"No. You seem to be." He puts on a look of concern.

"The way you're dressed. It's snowing."

He laughs. "You're dreaming. The sun is shining and it's perfectly beautiful. I took a swim before breakfast."

"Oh." I can't say any more.

"Dr. White and Jan send their best. They hope you feel better." He wore his professional voice.

I felt an alert. "Where are they?"

"They left a while ago."

"They were here?"

"They stayed the night."

I raise myself up and take my eyes off Tim. The sight makes my head swim. The gray brown walls of the hospital are now the soft golden tones of the Mexican hacienda's natural reed walls. Filmy white mosquito netting flutters around a bed no longer made of iron. Surf is crashing. "How long have I been sleeping?"

"Hours. You slept through the night."

I look down at my clothes. I still wear the white linen slacks I had on when I walked in the jungle. They're wrinkled and dirty. A dull ache in my head warns of a headache.

Tim sits beside me and rubs my neck. It feels better. He used to do that before everything deteriorated.

Reality has become confusing. Is any of this real? Is he really this loving with my head on his lap, this feeling of happiness? Panic rears its head again. Which is the reality?

What about Elizabeth, is she flesh and blood like Tim? Are they both real, or one of them merely a product of my imagination? Maybe Tim exists only at times like this, and Elizabeth is a reality when I'm with her later.

Doubt feeds my panic. I'm just not sure. Maybe this is a dream - but then again, this is the way my life has become - living events before they happen, regressing to past ones. Can I continue this sort of discombobulated existence? Is this a gift or a curse?

Tim rubs my temples and the nape of my neck, calming me. How I wish I could trust him, trust this moment as fact. But it doesn't feel real – it's too good to be true. Tears of regret come quickly for those lost moments we had that we'll never have again.

He kissed my forehead. "Feel better?"

"Yes. Thank you." He had never done that. It was so bizarre. I thought I had all these insights into what he had become but now he was comforting, contradicting my impressions.

"I had a vivid dream," I decided to tell him. "So vivid I can't believe it didn't happen. Unless that was the reality and you are the dream."

"Maybe I am," he grinned.

"Maybe." A cold shiver ran through me. I don't share his smile. "I thought I was in a sanitarium. You had taken me there. I had a friend, Elizabeth who was starting to show me strange things - like she could fly. I know that sounds strange, crazy perhaps, but I think I can see the future and have been shown certain truths. It was all so vivid, yet this is too."

I sat up suddenly. "My notebooks. Where are they?"

"There," he gestures toward the desk.

I get out of bed. My legs feel shaky, as though I hadn't walked in days.

Opening the first page of my red notebook, SOLID STATE CONSPIRACY, is printed in caps. I bring it to Tim and point, "have I told you about this?"

"You speak of nothing else. That's part of your whole conspiracy theory."

"Yes, in part, not completely. It's more involved than that."

He crosses his arms and waits patiently - too patiently, for me to continue.

Leaning against the bureau, grasping the notebook, holding it to myself I explain once again hoping he'll understand this time. "Technology has taken over - it's almost out of our hands, the hands that created it."

Tim looked amused. "Yes, you've said that, and I say we still have the on-off switch."

"For now."

"Have you seen a rerun of Kubrik's '2001? Has Hal the computer who took over, influenced you?" He said it as a joke, though he was dead serious.

"No, but that's what I'm talking about... The population is expanding and we're running out of food, and need I repeat what's happened to our water."

I draw him to me. "Whales are being slaughtered because they're the largest mammals that require large bodies of water. It's possible their huge brains carry the history of the universe if we could learn to communicate with them. Then maybe we won't repeat past mistakes. So what are we doing? We're destroying them! In the next century there may not be enough water for whales to survive. Don't you think it's possible that the powers who wish to take control of this planet don't want us to decode the whales?"

"Sure, Jenny. I hear what you're saying."

He starts to pull away, but I hold him tightly. "With the population growing and people living longer, where is everyone going to live? We're filling in the oceans and lakes and diverting rivers. For what? Better environments for technology because it thrives in arid, dry climates.

Tim put his hand on my arm. "Jenny, all you say is true but the context in which you're putting it is ridiculous."

I move away from him. "Tim, you know we're abusing the land, that soon we won't have fertile soil to grow food. There's almost none left. If this keeps up, I saw a vision of this planet without animals or plants. Technology pollutes and creates deserts. It all fits. As a planet, we're either slowly committing suicide or being consciously suffocated."

"Jenny, your argument is convoluted. With technology we are creating better lives, healthier environments and more nutritious foods to consume."

"On one hand, yes. That's the bait. But what is going to happen when there are too many people with nothing to eat and no place to live? It's the plan of the Solid State Conspiracy to get humans to kill each other. That's what happens when people are hungry and don't have shelter. Society reverts to a primitive level. Pure survival - survival of the fittest."

"Is that what you're dreaming?"

"It's not a dream, it's reality. It's happening as we're speaking."

He tried not to smile. "How do you know?"

"I told you, I've seen the future."

"Really, how?"

"If I tell you, you won't believe it."

"Try me."

"With a higher intelligence. My guides."

"Right." He turns away.

I start to follow him. "I know it sounds crazy and if the situation was reversed I might have problems if you were saying these things. But I know in every part of myself that this planet is headed toward destruction."

"Sweetheart, next you'll be wearing a placard walking up and down Times Square saying THE END IS NEAR." He took my hand gently and held it against his chest. "You're having vivid dreams that are creating an alien world because of personal problems you're having. You can't impose this kind of paranoia on rational minds. It isn't acceptable. I love you and I'm going to be honest so I'll tell you straight, you sound crazy. Do you understand?"

I just look at him as he continues. "I don't know what to do. At breakfast I tell you we're expecting guests and you disappear. You return from the jungle wrinkled, spaced out, messy, and totally surprised we have people here. Then you leave in the middle of lunch. Now you talk about an alien form of life parading in the guise of a lamp switch or a battery, anything technical is taking over our lives. That's schizophrenia."

"It may sound crazy but I know it isn't. For some reason I've been able to tap into the future and see the global mistakes that need reversal."

"Jenny, you're going to destroy your life long before this planet destructs. You've got to stop this."

"And you? What about the group that is grooming you for the Presidency?

"What group darling?" He smiles at me in his most charming and photogenic way. "Your conspiracy theories sound straight from the Sixties."

I force myself to stay calm. "I'm a problem, right? When we were younger my views were charming, but they're not now. I either have to be re- programmed or discarded. Dissidents don't work in American politics. Remember what happened to Martha Mitchell, the wife of President Nixon's Attorney General, John Mitchell? She called lots of reporters to expose what was going on. She died suddenly. Was her death a result of having a big mouth? Dissension is allowed only when it is popular and can attract voters."

"Well," he shook his head, his hand covering his mouth. "Your behavior has become a problem - especially for you."

I ignored that. "I'd like to think you're being controlled by something other than your own ambition. I say that because I love you and would like to give you the benefit of the doubt."

His face is turning white but he draws me close. " I love you, but you're not making sense. No one will believe you. It's nonsense." He kisses me.

I turn my head. I would like to believe him, but something tells me not to. His kiss isn't right, it feels angry. Turning to him words tumble out, "I'm being guided to counteract you. You and the people you're involved with."

"Why not?" He gets off the bed, his face a portrait of contained anger.

"I mean it Tim."

"I know you do. That's what is so upsetting. Your delusions are getting worse. It's frightening. I just can't think you really believe this. Perhaps it was the rape - if that really happened - but you need psychiatric treatment."

"IF that really happened," I repeat slowly. "You doubt that. Maybe you should doubt my existence. Maybe I'm not really here. Then you won't have to sell me out and send me to that hospital."

Surprised he stares at me.

"I've been there," I answer his look. "I've already lived that part of the future."

He paused another moment, then walked away. A hole opened in my stomach and started to spread. I bury my head in the pillow and cry.

The air changes. Its thinner and colder. The pillowcase is cold. I look up and I'm not surprised to see the gray brown walls of the hospital. Through the windows snow is falling. Yet I knew what had just happened with Tim had been for real. It wasn't a dream- the pillow is still wet from my tears. Do people cry in their sleep? I must be going through some kind of time warp. That has to be the answer.

Rolling over I stare at the ceiling, my face wet with tears. What should I do? I can be in two places at the same time. Suddenly a ripple of energy rolls through me and I roll to the side.

I see my body lying face up beneath me. Then I'm outside the building and over the lawn, looking at the few people bundled up and sitting on benches as I swoop down like a bird, but nobody notices.

I'm flying outside of my body. Does this mean I'm dying?

Suddenly I'm back in my room. I'm still lying quietly face up on the bed. I have such a strong connection with it I'm inside myself again. My arm is solid, my cheeks are cold and wet with my tears. But I'm feeling lighter, liberated, more at peace than I've ever been. A new sense of power is beginning to fill me with joy. I'm not sure where my body is supposed to be, in this room or in Mexico with Tim, but I know it doesn't matter. I can be anywhere in the past, present or future.

"*You need more training,*" the voice whispers.

"You mean I can't always do this?" I'm so disappointed.

The door opens and Elizabeth pokes her head in. She's floating. My body soars weightless off the bed and follows Elizabeth as she turns toward the open doorway.

Slashes of light slip through the doors of the darkened hall as I follow my special friend lightly and easily. Elizabeth stops and turns to me, her finger to her lips, and opens a door very slightly.

I peek in.

There's a modern lobby that looks familiar. As I think about going in, something starts to pull me. At the same time something in the opposite direction pulls me the other way by my waist. A tug of war ensues with me in the middle - Elizabeth is pulling me back and some unknown force is trying to pull me inside.

Without hesitation I will myself over to Elizabeth. The pulling stops. We both tumble backward with the impact. "Let's go." Elizabeth gasps, worn out with the exertion. She looks scared. "That was a close one."

"What was that?" I yell after her as we both fly down the hall.

"THE CITY OF MATERIAL DESIRES." Once you go in it's hard to get out. Don't ever go near there again if you're alone. Its pulls are very strong and you can get lost without someone else watching."

I touch my friend sailing down the corridor in front of me. "What is all this?" "How is this happening?"

"You're learning to go back and forth in time, to different realities and experience them without fear or comparison. Nothing is holding you back. You want to fly, you do it. You're getting the technique and it's becoming natural for you."

All this information is making me dizzy. I don't want to be rude, but ask, "what do I do to go back?"

"Ask."

"That's it?"

"Yep. Watch."

I find myself back on the bed staring up at the ceiling. Elizabeth has vanished. Outside the sky is dark with just a few stars sparkling. The snow has stopped falling. The moon is making its slow way up into the sky, its thin crescent cutting through the clouds surrounding it. Far in the distance a dog is barking. I wonder if its Christmas time. I have no idea.

I decide to visit Tim again and lay down to will myself back to him. But I'm not moving, I'm still on top of the bed.

I try again. I don't budge. A hand on my shoulder starts shaking me. I try to push it off, but it persists. A vibration is buzzing. The hand shakes me again. I open my eyes. A young woman in a blue suit and white shirt looks down at me.

"We're coming in for a landing. Please raise up your seat and fasten your seat belt."

Not again! I'm back on the plane again. Why? I push the button for the seat back that jerks me into a vertical position and feel under the blanket to make sure my seat belt is buckled. Tim sits across the aisle, engrossed in a book. I look out the window. Clouds are floating past. The flight attendant moves away. I touch my arm. Its real. I'm in human form again.

I reach out and touch Tim's sleeve. He turns and smiles. "You've had quite a long sleep."

"You seem to be saying that to me a lot lately."

"Well, you've been out of it for a long time. Are you feeling better?"

"Am I sick?"

"Don't you remember? You've had Jungle Fever. You collapsed when Dr. White and Jan were over. He gave you some medication and you slept through the rest of our vacation." He smiled easily. "It's been good for both of us, very restful." He turned a bit more serious. "Don't you remember getting up this morning and saying you were feeling better? That's why we were able to leave."

"No, I don't." I bit a hangnail on my cuticle. I can feel the sensation. "Did I walk?"

"Yes. You really don't remember?

I shook my head. The plane started to shake as it lost altitude. Everything is quiet. Leaning over I look out the window and only see my reflection in the glass staring back. The reflection bit her nails. It shook its head no and I see it take out the finger. Simultaneously my hand rests in my lap. The finger is wet.

Tim puts his hand on my arm and walks me off the plane with shaky legs as we go through immigration's bright lights, rushing people, baggage revolving on islands of silver, echoing voices coming through the air as we continue through customs.

"We've already done this," I tell him.

"No, we haven't."

"Yes. There's a long gray limousine waiting to take me to the sanitarium. You're not going because it isn't a sanitarium, it's a training center. The illness you said I had is an excuse to knock me out so you could get me here. I'm weakened from drugs and too much sleep, not Jungle Fever. A lie to get me to go with no resistance. I know what's happening, and I was hoping it wasn't true."

Tim grabbed my arm tighter and stared.

"How do I know?" I ask his surprised face. I told you, I've been here before. Been through everything. I'm a graduate. You're going to load me into the back of that car and stand and watch it go and I'm going to feel sorry for you because you look sad and lonely."

He faltered a bit. "Jenny, I feel like hell this is happening. But it's for your own good."

A sinking feeling of anger and betrayal flashes through me. He's trying to turn this into my need instead of his own interest. The ultimate tool to instill weakness and self-doubt.

"Darling," he leads me to a bench where I sat down. "You're having disassociation problems. You need help. You've agreed to it. Your realities are getting mixed up with your imagination. And your imagination is very powerful."

I don't answer. He's not going to talk me into being crazy.

"There is no conspiracy or desire to change you," he went on. "We want you healthy and strong. You seem to have lost all sense of time and become extremely paranoid."

I wish I could throw up all over him. Over his clean white pants and his immaculate white shirt. Over his strong tanned jaw and his deep-set eyes. He'd be horrified! I can't suppress a giggle. Mr. Immaculate with vomit all over him. I can't hold back the laugh. A smile touches his lips, he's about to laugh with me when something catches his attention. He straightens and stands up. My laughter stops.

The gray limousine has pulled up to the curb. Tim leads me to the inevitable. I want to scream and cry for help, but this is the past and future as well as the present. There is no changing it.

Tim helps me into the car. He quickly closes the door and steps back on to the curb. The big car pulls away. I see the replay of the scene I had been in before. Which is the real one, or are they both real?

The sad lonely man stands on the edge of the curb, his coat collar turned up against the cold, his shoulders hunched, watching me go. Same events, different tone. Why? I settle back and wait for the inevitable.

I find myself back on my bed in the sanitarium. "*You're going back and forth in space and time now.*" The words are so loud I jump. "*You were definitely there. You just saw aspects you hadn't seen before, but you were definitely there. Didn't it feel like it?*"

"Yes," I whisper aloud. "What if I want to go back to the experience now?"

The back seat of the limo is empty. The smoked gray Plexiglas divider between me and the driver is securely closed. I would not again try opening the window and turning on the light. They won't work. Again I'm being made to stay in darkness and silence on this long trip to the hospital. This time it's the same, but it's also very different. This time I knew exactly what's happening.

Truth and awareness are my tools.

CHAPTER NINETEEN

"Tell him Detective Parker has called for the third time and I want him to return my call as soon as possible," Parker slams the phone down. The officer at the next desk turns, surprised. Parker takes a deep breath. He has a sinking feeling about Jenny Webster. Something is happening, and it doesn't feel right.

Boyle saunters over. "What's the problem? You on edge?"

"Why is Jenny Webster in that sanitarium? She had been upset after her friend Mannie's death, but she seemed to be in control. What did we miss?"

"Nothing. Look Detective," Boyle snapped, "The Sebastian case is closed. It's for the insurance companies now. It was murder. End of story."

Parker turns his head away from Boyle's labored breath. He can't accept the official decision. Why did they want to wrap the case so quickly? It was the kind of case they usually like to draw out – flashy with lots of publicity in what appears to be a no brainer. Sebastiane was depressed and committed suicide and murder. Probably someone wants it closed before there is sufficient evidence that it could be linked to Anson Industries and their research.

"Come on," Boyle clapped him on the shoulder. "We have to see the Captain."

Parker relaxed his clenched jaw. "Sure," he exhaled.

When I saw Parker shiver I thought it might be cold in the police station or maybe he was anxious. Then I remembered that sometimes I make people shiver with my unseen presence, so I try to stay very still.

As they enter the Captain's office like Rudnik, the Captain is taking a long time loading his pipe in front of a "No Smoking" sign. I smile at the irony, or at least, I feel like I'm smiling.

"We have a compromised police officer in this precinct," the Captain was saying, tapping the tobacco down into the pipe's bowl with a small silver trowel. "Weapons and drugs. The brass want him before the media finds out. We don't want negative publicity, it's a matter of pride, we don't want this precinct tainted." He struck a match and sucked deeply on the stem of the pipe. "It's touchy Boyle, that's why we want you on this."

He looked over at Parker for the first time. You'll learn a lot."

Boyle rolled his eyes.

I peered at the three men. Something was askew. Smoke was starting to seep from Boyle's skin, leaking through his pores. The dark, bottomless pools of his eyes turned toward me and pierced me with understanding. In that instant I could hear his thoughts, feel his contempt, and see his devious plans. The suspect the Captain was describing is Boyle himself. And Boyle senses a presence. Not sure he knows it's me. But I do know Parker is in danger.

But how can I tell him? Maybe Rudnik? He always said he could read my mind.

I thought of Rudnick's rumpled white shirt, his loose tie, the ever- present cigarette in the corner of his mouth as the news program office came slithering into a wavy net of quasi-substance. But Rudnik wasn't at his desk and the air was clear of cigarette smoke. With the exception of a few writers and copy editors, the office was empty. I don't know why Rudnik isn't here. But then I'm not sure of the day or time, or even the year. It could be the past, it could be the future. I don't know till I get into it.

"*Focus on the person, not the place*," said the voice before I could think of where to go. "*Deal with his essence.*"

I go into Rudnick's office and sit in his chair. I try picking up a pen to write a note, but my fingers keep going through it. Then I remember my fingers are not attached to my hand, in fact I have no hand. At the moment all parts of my body are extensions of my creative memory and don't have three dimensions at all. Since I can't pick up a pen to write or use the computer to tell Rudnik about Boyle and Parker I'll have to get through to him subtly, through his feelings and intuition.

I focus on Rudnik's feelings and begin to get a sense of anxiety and frustrating insecurity. He wants to do the right thing, but he has to be practical, he has a family to support and he needs to keep working. His emotions start to take me over, binding and wrapping me inside of him and becoming one with my own self.

Suddenly I'm in the passenger seat of a car Rudnik is driving. I recognize the valley and the mountains that rim Clifton Sanitarium.

"Al?" I whisper. There is no answer. I doubt he would hear me even if I was here with him in the flesh. With a deep frown frozen across his face, I remember Rudnik hated driving and was forcing himself to concentrate on the winding road in front of him.

"Al?" I try again and touch his shoulder. He shivers and turns the radio on, but there is a lot of static. He pulls out a Henry Mancini compilation of favorite hits and puts it in the tape deck but forgets to push the START button as the road becomes even more twisted and narrow.

We pass farmland and forests as the car climbs higher, but Rudnik isn't sightseeing, he is trying to stay on the road.

I look at my hand – it's shimmering, light spilling from it. I love this feeling and the absolute irony that here I'm an invisible passenger traveling through space, defying the laws of three dimensions and gravity, driving to see myself with my boss.

Rudnik pushes a button on his dash and says, *office.* "Amy, what's happening?"

"Nothing unusual. Detective Parker called three times. Said it was important. Everything else seems to be under control. Do you want Parker's number or shall I give him yours?"

"Not now, I'm trying to stay on this damn road."

"Okey dokey !" she answers.

"Did you get in touch with Clifton and tell them I'm arriving?"

"Not yet. I tried calling and sending a fax and a text but their cable lines are down. I'll keep trying."

"I'll get there before you get through to them."

"I hope not."

"Me too." He hung up, stared into space, then swerved into his next turn.

I held my breath, then realized I had none to hold.

Rudnik picked up a memo sheet with the phone number and directions to Clifton Sanitarium. Balancing driving and making the call, he manages to push the number on his cell. There's no ring, nothing. He presses O for the operator and gets a busy signal. "Damn." He pushes the on button to his tape deck and settles back to Henry Mancini.

My transparent body is leaning against the car door-practically through it.

Suddenly Rudnik hits the brakes, throws the car into reverse, and turns into Clifton's unmarked driveway and a huge iron gate. He gets out of the car to use the intercom embedded in the concrete fence poles and pushes the RECEPTION button.

"Yes?" a metallic voice answered sounding not entirely human.

The voice makes Al pause a moment before talking. "This is Al Rudnik, Los Angeles News. You have Jenny Webster here. I'm scheduled to see her."

"Do you have an appointment?"

"That's what "scheduled" means. It was arranged yesterday and confirmed." His face is starting to puff. Al Rudnik is growing impatient.

"I'm sorry, you're not on the list and there is no one available."

"Look, I'm the Producer of Los Angeles News. This was arranged before I left. My office called to re-confirm and your internet is down. Let me talk to someone in charge."

"I'm sorry. No one is available. You'll have to call back tomorrow for an appointment."

"What are you, some kind of robot? I just said I have an appointment. Look at your list and open this gate."

"You'll have to call for an appointment and specify who it is you want to speak with." The operator sounds more like a recording.

The line goes dead and Rudnik slams his hand against the call button. "I don't believe this!" He pushes call again then every number on the board but there is no further response. Like a child at the zoo he grabs the iron bars of the gate and peers in. The long winding road does not offer a view of any buildings. Only a single lane dividing the edge of the forest and meadow. Rudnik notes a multitude of wires leading into the interior, the landscaping designed to both expose and conceal. Sophisticated surveillance is in effect. This is not for the criminally insane and very sophisticated for a sanitarium that is supposed to be for depressives, substance abusers, and garden-variety psychotics.

A four-wheel drive vehicle charges up the road to the gate in a cloud of dust. Two hulking giants barely seem to fit inside. One of them peels himself out, his hand resting lightly on the gun at his hip. "Got a problem?"

"Yes. I have a scheduled meeting with one of your patients. I made the necessary arrangements and now I can't get in. Would you please open this gate."

"You need permission from the attending doctor or supervising physician."

"I have it."

"May we see it please?"

"My office took care of it. Call someone and tell them to look for it."

The taller of the two hulking giants comes close to the bars. His round little eyes do not reveal a higher intelligence, however his bulk and well developed muscles prove a kind of compensation. "You need a letter from the head Doc here, otherwise we can't let you in."

"That's ridiculous."

"It's the rules."

Shaking with anger, Rudnik pulls out a card and gives it to the giant. "Give this to your head guy. I'll wait."

"It could take days."

"Then I'll call damn it."

I felt so sad for him as he went back to the car and slammed the door. A swirl of dust rose up and enveloped me as he peeled away. I want to be in the car with him, talk to him, but somehow I can't and it would freak him out anyway.

I'm caught in a milky white thickness and can no longer see.

CHAPTER TWENTY

Tim paced in his office. He opened a small refrigerator in the wet bar, but slammed it shut. He tried to read the contents of a folder, then aimlessly wiped off its dust. Picking up a "Law Review" he swatted an imaginary fly, then threw the Review across the room missing a chair and letting it stay on the floor where it landed. He picked up a picture of Jenny, sighed heavily, and put it face down. Suddenly his fist banged down on top of it which he withdrew accusingly as if it had moved on its own.

Grabbing a small overnight bag out of the closet, he changes into a pair of Levi's, a wool Pendleton shirt, and canvas hiking boots. Speaking into his Smart Watch he calls his assistant. "Roxanne, I'm going to the cabin for a few days. No one is to know where I am except Jenny." He starts to leave then pushes the button again. "When I get back, we need to talk. Schedule it."

Revving the engine of his black Astin Martin, Tim caresses the steering wheel like a woman's shoulders, leans back, grabs the knob of the stick shift and pushes it forward. The car jumps to his command.

Showing its stuff on the empty country road the speedometer shows 105, 110, 115 mph. Racing past horse farms and mountain passes he gets off the highway on to a steep and winding road. The sudden shock of clean fresh mountain air envelopes him when he stops for gas. In seconds his face is stung red by the cold, filling his dry lungs like a spring of fresh water and invigorating his soul.

Trying the number for the hospital once again there is a busy signal, so Tim goes inside the gas station to use a public phone. But once again he gets the message the circuits are busy. "Damn." He puts his head down and sprints back through the cold to his car.

Roxanne plays Tim's message then erases it pushes a number into her phone."He's going to Winrock, his cabin in the mountains."

My hand drops off the bed and is touching the floor. Just waking up I feel so relaxed I don't want to move. My body starts to vibrate, but I stay quiet and watch what is happening. I don't want to go out of body, I want to rest.

It's dark and very cold by the time Tim gets to the cabin. He stacks the few remaining logs from the cord of wood into the fireplace and tucks some old newspapers beneath them. The matches are damp and refuse to light anything. Starting the first fire in the fireplace had always been a race so he and Jenny could cuddle, get warm and relax. This time is different. Jenny isn't here, the wood is wet, there doesn't seem to be any other matches, and the butane fire starter is out of butane. Annoyance grabs him. Why does the simple act of lighting a fire have to be so difficult? He throws the lighter across the room. Tears of frustration crop up in him. He never allows any emotional display - not since he was in diapers. His father wouldn't allow it. Almost from the first, he knew his father was right about that. Tim accepted everything his father demanded of him because he knew that his strict discipline would help him achieve what they both wanted, the Presidency of the United States. But why, after years of such strict discipline is he suddenly having uncontrolled emotion?

"Where in the hell is the butane refill?" he yells and hits his hip against the side of the stove. "Where are the god damn matches?" he demands. "Where did she keep the god damn matches?"

He turns the gas jets on the stove - at least they work and trys to go outside to find some dry wood. But the door is stuck. He pulls and bangs, but he can't get out. He looks for the axe but can't find that either. He trys opening a window to climb out, but the windows are jammed shut. He stands still, trying to shrug off a cold fear shooting through him. Why is the door blocked? He just came through it.

He doesn't notice the flame on the gas jets have gone out.

Crouching in front of the cold fireplace, Tim surpries himself with tears welling. "Jenny" he calls to her. With the silent response comes tears of frustration that quickly turn to hacking sobs, an epiphany, a release from a lifetime of repression.

He grabbed a piece of charcoal and scribbled on the wood floor:

Jenny, he writes. I tried taking the short cut. I destroyed what we had. Forgive me. I love you forever, Tim

A portrait of remorse and despair, he collapses in front of the fireplace.

Something bumpy hits my hand as it goes through the floor and continues to grow down into the room beneath me. I ask my hand to return and it comes back easily, it's outline glowing phosphorescently.

Toward the corner of the room a gray cloud gathers and starts to take shape. I'm filled with curiosity. What is it? It materializes and I'm amazed. It's Tim ! But something won't let me go near to touch him. Coldness is emanating from him and I sense great fear. "Tim," I call to him.

"I don't know what's happening," he cries out. "I don't know what to do."

His terror grabs and paralyzes me

"They want me dead," he whispers. "I'm scared."

I want to run to him. All the anger, all the resentment I 've been feeling, evaporated. He is so vulnerable, I want to put my arms around him, take care and comfort him. But something is warning me not to off-set his precarious balance. I wait. Whatever is happening to Tim is something he has to go through and I can't help him. On the contrary, I have to stay clear. "I love you," started going through my mind - wanting to connect with him. "I love you," I call to him soundlessly. He doesn't seem to hear.

"They've trapped me," he calls out desperately. The tone of his words match his unworldly ethereal shape. "I don't know what's happening," he calls out with shattering terror. "Am I dying, or am I dead? I'm in two places. I can see myself on the floor of our cabin, but I see you with me in some bedroom. Why is this happening?"

"It's what I've been trying to tell you," I answer with my thoughts. "We're on another plane, another level, no longer in Earth's reality." You can call it spirit or think of it as pure energy that is coming from our souls."

"Does that mean we're dead?" He doesn't wait for my answer. "They locked the doors and won't let me out. From the moment I left the office I realized how much I needed and wanted you. I treated you badly. Can you ever forgive me?"

"I always forgive you. I love you. Love is about understanding and forgiveness. Don't be frightened. You'll be all right."

He starts to turn back into that gray cloudy form hovering in the door of my hospital room. I still hear his thoughts.

"I needed to be alone to think," he was saying. "You were right about everything. I wanted to call and tell you that, but I couldn't get through. They kept me from contacting you and now they've trapped me. They followed me and they won't let me out of here alive."

"That isn't important anymore. You're with me now. You're still thinking, they haven't taken that have they? Please stay calm, stay centered and let's see if we can get you through this." I keep my voice quiet and calming and hopefully reassuring.

"I don't understand whats happening. It's like they're pulling me away from my body. I can see myself on the floor near the fireplace. But I also see you in that room...." His voice rises with panic.

He's starting to freeze in midway position, attached to Earth - to life, yet out of his body and unable to get back to it. This is how ghosts are formed. Souls attached to Earth who don't want to leave the atmosphere, bodies or homes they loved, explains the voice in my head,

I know Tim won't willingly give up his body but I want to save him, free him from being trapped in this ghostly place and wish I could help him return to his body and living. But I'm not sure how to guide him and Tim doesn't know what to do. "Will the voice in my head please help me," I plead to myself.

"*If Tim returns in this panic,*" the voice answers, "*he might have physical or psychological problems. You are open to consciously leave and return because you trust,*" the voice continues. "*Tim doesn't.*"

I put my arms out to him. Perhaps I can guide him, but he shrinks away.

"Please darling, let's go back to Winrock so you can get back in your body. Join me."

He recoils in terror from me.

"Please," I call to him. "Let me help you."

The puff of gray matter grows fainter and fainter. Fear is not letting him release his pre-conceptions.

"*You must give up your attachment to having Tim on the planet*, the voice inside me says. "*Help to guide him to the place where true freedom awaits him.*"

"You mean kill him."

"*Give up your physical attachment to him. For his soul's sake, you must guide him and release him.*"

I close my eyes and try to picture Winrock. I can make out Tim lying on the stone floor next to the fireplace. The scene is desolate and cold. I pull up and away from it and settle into a soft white cocoon that could be a cloud. "Tim," I call to him. "Feel yourself out here. Visualize me surrounded by soft white. Come to me. Don't be afraid. You don't need your body. You're energy, pure consciousness. Energy can't be destroyed."

He whines like a puppy. "I'm afraid."

My heart goes out to him. I can feel his grayness trying to merge with me. Then I find myself enveloped in a pulsation of movement, a sexual, sensual ripple like passion. A squall of warmth and wet thrusting energy explodes as Tim merges with me. We shake and vibrate in a series of love so explosive its almost too much and we force ourselves to separate.

Vibrating as if he is still a part of me, I float toward my body lying on top of the bed. It looks smaller than it feels when I wear it, smaller and more vulnerable. Flying into it I hug myself gratefully as I assimilate and assume my shape.

Suddenly the realization of what just happened strikes my consciousness. OH MY GOD! Tim is going to die! Fear and panic seize me as I run to the door. I don't want him dead. Why hadn't I been able to help him get back to his body consciously? Am I responsible if he dies? Did I kill him?

Charging through the empty hallway of closed doors and dimmed lights to the brighter light of the guards' area, a lone cone of light surrounds Leo, the night guard who sits reading a magazine. The brilliance of his white shirt and pants seem to be glowing. His large feet propped up on the desk quickly slam down when I call to him, "Please...."

Having lost his composure he angrily pulls it back.

"You've got to call the police," I cry.

"Sure" he smiles sarcastically. "And after that I'll call the Queen."

"I mean it, Leo," drawing shreds of my former dignity around myself. I lost all veracity when I became a patient here. My choices are backfiring. Am I crazy? Is this all my imagination? Scanlon had been right. I must get out of here.

"You're my first 'call the police' request tonight."

"I'm not crazy, you don't understand," I yelled, hysteria growing with the horrible reality. "You have to call the police. My fiancée is dying. He's unconscious and can't get back to his body."

The guard's mouth twitches with laughter. His eyes are cold.

"Look, I know what you're thinking, but you've got to understand." I grab his hand, pleading. He pulls it away.

"I can see the future, see things that are happening far from here. My fiancée, Tim is in a cabin alone. The doors and windows are locked. He can't get out. He can see himself unconscious on the floor and he's panicked. It's horrible and cruel. Please, you can save him."

The burly man pushes himself out of the chair and towers over me in my thin nightdress. "Please," I shiver from fear, and emotion. "He can't get back to his body. He doesn't know how. He needs someone there to save him. Otherwise he's gone."

The man yawns. His breath smells sour. Muscles ripple in his shoulders and throat. "Want a tranquilizer?" He picks up a clipboard and flips through the charts. "You're scheduled to have one if needed."

"Please, I know what you think. But you have nothing to lose. If it's true you will have saved someone, if not, I'm crazy. But if it's true and you do nothing, then you're partially responsible."

"O.K. Jenny. I'm responsible. I'm a dirty rat. Now get back to bed." He takes me strongly by the arm and leads me to my room. I'm helpless with rage.

Shoving me roughly to the bed he hands me a small pill and paper cup of water and demands, "Take it."

I take the pill quietly and place it in my mouth, then take a swallow of water. As I start to hand the paper cup back he slaps it out of my hand. It flies across the bed, water splashing on me as he grabs me by the hair, pulls my head back, and sticks his fat tobacco stained finger in my mouth. He finds the pill and shoves it to the back of my throat. I choke but he keeps my head back till I swallow it. Satisfied he lets go and lumbers out of the room, locking the door behind him.

"*You're not thinking clearly,*" comes the familiar bell-like voice. "*You're caught up emotionally.*" Soothing breath pumps through my body. Every pulse, every movement becomes strong. "*Go to him now,*" the voice said. "*Guide him.*"

I concentrate on the center of my forehead, my pineal gland, as shudders come up from my toes to a familiar pulse in my genitals, a quickening excitement before I take off.

"Tim," I concentrate strongly. "I want to go to Tim".

Remembering the feel of his skin, his hands on me, the sense of his smell I feel the weight before I see his shape cradled in my arms in front of the fireplace. I stroke his face softly.

"I set you up," he whispers, tears falling softly down his cheeks. They mixed with my own.

"It's all right. You did what you had to do."

"I've caused you great suffering."

"It's brought me great strength. I've discovered inner peace. I bless you for it."

"They think you're crazy."

"Only for now."

"No one will listen to you." His voice was plaintive.

"They will," I said. "I have powers that go beyond anything that can be used against me."

"Not possible..." his voice starts to fade.

"Everything is possible, beyond your imagination. Tim I can leave my body. That's why I'm here with you now. Can you understand? You're more than just body. You're pure energy. You're spirit." My voice is distant and drifting.

"Are we both dead??"

"No, not yet. But I think it's too late for you, you've been out of your body too long. I think you're supposed to leave."

He shudders with terror.

"What will happen?" He sounds so distant, so scared. He is so unprepared.

I call to him. "Your mind will rule. You can create any place you want to be. Even with me right now if you trust."

"Where are you?" he calls out in the very far distance.

"At Winrock, with you."

"Will you find me after I leave?" His voice is growing more and more faint.

"Of course I will. I'll always find you."

I will also find the cause of his murder, find out who is killing everyone who might be in their way. I lost my best friend and now my love, the man who would have been my husband. I vow on Tim's expiring life I will find the core of this nightmare and expose what is happening.

Tim suddenly appears close to me. He seems whole again. We hold each other and he seems to be calm. Lifting his head close to mine we kiss lightly, gently, full of love. I'm joyful.

"Good bye." His eyes close.

I feel his head on my lap, his limp body heavy in my arms, empty of the essence that was Tim. It was then I become aware of gas. So many sensations have been bombarding me I hadn't noticed till then. I try to lift Tim, but he's inert and heavy. I try connecting with him but there is no longer any part of Tim inside his body nor in the atmosphere around me. He has gone off far away.

There is going to be an explosion, a big one, says the voice.

"But how will it affect me?" I question myself.

"*Don't find out. Don't get caught in it.*" says the voice in my mind. "*Get out of there.*"

Fatigue is closing in. I bend and hold Tim in my arms one last time and kiss his flesh, the only part left of him, then ask to return to my body.

His weight disappears and my body lay twisted in a semi-fetal position on the bed. A headache hammers. The medication the attendant had given me fights for attention. It wants me to sleep. I give in to its persistence, close my eyes and drift.

CHAPTER TWENTY-ONE

Dr. White walks somberly into the dining room. Heading toward me, eyes cast down, his shoulders drawn together, I fight the dread that threatens to come. This is a time when I hope my truth is not reality.

White clears his throat and sits down next to me.

I try to collect myself. I had been hoping it was only a vivid dream. But White's face and posture broadcast that it's real.

Tim is dead. I feel my throat closing up. The heavy pain that fills my heart to know without doubt he will never walk on this Earth with me again. I'll never feel his touch, we'll no longer have those private laughs or our serious talks. My trusted friend, another one, gone. Grief crashes in on a breath-taking wave. It has become too familiar, will it never go away?

"*Re-focus,*" I hear the voice command. I sit up straighter and measure White carefully. His furtive eyes give him away. He resents my probing. He knows I see his insecurities.

Picking up my unused fork I turn to him, innocence and openness my weapons. He must not know what I'm feeling.

"Good morning, Dr. White. Joining the inmates for breakfast? You can have mine if you'd like. You know I don't eat and this isn't quite cold yet." I offer the fork and push the plate of scrambled eggs in front of him.

White twists and turns, uncomfortable with his body as he waves away the fork and tries to pull himself into a semblance of power. I smile at his discomfort.

"How are you this morning?" he focuses on the sugar dispenser, pouring globs of it into his coffee.

"I've read sugar could cause schizophrenia." I say sweetly.

He puts the sugar dispenser down and juts his head like a brontosaurus. "I want to speak to you in my office."

"About Tim?" A strange euphoria is building, like I'm about to float out of body. But I want to stay grounded and command myself to stay that way.

"You know," he utters both the question and answer.

"Didn't the attendant tell you what happened last night?"

He looks at me evenly. "You woke up in the middle of the night and required sedation I immediately receive reports of uneven behavior."

"Uneven behavior." I work to keep the bile of outrage down.

His lip curl. He knows he pinged me. "A patient gets up in the middle of the night agitated, requests the attendant to contact police to investigate somebody who might be dying because he can't get back to his body. We videotape everything, otherwise I would have thought the attendant was having hallucinations." He shifts trying to make himself feel stronger.

"Dr. White, in all your years of research and study, you must know something about out of body experience, Isn't that what you're trying to achieve here? "

"There are books recording near-death experiences in which people believe they are out of body. But there are many explanations for that," he explained defensively.

"Yes, and there are many that have almost the exact visual and emotional experience - whether it's an eight year old child on one side of the planet or an eighty year old person on the other."

"Well you obviously have read books on the subject."

"Not really."

We look at each other. I don't want to say any more but the voice has taken over for me and is doing it's own talking. "*Dr. White, research in the manipulation of human behavior is considered by many to be professionally unethical.*"

"I agree." He looks straight at me.

I try to control my building anger by joining the conversation. "It isn't legal either."

"What are you saying?" His tone is getting aggressive.

"You're putting peoples' rights in jeopardy."

"Jenny," White is slow and precise. "You came here for therapy. You signed yourself in. Your rights aren't jeopardized."

"Few people sign themselves in here, although on paper it says they do."

He doesn't move a muscle. "You can't prove anything, Jenny."

"Maybe." I look at him and smile.

White shakes his head grimly and pours himself another cup of coffee using the rest of the sugar. "Jenny, we know you have a vivid imagination, but save it. We don't fit your manufactured fantasies. We're trying to help you live a more fulfilling life but you get too agitated."

I can't hold myself back. "I don't know for sure what you've done to me, but you haven't succeeded in changing the way I think. You don't know me, can't even see me most of the time."

I shrink from his reaction to what I should never have said. I better change the subject. "Why did you keep my Producer, Al Rudnik, from coming in here?"

"When was he here Jenny? I wasn't informed."

"Of course you were. He called before he came and was told he could get in. Once he got here he was denied entrance."

He looked at me steadily. "He wasn't here. He never came. It's your imagination."

"Want to tell me Tim is my imagination? That nothing happened to him?"

He ignores that. "Al Rudnik never sent me any correspondence. I'm sorry Jenny. I'm sure you would have liked him to do that for you."

I look at him steadily. He's not going to pull that with me. "All you managed to do is make Rudnik angry. He has probably set a huge investigating team in motion by now. You're going to have major problems if anything happens to me. Destruction of the mind is worse than physical death. There are people who know what you're doing and are ready if anything happens to me to expose you. They have all the information, all of your research and the corresponding work of Anson Labs. I made sure of that."

He was calm, almost passive. "Jenny, you had a nervous breakdown when your friend Mannie Sebastiane died."

"Did I?" My tone is incredulous.

"Jenny dear, you're very upset."

"Don't call me dear. Its condescending and patronizing."

"Maybe you should have another sedative."

"Don't you dare." I used a tone in my voice that came from such a power source I surprised myself and thanked it.

He paused a moment, considering. "You've reached the wrong conclusions because you're upset." He isn't smiling.

"All your chemicals and technology are not working with me. I've connected with something stronger and that is protecting me. Something you will probably never understand because you're not sensitive and don't want to be. That's why you have no right to mess with peoples' heads. You don't have the capacity to understand that which you try to control."

I probably shouldn't have said that but I'm glad he knows how I feel. He knows I'm smarter than he is and I see that he's failing.

White bends toward me, sinister, speaking softly, a low monotone. "As long as you believe the fantasy, that's fine. It's a nice positive attitude. Better than despondent. Anything that keeps you comfortable while you're recovering."

His breath and tone are almost more menacing than his words.

"That's destructive intent, Doctor White. You can't make me insecure with drivel like that. You've got to do better."

"We will. That's why you're here."

Fear shot up my back. He almost got me. I can handle him, but I'm not sure how I can tolerate more of the treatments I already had. What if I lose my ability to go out of body? What if there is no conspiracy and if everything I believe isn't possible?

I remind myself that there have been travelers that had taken a similar path and expressed their journeys through the arts, one way or another. Personally, those various areas of vision and knowledge have made me stronger to recognize I'm not crazy, I'm not alone. I belong to a secret society unbeknown to each other, who receive information they feel is important to share. Sometimes we recognize it in others, but usually we go it alone – a lonely and sometimes difficult journey.

White shifts in his chair and pushes it back. He's about to leave.

"Just because some see the world differently, does not mean they're crazy Dr. White. It's useless to destroy anything that is different from your own perspective. Truth always finds a way out and always wins. Why don't you work for the good?"

"I understand how upset you must feel." He ignores my question. "We expected this when we learned about our dear friend Tim."

"Upset?" I fought to hold my temper. "You call my reaction to seeing him unable to get back into his body, 'UNEASY BEHAVIOR!'"

"How did you see that Jenny?"

"Some of us are able to do what you're trying to do chemically. I know what you're doing."

White stood impassive, unresponsive. I try to keep my voice low and contained, not let him see me shaking or draw attention to our exchange. "Tim died. It didn't have to happen. Or was it planned because you lost control of him? Was he feeling remorse? Was it the second thoughts you didn't think he could handle?"

White visibly hardened. "If you were there with him, why didn't you save him if you have such extraordinary powers."

"That doesn't mean I can overturn destiny." I gaze at him steadily. "Why the explosion? That was primitive and unnecessary, Tim was dead already."

White smiled sadistically. "Accidents happen."

"That was no accident. I'm not sure how you killed him, but my guess is you used a drug that attacks the nervous system. That's why he was so panicked. He had lost his body and had only his mind."

White tried to keep his expression even, but his seething anger felt ready to explode.

I decide to take a chance. "The police and press have information about Mannie's research. Your people were sloppy and left a lot behind. You and Jan should co-operate now, it might reduce your prison sentences."

He ran his finger across unsmiling lips. "Unlikely." he smoothed his bristly scalp and scraped his chair back loudly. "Come see me after breakfast. Let's talk about your discharge."

"Sure." I pushed the scrambled eggs around on the plate. The mushy bright yellow glop looks like soft cardboard. I can't touch it. I hadn't eaten in days, or has it been months?

CHAPTER TWENTY-TWO

I reach White's office before he gets to it. He doesn't see me or react to my invisible presence as some do unconsciously. He flicks the switch on the intercom. "Jan, come in here." He drums his fingers on the desk. "We have a problem."

Jan comes in from the interior office, concerned when she sees White's face. "What's wrong?"

"Tim Jenkins is dead. There was a gas explosion at his mountain cabin. Everything was destroyed - pulverized." He looks at her steadily, questioning her prior knowledge of this. She doesn't react.

"Jenny Webster says it was murder. She says Tim was separated from his body by some artificial means and he couldn't get back to it. She said he was dead before the explosion." He takes a deep breath, his face contorted with worry. "Can the coroner determine that?"

"I suppose so." Jan reasoned calmly. "If there is enough left of the body."

He shakes his head. "I don't know." He exhales deeply. "Jenny said explicitly, he was out of body !" He took another deep breath. He was having some trouble breathing. "Can she know what we did to him?" He holds tightly to the edge of the desk and leans in to her. "I don't know, but she practically said she did. The way she looked at me.." he shivers convulsively. "I think she knows everything."

Jan shrugs. "So what? What can she do? She's crazy. I don't know why you're so upset. It's good this happened now before we went further with either one of them. We need perfect specimens. He was flawed. Sentiment was overtaking him."

"You're in denial. You're not hearing what I'm saying. Jenny may have been with him out of her body. She says she was and knows how to do it ! Everything we've done to her has turned to her advantage. It's all gone wrong." Wringing his hands his face is white as stone. "What about the coroner's report?"

"Stop worrying. Nothing is going to happen. We can take care of that, it's Stanley Smith. If nothing has happened so far, it isn't going to happen."

He looks at the wall beyond her. "We made a mistake. Her reports didn't compute well enough. She should have been re-programmed by now. Do you realize what we've given her? How much more can she take? You wouldn't have believed our conversation just now. She is completely even, barely reacting to Tim's death. She had time to grieve because she was there when it happened. She was so composed when I gave her the news."

"Will you stop !" Jan banged her hand on the desk. White jumped and looked at her in amazement. She hadn't shown that much passion in all the years they'd been together. "None of that is important. What's important is to decide if we should keep her or kill her."

"We can't keep her much longer, that's for sure. Her army of lawyers want her out." He pauses then points his finger for emphasis. "Make sure her admissions sheet is signed and says voluntary commitment due to job stress, do not mention anything about a rape."

I listen, mesmerized. These people are such scum.

"We must determine the extent of her powers before we release her," White emphasized.

"Why?" Jan shook her head in disagreement.

"She can cause problems."

Jan shook her head. "No she can't." Her voice is soft, calm, soothing. "She's in a mental hospital. What is she going to say? We kept her here against her will? We did things to her mind? That's paranoia. You're not looking at this logically. Anything she says will make her sound crazier. Or we can just kill her. Make it look like suicide – though that might put unwanted negative attention on this place."

"She said she left information behind if anything happens to her. It's too risky. And I can't accept she hasn't been affected by what we've done to her. Those who have gone as far out as she has, usually don't come back. The few that have, are no longer able to function. She can. You should have heard her at breakfast just now."

"Was she eating?"

"No. It's been more than three months and she still looks healthy. Maybe healthier. I don't like it."

"Hmmm - " Jan was pensive, not liking it either.

I watched from the corner, afraid to move, I don't want my energy to rustle anything. A movement could cause detection. They can't see me, but there is a chance they can feel my presence. Sometimes when I travel out of body, especially around the hospital, I notice a few people seem to experience my presence with a chill. Do the Whites know those signs? What will they do if they recognized them?

White looks harassed. "Do you think it's possible she has the power to do naturally what we're trying to create artificially?"

"Not really. She may have dreamed something was happening. The time bending we have been working on is a chemical reaction. I don't see how it can occur naturally. Maybe we've been more successful with her than we realize and she's just not sharing where she's been. Maybe her zombie – like behavior after we took her out of the rooms is an act."

White looks out the window then back at Jan. "You know that she alerted the attendant about Tim."

"No, I didn't."

"It was that stupid idiot, Leo. Have him fired."

Jan pats him on the hand and tries to soothe him. "Calm down. If we fire him it could cause suspicion."

"Quite the contrary. We accept prescient vision. One of us should have been consulted."

"It was the middle of the night."

"I don't care."

"You're being unreasonable."

"I'm being cautious."

"All right," she sighed. "Maybe we should just kill her."

He shook his head disbelieving. "We may finally have someone with the ability to go out of body and return to it consciously. The problem is that we haven't conditioned her sufficiently. It would be a terrible waste to kill her! We have to step up the programming - change her way of thinking, create vulnerability and dependence, then we can use her !"

Rebuked, Jan cast her eyes down. "You're right."

"If we can harness her, she's an incredible tool. I think we should try stronger doses of chemicals in conjunction with hypnosis."

I went behind White and sat down next to him. He didn't seem to notice.

"What we have to do," he said, "is make her feel safe and comfortable. Complacency is a powerful tool. But I also think we need someone to go out of body with her, to control her."

Jan looked at him evenly. "Give me the preparation, I can do it."

"You haven't been trained or tested. Forget it. No one's done it except those transients and illegals we brought in here. Need I remind you what happened to them?"

"Yes," she sounded impatient. "But we did consider keeping some of them when they came back. The chemicals work. Look, Jenny is beginning to trust me. You read her psychological profile. She wants to trust. She's already started."

White shakes his head. "There have been too many failures. You forget the amount of sacrifices."

"Consider the genetic types." Jan shifts in her chair, re-crosses her legs. She seems to be losing patience. "Am I hearing remorse?"

"Not at all. I'm talking about the independence factor that can't be controlled. There is something out there that empowers people. Makes them more than what they were. That's why we have problems if or when they return. It happened with some of the astronauts. And you know how disciplined they are."

"You're displaying remorse." Her eyes narrow. "It's time to let me go. Then we'll know everything firsthand. My allegiance is to you and everything we're doing."

White doesn't look at her. He's angry about her accusation.

"It's my choice, " she continues. "You need me out there. I know the consequences and I'm not afraid. You know how dedicated and devoted I am. This project is my life and I'm one of the few you can trust. We are going to have to use someone from the group and it may as well be me."

White weighes her words.

Jan sits closer and uncrosses her legs. She smiles and leans in closer. "I keep my loyalties. I should definitely be the first of our group to go out of body."

He rubs her knee. She smiles at him. He pulls away. "Too many things can go wrong," he says. "Look what happened to Tim.

"Are you comparing me to him? He wasn't strong enough." Jan puts his hand back, high on her thigh. "We've done enough experiments with the Disposables, the only thing that ever goes wrong is personality control. And you know mine." She smiles and brings his hand closer up her thigh. The last vestiges of his resentment melts as his fingers move up between her legs. As he starts to wiggle his fingers she pulls away. "Let me try to go out of body with our chemicals. Only for a few minutes. You can regulate it. It's necessary."

He pulls his hand out from under her skirt and picks up a chart on the desk, making a pretext of looking at it, sneaking a whiff of his hand.

"Do you notice anything strange in here?" he suddenly asks. "Something has been bothering me since I came in." He takes a black rod from his desk and points it around the room. I lean so far into the wall I'm halfway through it.

Looking around he opens the door and shuts it. "Funny. I just had a strange feeling we're not alone. We're not bugged, that's for sure. There is no way anyone can get through these defenses."

Jan remains still, waiting for White's decision.

"I guess you're right," he concedes You're the one I can trust. Let's do it."

Jan smiles relieved, excited. "Now."

He nods.

They go through an inner door of the office into a small laboratory. Jan goes straight to the white metal table at the end of the room and sits on it. White prepares an injection with a clear fluid then rubs her arm with alcohol. "We'll start with three minutes." He leans down and kisses her on the cheek. "Thank you." He injects her with the shot. She immediately sleds into unconsciousness. He helps her lie down, then checks her pulse, the time, and records it.

I stand by the table where Jan lay, ready to meet her when she emerges from the physical. But she doesn't come out. She merely lays there, trapped in her body. I check the woman's aura. It's gaining in brightness, growing and spreading, leaking out of her. I watch in amazement as everything goes out of control. Jan's ethereal body is separating and taking off without her.

I try to intervene, to send a message to be aware. But I know I'm throwing my energy into the void. Jan's disappearing light, her essence, is streaking into the cosmos. I know without asking my inner voice that I must not follow. There is no coming back from the realm she's going.

I go over to White and try to get his attention. He's watching Jan from a stool, checking his watch, making notes on a pad. He can't see the light almost gone from her body.

I throw all my energy against him. He shivers a bit then gets up and goes to the prone figure on the table and checks her pulse. She has none. He pulls back her lids. Her fixed eyes stare straight ahead. He puts his ear to her chest, then starts artificial respiration pushing and using his whole body for power. He stops, hands trembling and rushes to the medicine cabinet where he prepares a hypodermic. On the way back he punches the intercom, yells CODE RED, then injects the syringe directly into Jan's heart. There is no response. He starts pushing on her diaphragm desperately, then breaths into her mouth. Nothing. She doesn't respond.

I watch as the last remnants of light leak from her body. She is completely gone, gone so far she has skipped the fourth dimension where most people go when they first leave their bodies. I will myself back to my physical body and find I had put my head down on the table in the dining room as if I had been napping.

All the people and breakfast dishes are gone so I get up and start down the hall. A few nurses and orderlies rush past. I knew where they're going.

Going back to my room I sit cross legged in the middle of the bed and close my eyes, resting my hands palms up on my knees and ask the voice for guidance.

Al Rudnik comes to my thoughts. "Can he be trusted?

"*Not really,*" says the voice inside me. "*He's too frightened to think clearly. Go to Detective Parker. He's sensitive and a clear thinker. If you keep your thoughts simple and pure, they'll flood him with inspiration. Just stay where you are and focus on him.*"

I hope I can remember Parker well enough. There is a quickening inside when I think about his crooked smile. But his face isn't too clear to me. I remember his red hair and thin face and penetrating eyes. So penetrating I start tingling and warming inside, strong stirrings - not the usual out of body ones, but physical and maybe a little bit sexy.

Parker is appealing in a sensitive, intelligent way. I had always preferred to be with smart men. We communicate better. Smiling I think of Parker's freckles, the way he looked at me that made me tingle. When my life was in turmoil and he smiled at me with compassion and warmth, it made me feel better.

Drawn through a vortex, soaring through the air like a bird, I find myself just above the Hollywood Bowl in Los Angeles and land in an apartment close by that is essentially the opposite of my own. This one is dingy and covered with simulated wood paneling, ancient overstuffed armchairs and a sofa bed with a cover from decades ago. In the center of the threadbare sofa bed sits Detective James Parker. I can read his mind and he's thinking about me! He's concerned. I feel a rush.

Red and blue lights flicker from the neon sign outside the window, creating a multicolored warrior's mask onto his thin, pale face. He looks weary.

"Nothing is going right with the Webster case," I can feel him thinking. "Why are they stalling the investigation? If they want to indict her, why haven't they brought it to the Grand Jury ? Something isn't right. There's foot dragging. What's happening?

Notes are scribbled on a pad next to him. "Cover-up is scrawled at the top. "Set up? Who? Why?" had been written.

"I like what she's made of..." Parker is thinking.

If I had a face at this point I would be grinning, probably blushing. I like being able to eaves drop on him, but the irony doesn't escape me. What I fear and want to expose is exactly what I'm doing. I had vowed never to take advantage of this extraordinary privilege, and yet, here I am, doing exactly what I want to be fighting. Hypocrisy for the common good?

I almost turn away as Parker absent-mindedly starts to stroke himself through his seersucker pajamas. He's reminiscing how grateful for holidays and birthdays because his mother always sends him practical things like underwear or pajamas that he would forget to buy for himself. These blue and white seersucker pajamas were Mother's gift from Easter. This was the first time he had them on. They feel scratchy and not particularly comfortable. He wouldn't wear these with Jenny.

I giggle, embarrassed. I shouldn't be listening. But I can't help it!

What would I wear with her, he mused. Silk? Boxer shorts? A robe? Nothing? Where would he wear nothing with Jenny? He stroked his penis as he saw her in his mind, fantasizing that she walked toward him wearing only a smile. Her hair is shining, she's laughing-beckoning... But he's dressed. He can't take off his clothes. He can't be nude with Jenny. Not even while he's dreaming.

I can't help watching as he strokes himself growing larger and harder.

I'm so glad I'm out of my body.

CHAPTER TWENTY-THREE

Grainy lines form a head squeezing out of the printer at Santa Monica Police Headquarters. Rolling out is a picture of Timothy Jenkins, followed by his curriculum vitae and all other available information.

Parker studies the aristocratic face. There is no softness in the handsome portrait. The eyes appear to be cold and calculating, the lips turned down in what could be interpreted as a sneer. Some women like that. Jenny obviously did. Parker caught himself. Why was he making these judgments ? He never met the man and now he's dead.

There are no leads and not much had been left of Jenkins body except a few charred bones. Finding the exact cause of death will be impossible. He had to find out if it really was an accident. Two fiery deaths like Jenkins and Sebastiane's can't be coincidence. If they are linked, then they point to Jenny possibly being the next victim. A death staged as a suicide in a mental institution would be easy. Parker had learned in philosophy class that the obvious was always the most difficult, and he had an unsettling feeling he was overlooking the obvious.

Boyle sauntered over to him. "I've got a surprise for you college boy," his grin borrowed from a Cheshire cat.

"What is it ?" Parker asks.

Boyle bends and whispers in his ear, "We're doing a sting tonight."

Parker leans away from him.

"A cop's getting a pay off. We're not sure who he is, but our informant will be there with the connection. Ready for it college boy?"

Parker is excited. Except for the short time he had been a uniformed policeman he hadn't seen much action. The Sebastiane and Jenkins cases require detailed research and investigation but it's mostly paperwork and conversation. Tonight he'll be in the trenches, a foot soldier once again, adrenaline pumping, mind and body sharpened. "When does it happen ?"

"We gotta talk to the Captain first." Boyle claps him on the back as they head for the Captain's office.

Pounding rouses me from my dream. Or is it a dream? Unsettled I rise shakily and go to the door. I don't make it all the way before Dr. White comes barging in. "Happy?" He's seething. "You got rid of both of them."

"What are you talking about?" I'm still groggy from sleep.

"Your boyfriend and my wife," yells White, nearly out of control.

Starting to speak, reason stops me. White is irrational. I'm not going to join his dance.

"You're being investigated for both murders."

I can't make any sense of his words "It isn't possible. Tim just died. How could I be a suspect?"

"You don't remember much do you?" White's lips twisted in anger.

"Remember?" Panic joined dismay. Am I going to sink?

"You've been sleeping," he spit the words at her, "a month," he added sadistically.

I sat down on the bed, shock threatening to collapse my chest. I can't breathe, I can only whisper, "Bastard."

"You were hysterical. It was for your own good."

I fought to calm myself. "Before or after Jan died?"

"After."

My lips play with an ironic bitter smile. I can't hold back. "Because she died?"

He looked at me steadily. "Yes."

"Suspicion?"

"There is evidence someone changed the labels on the drugs. Jan was having a seizure. When I injected her, it was with the wrong drug. She died. But of course, you know that."

"You obviously made a mistake."

"You say you can go out of body. It's a metaphor for being able to get in and out of places like a cat burglar."

"Blaming me for your mistake won't work. Do you have surveillance in your lab? Then you would see me do it."

White's eyes glowed. A chill ran through me and I decided not to say anything more. I remember my last meeting with Scanlon - how he had begged me to leave. How much time has passed since I had been with him ? Everything is so jumbled. I've lost all sense of time and place. I know the events, but not their sequence. Dreading my next question but needing to know I ask. "Was I in the sleep room?"

"Yes."

"Bastard." I want to slap him. "How long?"

"Since you changed the labels on the bottles. You were out of control. We had to do it."

A scream of anguish was bubbling in my chest, but I force it to stay down. I have to know the rest. "Electroshocks?"

"You signed the consent."

"Liar," I'm unable to hold back.

"You blocked Jan's re-entry." He stared at me his mouth twisted with contempt.

"You're crazy." I want to scream but hold myself so tight I start to shake badly. I don't know how much time I've lost, how much memory. I thought I remembered most of my out of body states, but when had they happened ? How long have I been suspended? Scanlon had been right. They were going to try to take everything away from me. They hadn't yet. I can still use deductive reasoning.

"You killed her," White kept saying.

"You injected her, Dr. White. Maybe an overdose? On purpose."

"I want you out of here." His anger fills the room.

I feel a power within me as I watch his tantrum. "Walking or on a slab?"I ask the strutting man muttering a monologue I tr to ignore.

"We're not going to kill you. We already own your brain."

I heard that loud and clear. To keep from shaking I tell myself he's bluffing. If he had been successful, I wouldn't be questioning him. But what if I hadn't always been self- aware? Could my mind have been grabbed then? Were my out of body experiences created by others and only put in my head? Was I immersed in a virtual reality machine while the Whites and their staff twisted my dials? Did I underestimate his power, his destructiveness, his evil? Is my inability to accept the extreme cruelty of others to be the cause of my downfall?

Doubts continue to pour through my mind. If I'm wrong about the out of body, maybe the rape didn't occur either. But I had the bruises, the contusions on my skin. I know they had tried using chemical hallucinogens and they had the technical ability to project three-dimensional programmed dramas into my eyes to affect my mind. It's growing more possible that my own beliefs and truths could not be my own but are implants from other sources with the use of virtual and chemical reality.

"The police want to talk to you."

"First I talk to my attorney. Let me use the phone."

"The lines are down"

I know he's lying.

"I want to know how Jan died," he was saying. Tell me what you saw."

I shake my head.

His lip curl. "Tell me what you saw." He was on a platform he won't step off.

"What makes you so sure I saw anything?" I ask evenly. Calm on the surface I feel split in half, half filled with dread that I may have said something when they drugged me, half hopeful my higher resources will keep me from trouble.

White paced the room, a crumbled, discolored fish out of water. "Leave. There's nothing more we can do for you."

"All right." I hadn't expected this.

He jumped to attention and started to speak, then changed his mind and walked out, slamming the door behind him.

Almost as quickly Elizabeth walked through the door without opening it. "You keep making me manifest myself when you have these stupid doubts. You've got to trust your higher self and know what you're about. It's good you're open to others, but you must learn to listen to yourself."

"Did they do anything to me? Program me?"

"They tried."

"Did they succeed?"

"Only you know the answer to that. You're the student and you're also the teacher. Mix all your information with your intuition - it will come out right."

I adore this girl. Love pours off her like a waterfall.

Elizabeth continued. "Don't you want to get off this planet? It's the pits. It's always in chaos, there's always a commotion. I'm getting tired of coming here. This Urban blight and bad energy is lousy for my aura. I've got to do a major cleansing whenever I leave here."

I laugh, "are you for real?"

"Are you?"

"That's part of my current crisis. I'm not sure if I'm making you up. You could be a dream, which would be a lot easier. Or maybe I'm manifesting you for myself which makes me certifiably crazy."

Elizabeth hugged her. "How do I feel?"

The girl's energy is literally electrifying. "Good." My fears are arrested.

"You're on the right track with Detective Parker," Elizabeth declares. "He'll get you out of this mess. Keep him in the positive and perceive him as working with you. That's important."

Although I'm not sure if Elizabeth is a figment of my imagination or a spirit from another world, she is such a positive, reinforcing energy, it doesn't matter. "You make it sound so easy."

"It is. That's the fun of it. Remember when you were a baby, you had no concept of time or space? Your needs were pure and you could summon your changes; food, dry clothes, heat, cold, by crying or screaming ? You're doing that again, but in another way. Only this time your demands are more complex and the way you ask more devious and sophisticated. Then, to complicate everything, the minute you learn something, you want to run and blab it all over to save the world. But the world doesn't always want to be saved or see the future. Change is frightening, especially with unseen forces."

Elizabeth sits down on the bed next to me. It bounces with her weight. I want to hug her but restrain myself and wait.

"Think you should call your lawyer? Get signed out of here?"

"YES!"

"Then come on, time to go. Let's get this show on the road. Follow me."

We fly through the hallway and enter a small office in the back of the administration building through it's locked door. The room is empty except for a desk with a telephone.

"Is this for real ?" I ask Elizabeth.

"Call Scanlon. You'll see."

Scanlon is surprised with my call. "Jenny, hello!"

"I want to get out of here Uncle James. You were right. I need to be free."

"Get a release from White this instant. Go to his office and get out today."

"Will you call him first?"

"Yes, of course I will. Jenny, are you frightened?" Scanlon sounded concerned.

"A little. White told me he wanted me out of here," I told him. "But I want to walk out and not be carried horizontally. He said I was responsible for his wife's death, that the labels on her medication were switched. I wouldn't know what to switch, the accusation is ridiculous. But so much of this is. I'm accused of murdering two people. Uncle James, you've been so right. I desperately need your help."

"Don't worry, we're doing everything for you. You'll be exonerated."

"I only watched." I start crying.

"Watched what ?" He sounds alarmed.

"I saw White give Jan the injection that killed her. It was an experimental drug they were working on that would propel people out of body. They know I can do that and they wanted to counteract me. But her death wasn't my fault. I only watched. I didn't do anything."

There was a long pause. "Did White see you?"

"He couldn't. I was out of body."

An intake of breath as Scanlon hesitated.

"I know you think I'm delusional Uncle James, but you have to believe me. Out of body pheromone can happen. It's been proven. I'll try to show you one day, I promise." I liked calling him Uncle James, it made me feel comfortable.

"Jenny, listen to me. Don't say another word about that. If you say you can leave your body, they won't let you out of there."

Elizabeth snickered. I motioned for her to keep quiet, but she laughed out loud making me giggle.

The attorney's silence continued.

"Look, I know what you think," I managed, "but it's true. If there had been an autopsy, it would be proven."

"There was an autopsy, and there was evidence of a strong tranquilizer that is used for hyperkinetic children and nerve spasms. It wasn't enough to kill her."

"What if it was mixed with something undetectable, and the two together were toxic?"

"Possible. We have a lab working on it."

"Will you call White and get me out of here?"

"Yes, and I'll send someone from my staff to get you. My plane is nearby."

"I adore you! I promise I'm going to start living again."

I hung up the telephone and hugged Elizabeth.

CHAPTER TWENTY-FOUR

The moon is low, the street very dark, as Boyle and Parker wait in their unmarked car at the top of a block that dead-ends at a wall of warehouses. A single streetlamp at the far end paints a glossy sheen of light across the bricks of the buildings, splashes of red and green gang graffiti is the only color in the chiaroscuro setting. The air is thick with deathly stillness in the total desolation of the urban canyon. Even though Parker knows SWAT teams are posted on rooftops and inside vans and doorways, he wipes his hand once more to keep his heavy gun from slipping.

A shadowy figure emerges from between two buildings. Parker is sure Boyle can hear his heart beating. Boyle is smiling.

"Ready?" Boyle asks him.

Parker takes a breath. "Yes," he exhales as he puts his hand on the door. "But shouldn't we wait for..." He doesn't finish. Boyle is already out the door, hissing over his shoulder, "come on..."

Boyle walks down the middle of the street, his gun drawn, toward the figure in the shadows.

Parker lunges for the car door, but something stops him. He can't see me blocking his way, using every amount of thought and force I possess to keep him from getting out. He can only watch as the shadowy figure whirls, gun raised, and pulls the trigger pointed at Boyle.

Boyle hesitates, then in slow motion crumbles to the ground, a spray of blood beginning to cover the belt buckle engraved C.O.P.

Bright lights, screams: "DON'T SHOOT! "FREEZE, DROP YOUR GUN..." stop Parker before he can fire. He runs to his fallen partner and tries to find a pulse. His heart sinks by the look in Boyle's eyes. They're vacant.

Someone takes Parker's arm and leads him away. "Sorry," says another as a crowd of policemen close rank around the fallen figure.

Unthinking, unfeeling Parker turns and goes over to the prone suspect handcuffed with his arms behind his back. He looks like a transient. Parker stands over him, holding his gun, wanting to pull the trigger, but keeping it down. A hand pats his shoulder. It's the Captain. "Come on," the hand tightens on his arm as he leads him away, "there's nothing we can do here. Let's have some coffee and talk till he's booked."

The smell of disinfectant in the small coffee shop is making Parker nauseous. He waits while the Captain lights a cigarette and stirs cream into his coffee. "Why did Boyle get out of the car ?" he finally asks him. "You had orders to wait till there were two suspects."

Parker shakes his head. "I don't know. Boyle asked me if I was ready, and I said yes, but then I said shouldn't we wait for - but he didn't let me finish. He got out of the car, before I had a chance to say more. I don't know what I should have done..." He started to choke up.

"You did the right thing. You followed orders."

"Parker shook his head in despair. "It was all wrong. I knew it while it was happening, it was like," he paused for a moment, started to pick up his coffee cup, then decided against it. He looked straight at the Captain. "It was like he did it on purpose. I don't understand why he did that..."

"I had the same feeling. You have to go for counseling," the Captain said.

"No, I'm all right, really. Let me interrogate the suspect. I'll get the truth out of him."

The Captain shook his head. "I said counseling, not therapy. We can't afford rough stuff. We go by the book on this one. I want the guy convicted. Murder One-Special Circumstances. I want him receiving a lethal injection, compliments of the State of California. A case like this is procedure. You gotta talk to a Counselor."

"I was a psych major before I went into jurisprudence, I don't need a shrink to tell me what I just went through. I know. Let me interrogate the sun of a bitch. I won't use force, it's not my style. Not physical force."

The Captain took a long drag of his cigarette and blew out a perfect smoke ring. "I watched you when you went over to the suspect. I knew what you were thinking. I would have too. You showed good discipline." He appraised Parker through the smoke. "We want this guy to talk. I don't think I could handle it if it had been my partner."

"With all respect Captain, I think I can."

The Captain gave him another long appraisal. "All right, we'll try. I'll put Jimmy Grady on with you. He's a good cop, level headed. But remember, the minute you start to lose it, you're off. Clear ?"

"Yes sir," Parker answered, anxious to get back to the station.

Tracey Seebert, a slick young lawyer from Scanlon's retinue, is noticeably tense, her fine wool crepe Armani draped shoulders were drawn up close to the shiny gold Paloma Picasso x's pierced through her ears. Rubbing her manicured fingers together she seems to forget her usually perfect posture and is hunched on a chair, watching me pack.

Tracey had been sent to pick me up and expedite my departure. But she obviously doesn't feel comfortable here and wants to get out as soon as possible. A few miles away Scanlon's private plane is waiting to take us to California.

Shutting the suitcase the lock clicks with finality. Now I have to find Elizabeth to make sure I'll see her again. I love her so much – feel such gratitude for what she has taught me.

"I love you too." grinned Elizabeth as she materializes and takes my arm. "Congratulations, you're getting out of here."

"How do you know?"

"Do I really have to answer that?"

We giggle. Tracey turns and smiles at the laughter but doesn't see Elizabeth. "We've got to get going," she says with an apologetic smile. "We can't keep the plane waiting." Her tone doesn't match her smile.

"Why don't you take a walk on the grounds while I finish up here," I suggest. "It's pretty" I want to be alone with Elizabeth and I can't talk to her with Tracey in the room. She would think I was crazy.

"Is it safe?" asks the young attorney.

"Don't worry, the ghouls and real crazies only go out after sunset."

Tracey's eyes go wide with calculation as she processes my words. Deciding I'm joking she's still holds back. Not sure she'll be safe.

"I'll take a quick peek out the front door." She slowly goes out the door, looking both ways before she steps into the hallway.

Elizabeth and I laugh when Tracey is out of sight. We had read her mind together. I feel a twinge of guilt. I eaves dropped again. I hope I'm not abusing my newfound powers. At the same time, Elizabeth thinks the same. We look at each other and erupt with laughter. I scold myself not to behave like this as Elizabeth shakes a finger at me.

We laugh again and feelings of love swell inside me. "I'm going to miss you." I wipe one of the tears that escapes from my eyes.

"You don't have to." Elizabeth hugged me. "I can always be with you. Don't forget that." Her shining smile is enchanting, lines of golden energy radiate around her, stretching into a radiant halo that outlines her body. "Our relationship is special," she comforts me. "We're soul sisters. We can always be together."

"But what about when I'm gone from here?"

"I'm not here anymore." She bounces down on the bed nearly toppling me. "Look, I can always be with you, I'm a time traveler. All you have do is call me and we'll be together - whatever, no matter."

"But what if I forget?"

Elizabeth frowned. "That's a problem." She seems to turn pale as she thinks about it. "You will be entering major interferences as you live life as an Earthling – a planet regular. If you talk about me or the things that you've learned here, most won't understand it and they'll get scared and call you crazy. You'll have to be careful because if that happens, then nothing you say will be believed or taken seriously. You'll be separated except for a few sensitive beings."

"That will be lonely out there," I say with sudden misgivings.

"Perhaps - maybe frightening." Elizabeth walks toward the window. "I hate to lose you for now, but I don't want to compromise your time here either. When you were asked in the other world why you wanted to return to Earth, you said you had work to do and must continue. You have to find ways to do it. But remember, always stay with truth and that will make it easier."

"Can I work at the television station and use what I've learned? Go out of body? See the future? What a way to investigate stories!"

"That's dangerous. Too much visibility. There are people who have to believe they're in control. If they think you have more power than they do, they'll throw everything they have at you and try to annihilate you. You'd be a threat and they'll do anything to silence you.

You've had a taste of that already - that's why you're in this hospital. You are going to have to use the utmost of discretion to accomplish your mission."

I shrugged. "I can't worry about anything personal. When my time's up, I'm ready."

"No fear?"

"Why? I know what's waiting and it's beautiful. I just don't want to have to go through another hell like the one wrapped around this learning experience. It was awful."

Elizabeth shook her head, a tiny frown of worry creasing her forehead. "Maybe, but you used it positively and learned a lot from it. There are no guarantees. But don't leave your body completely till you've accomplished what you set out to do. Always go back to it. Otherwise, your life and all you've learned will have been wasted and you'll have to come back to do it all again. You know what you must do and you'll join with others to accomplish it." She reaches over and gives me a hug and kiss on the cheek. "And hurry up. I don't want to have to keep returning to Earth for you. This time should be enough." She starts to leave, then pauses. "Remember, even if you forget me, I'll always be there for you - in some way that knowledge shall be your security and your foundation." She blows a kiss and swoopes through the window where she begins stirring up wind around Tracey.

I laugh , tears stream down my face.

Parker shoves the filthy man up against the wall. "Son of a bitch..." He draws his fist back to hit him but Detective Grady grabs his arm.

"Don't."

"Dirty Bastard. Let me at him. Boyle was going to retire soon - son of a bitch - I want to kill him."

"You almost did," said the other officer, holding Parker back as he flexes and strains against the officer's hands.

"I'll make you a deal," the filthy man said.

"What? Take a bath?" Grady yelled at the prisoner. "You stink like shit."

"No lawyers. No trial. I plead guilty - second degree — do some time, plastic surgery and that's it. No publicity."

"Second degree - you got to be kidding. If I don't kill you with my hands I'll personally inject you." Parker feins an attempt to go for him again.

"Cool it - he might have something to tell us." Detective Grady takes Parker out of the prisoner's hearing. "Good show, but back off a little. He's scared. That smell is coming from his pants."

Parker walks over to the man and motions him toward a chair. The man backs away and sits down immediately. Parker opens a window and the door. "You stink. How can you stand yourself?"

"Close the door if you want information." The man had lost his cower and his voice, no longer trembling reveals a sophisticated persona beneath the stench and rags. "I was paid to do that job. I did you guys a favor. Boyle was dirty. He was going to pin it on someone-probably you," he gestures toward Parker. "He's been on the take for years and my employers were afraid he was getting too hot."

"That's bullshit," Parker yelled, about to go for him.

The man kept talking. Parker settled down. "Think about some of your partner's actions. You're lucky you're alive Detective. That man was dirty. Greedy. Did you ever wonder why he overlooked details? About the way he sucked up to powerful people? Ring a bell? Huh?"

Parker doesn't answer but stares, his fists clenched.

"He was going to be investigated - drugs, arms - you name it. He was in a lot of people's pocket. He was stockpiling money for retirement. This is one cop whose family won't need a benefit. They're very well taken care of - if they know the number of the bank accounts."

"You're full of shit - literally," said Parker.

"Keep going," said Grady.

"Look, you got me. I have nothing to gain from this besides helping you guys. Your partner would have been a big embarrassment to the department, and he could have dragged you down with him. You're lucky."

"Cut the crap. You have something real to tell us ?" Parker says to him through gritted teeth.

"I work for a group who like to have things their way. They say they're non-violent, and only guard their privacy. If you cross them, their punishment is fast and lethal"

"Why are you telling us this?" asks Grady.

"Because the minute they find out I'm arrested, I won't get life insurance. And I don't want to be tortured before I die."

"What do you want?"

"I give you solid gold information, make you look good and you protect me. new I.D, plastic surgery from the Dr. of my choice, second degree charge and I get lost in the prison system of my choice for a few years, nothing more."

"No promises. Give us a preview. We're going to record it." Parker nodded at Grady who turns the tape recorder on.

"It'll help me write my memoirs," a smile plays at the corner of his lips. It ends with Parker's look.

"Remember the television newscaster who killed himself on the 6:00 evening news?"

Parker nodded, "Go on."

"That wasn't suicide. It was induced by hypnotic suggestion and a new drug in development. Very suggestible drug. Works well, huh ? The suicide served two purposes. He was a field test and my employers thought it would be good for their ratings - vested interest

- but I don't want to get into that. That's not what this is about."

"Get to what it's about," said Parker, practically on the edge of his seat.

"Not long ago some girl, a scientist or something drove off a cliff in Santa Monica on to rush hour traffic. Neat huh?"

Parker froze. The other detective snatched a look at him and motioned the man to continue.

"No one expected the bitch to take so many with her. She got shot up with a version of that same drug and we were going to pull her into a van. But a cop car came along and I had to let her go. She got into her car and I guess you know the rest." He paused and looked at the other detective then quickly at Parker before he continued. "They had factored in a time provision for an unforeseen event and figured the worst that could happen was if she endeder up driving she'd hit another car or a post or something. The chemicals were too hot. They should have taken longer to kick in. They were supposed to be timed to take fifteen minutes but..." he shrugged and grinned. "Shit happens. Someone fucked up."

Parker made a note that the man had incriminated himself with the word, "I". Grady saw the note and gave him a sign he too had picked it up. "Anything more?"

The man shrugged and shook his head.

"We sent your prints to DC They're being put through the main frame now. You may as well tell us your name, it's just a matter of time."

"You won't find anything. I don't leave prints around. They can be changed - you know that. We're professionals - not common slobs like you guys."

A flush worked its way up Parker's neck. He used his discipline to keep from exploding. "Want to give us something to call you besides dead man?"

"John."

"Like in Doe?"

"You got it."

"You're pushing me..." said Parker, half out of his chair, ready to go for him again for real this time.

"You got the first two - guarantee me protection, second degree charge with parole, and put out a press release that I was killed. Then let me get lost somewhere."

Parker would have liked to smash the man's arrogance, wipe out his face, but said to him instead, "We need names, more than what you've given us."

"You'll have them. It's all tied up with the group I work for. They have interesting plans on the drawing board for your futures. The clock is ticking."

"Sure, John. A conspiracy. How about a global one, just like in the movies." chuckled Grady. "That's always a good one."

Parker pushed his chair back, his fists clenched tighter. Since the filthy man mentioned Mannie, Parker wanted to grab him and pry every bit of information out of him. He knew he would be able to link Tim's death with this guy. It was almost the same M.O. as Mannie's. This guy might have information about Jenny too. What a strange piece of luck.

The man smiled and Parker leaped over to him and grabbed the front of his shirt, ripping it more than it already was as he leaned back to turn off the tape recorder. "Don't you even think of smiling, dead man. Understand? Just tell us what you know." He turned the tape recorder back on.

"You got the introduction. I don't give the rest till the deal is done."

"We can't promise you anything, cop killer, you know that. Your murder killing a cop was filmed. MURDER ONE with special circumstances. Santa Monica has eighteen more murders with your name on them now that you cleared Manuela Sebastiane."

"I didn't do that."

"You admitted you injected her. It's on tape. You used her as a weapon. Very special circumstances."

The man stayed silent. He wasn't about to say anything more.

"You don't have a glimmer of hope until you give us enough information that could bring down the Pope."

"I have some Vatican scam material - but nothing about the Pope. He was on vacation," quipped the man. Parker pushed back his chair but before he could get out of it the prisoner held up his hands, "just kidding! I'm talking about the government and the garbage that surrounds it."

"Yeah, you and every other two bit criminal." Parker didn't mean it. The guy might have something. He had mentioned two sensational deaths that looked like suicide. He would check out the coroner's report and see if there had been any evidence of drugs found in the newscaster.

"What about Tim Jenkins?" Parker decided to ask. "Know anything about that?"

"Detective Parker. You want me to give away the jewels before the deal is negotiated. That isn't good business."

CHAPTER TWENTY-FIVE

Southern California has been having one of its infrequent thunderstorms as the private jet bumped its way through the clouds covering the city. The flight had been incredible, and I had discovered near the start of it I was very hungry. I hadn't eaten in months. Although I tried to be cautious and not over-do, the steward was delighted with my enthusiastic responses to his cooking and created a dinner that I told him was "the best I've had in ages." I didn't mention that actually it was the first one in months.

After eating I had a different feeling, my body was attached to me again. I was no longer living in my head. To help me move outside my thoughts, the plane had a choice of first-run films and audio books to choose from. Anything I wanted was there for the asking. The flight seemed to zoom by so fast I was disappointed when we started to land. It had been pure luxury, this floating carpet for the rich could be easy to get used to.

When I reached my apartment, I was relieved that Clarita had been there and cleaned everything. I opened the Oriental window screens and fresh air entered the apartment. Everything seemed clean, sparkling and fresh, yet there was an undercurrent. Is it the memory of what happened here?

I didn't think I would want to move. I thought I could handle it. The apartment had been leased from a writer going on foreign assignment. Geographically centered between the studio and Tim's home it was to be used as a place to spend time when I wasn't with him. But then the writer decided to stay on the foreign desk in Europe and Tim surprised me with tickets to Europe for a shopping spree for my new apartment. Some of my hopes and dreams dimmed a little when I ended up with marble tables instead of an engagement ring. I silently resented part of his election plan was to postpone the engagement till the end of the campaign and right before the election pop the question in a very public way, perhaps on a popular talk show like Steven Colbert to give Tim an extra glow. But that's history and I have my new future to navigate.

I put the chain lock on the door. This is it ! I'm home! My beloved desk, my computer. Maybe I'll get a cat or a dog! I can hardly wait to sit down and write - there is so much to say, so much to deliver.

Yet – will I be allowed to write what I've learned? Seeing the destruction of this planet had been an invitation to add my voice to the growing concern that Earth's resources are not being respected. At one time I had studied the myths of Atlantis, a civilization said to have inhabited Earth thousands of years ago. In terms of sophisticated technology it was believed this highly evolved society had been far superior to the present one on Earth. Supposedly it had harnessed crystals to the power of the sun. Allegedly this linkage led to a series of great explosions that caused earthquakes and volcanic eruptions among other disasters that ultimately destroyed not only Atlantis, but most life on this planet. If the myth is based in truth, then the fate of Atlantis could be a window for our time and a metaphor for our future. History repeats itself.

If I reveal these thoughts people will call me crazy. I 'll probably be shut out of television news, my public forum.

But that won't stop me from doing my best to produce what I believe is necessary for the world to know. Clear thinking is adversarial to destructive behavior.

"Most people won't believe it," reminds the voice in my head – a voice as separate from my own thinking as my body is from this chair.

Defiantly I pick up the phone to call Rudnik. But the phone is dead. It isn't supposed to be turned off. What's wrong?

In the kitchen I try the other phone. Its dead as well. A cabinet door is partially opened and I look inside. It's crammed with groceries. Who would have done that? I rarely ate at home.

Something isn't right. Everything feels different. Perhaps I'm the one who has changed. But I can't be sure of that, not yet. Maybe this is just another hallucination and I'm out of body again. Maybe this foray back to what is called home and reality isn't real at all. Dread starts to take over. "*Get control,*" yells the voice. "*Don't get scared, stay strong.*"

Taking a deep breath I allow the usually annoying sounds of my neighborhood - children yelling, horns blowing - to comfort me with their familiar sounds. At least something has remained the same. I start to feel better. The doorbell rings.

Fear clutches me. I go to the door, praying the nightmare I hope behind me has ended. Through the peephole Detective Parker, a smile on his face, stands with a bouquet of flowers. As I open the door, an instant flush of comfort covers me. I feel better now.

"This is probably against regulations, but, welcome back," he hands me the flowers.

"That's so sweet. Thank you. I won't tell! It means a lot." I can feel the color rising in my cheeks for the words I've just said. I hadn't expected to say them, I was just so surprised.

I motioned him to sit down, "These are beautiful. I'll put them in water. Can I get you anything? My kitchen is mysteriously filled with food. I've never had more choices to eat in my life."

Its Parker's turn to blush. I think he's glad I'm in the kitchen. "Ah, the department, actually, I did that," he stammered.

"You did?" I popped back into the living room. beaming with pleasure and surprise.

"I thought it would be nice for you to come home and not worry about shopping and have something to eat. Guess it is my mother's influence. The manager let me in. One of the perks of Law Enforcement," he said with a heart-stopping smile.

"That's so lovely, thank you." I came over to the sofa and sit down on the other side. "And thank your mother for me. I have to admit it scared me a little when I saw everything in the kitchen. I couldn't imagine where it came from."

"I'm sorry."

"No, I don't mean it negatively. I'm thrilled. It's only because I was having problems with time when I was in the hospital. I could go from one reality to another, so I'm still a little afraid I'm not really here, afraid I'm going to wake up and find myself back in that terrible hospital again. What you've done could be a wonderful fantasy and if it is, I prefer not to wake from it."

"You won't, this is real, I promise." Parker's smile is warm and gentle. It soothes my nerves.

"I can assure you, you're very much here." He starts to put his hand out to touch mine but draws it back abruptly, clears his voice and stands up. "This is actually an official visit. We would like you to come down to headquarters and look at a line-up. We have someone that we thought might have a connection with Mannie's accident. If you recognize anyone, perhaps it will strike some memory, some detail to connect with the last night you were with her. Think you're up to it?"

"Absolutely."

He started to go for his cell phone then changed his mind. "I don't get good reception here." He picked up the kitchen phone. It was dead. Then he picked up the cord. It hadn't been plugged in. Tears of relief quickly sprang to my eyes. I was so grateful to him I almost couldn't stand it!

For the first time in my life I experience the meaning of topsy turvy. I'm was feeling that way and it's a terrific feeling.

Parker put down the receiver. "We have time for coffee, then they'll be ready. Okay?"

I shook my head affirmatively. I can't believe this is happening. I'm scared, but happy, and also hungry.

The bright lights and noisy din of the police station almost throw me into a panic - the raw emotion and the contained violence reach out and envelop my senses. Its only because of Parker's hand on my arm do I feel stability.

Holding me tightly, guiding me through the maze of victims and perps, jailors and noise to a dark, quiet room, a sanctuary, till a flick of a switch transforms it to a bright cube with an interior window running the length of one wall. On the other side is a slightly larger room with a raised platform for line-ups.

Although I know the glass is one way as the six men file in, I feel uncomfortable, almost conspicuous. Like they can see me, though I know they can't.

They're all of similar height and weight - some scroungy, terribly so, and most look like convicts. I assume most are policemen.

But there is one man, so disheveled and filthy it seems I can smell him. He makes me very uncomfortable, like I'm dirty. I feel like he can see me through the glass and can touch me. He wears the ragged garb of the homeless, but something about him belies his looks.

My eyes must be widening as I study him and shudder with what I'm thinking. Oh God. Can this be possible? My blood is surging, cold dread wins again. I know who he is, I recognize him. Like Jan White there is no forgetting who he is, no matter his costume.

Parker is looking at me but my eyes are locked to the window.

Truth is staring at me, waiting for me to reveal him. Dare I face it? Can I turn to Parker and speak it? Is it possible to tell the detective that on the other side of the glass is a filthy man who had stripped me to my primal essence, who had physically entered my body and had sex with me ? I try to take my eyes away and look at the others, but I can't. It's futile. I know who he is and I have to tell Detective Parker.

My hands clammy, my body both shivering and perspiring, I lean toward Parker. "Is it possible to have number three put on dark glasses?" My voice is thin and sounds skittish.

Parker is placid professional, making no judgement on what I had asked for. He lifts the intercom and makes the request. Someone on the other side of the glass goes over to the man at the place marked "3" and hands the vagrant a pair of dark tinted sunglasses and puts them on him.

The man who was in my apartment, who had approached me in bright daylight on the street and who had grabbed me in the garage. The one who blindly followed the orders of Jan White, who killed my best friend, Mannie a few hours after he tortured me was no longer hidden beneath this costume of a homeless man. It no longer hides this sadistic rapist and killer who is so close on the other side of the glass wall.

Revulsion and fear makes me speechless. I hadn't known the horrible truth till this very moment. The filthy man was my tormentor and rapist as well as the blind man in the Deli who must have killed Mannie. There is no mistaking him as I had before. He was both men and I hadn't known it, hadn't connected it till this actual moment.

Questions piled on questions. How could I not have recognized him when I saw him in the deli? How could I not have sensed he had been my attacker? Had I been that rattled, that out of focus ? Why had I not put the facts together when I was out of body - if that really happened. How much had I missed, how much more had I misinterpreted? Pin pricks of dread started to pepper my mind.

"Does he look like anyone you've seen?" Parker asked again.

My head refused to move. Shame and anger kept me rigid. I wanted to run, the man still scared me What would he say – we had sex at my encouragement. Did it matter ? Anything he said would defile and mortify me. I'm skidding into denial, what can I be thinking ? Tears no longer threaten, they stream down freely.

Only a thin piece of glass keeps me separated from that man who knew me naked, had rubbed his own naked skin against mine, had felt my shudders, saw my pride and knew the tolerance of my pain.

Sickness and conflict rage brutally inside me. Once again, he would mock me, once again expose me. I don't want Parker to see this. Everything I had gained, I have lost. If I had recognized this monster earlier I could have saved Mannie.

As a sigh comes through me I take a deep breath. I have to tell the detective the whole truth of what happened. What this man had done to me and expose the dark places that had been opened to me and what I used to survive. Did it matter he changed me forever? Stripped to the marrow and exposed as I had been, my vulnerability will forever be raw and open to terror. I now live with fear daily. I don't want to tell him, I feel so ashamed. I'm still that man's victim. He's haunting me and I'm afraid to accuse him. Can I say only that he is the blind man in the deli? Turning further away I'm mortified by my own thinking.

"Who is he?" insists Parker.

"He's the blind man in the deli. I think he killed Mannie." I paused, then "He has other connections."

Continuing quietly, "he wore dark glasses - had a red-tipped cane. He was the blind man that I told you who kept watching us and made me feel uncomfortable. I guess on some level I knew he could see us and in some deep level of consciousness I knew who he was. But I was afraid to admit I knew who he was, how I had seen him only hours before."

Parker looked surprised.

"Not in the restaurant. I was too bombarded with my own terror and of course, Mannie's emotional journey."

I stop to take a breath and calm myself. quickly, "but now," I take a breath. "I know who he worked for and I know a name he used."

Parker is almost wide eyed with surprise at the extent of my knowledge.

"What is it?"

"Larry Martin."

"How do you know that ?"

Time stopped. I had to continue. "Because, he was used by..." I opened my mouth but nothing came out. Parker waited.

"I know..." starting then stopped, looking at Parker whose kind eyes are sympathetic and encouraging. Dizziness is overwhelming me, making my story less concrete and difficult to tell. The truths of it are loathsome.

"He kidnapped me outside Anson Industries and raped me in my home under the supervision of Jan White, one of the head doctors at the psychiatric hospital where I had been hospitalized after the rape."

So light-headed with telling this, I seriously think I could pass out.

He looks at me steadily which surprisingly gives me strength as he picks up the phone "Number 3."

Smiling gently he leads me from the room. "Let's talk." We head toward the coffee machines.

"Can I go home?"

"In a little while. I need some clarification on what you just told me. You dropped a bombshell. How about hot chocolate, it makes everything feel better."

I nodded and he pushed the hot chocolate button.

"We want you to sign a paper with your positive identification. He paused and motioned me to sit next to him, handing me the paper cup. "Did you report the rape?"

"No," I answered. "But that was a reason they put me in the sanitarium. They said I attempted suicide, that *my reality testing was impaired* - medical double talk for not behaving the way others think I should act."

"Could that have happened?"

Fear stiffened to anger with his question. "I was set up," I said curtly, "I know what happened and why, but if I tell you, you might think I'm crazy. It's so outrageous and insidious, that if I were on the outside maybe I would have trouble believing it." I turn away. I had thought it was all behind me and I no longer had to justify my behavior and feelings, but here is someone I thought I could trust, and now he too questions me. Will I ever find peace? Does truth have to cost so much?

"Jenny," he said softly, leaning into me, sending me comforting feelings. "I know how terribly difficult this is for you. Your life these past months must have been a nightmare. Keep yourself strong and you'll endure this. You're on the last lap now and it will soon be over. But I need you to tell me as much about that man as you know. It will help our case as well as your own sense of security. Trust me, I know it's difficult, but I'll try to lead you comfortably through this."

I'm not sure I can believe him. I just want to go home, and sleep till it's over.

"Your conspiracy theory is checking out, it's valid."

I look up. Am I imagining this? Is there a light shining around him? No, it has to be my imagination. It's the glare of the overhead fluorescence.

"The man you singled out is the one we have in custody. He's a hired gun," Parker said. "We've got him on other charges. He shot and killed my partner."

"Oh no!" I shook my head. "I'm sorry."

Parker went on. "We might be able to get him for Mannie's murder as well as all the others. Your testimony can help get him a lethal injection. But first we want to know everything about who hired him."

"He was part of a team to make me psychologically vulnerable," I anxiously tell him.

"Rape as a political tool," he says as he writes it down. His fair skin has turned red and I notice he's gripping his pen tightly.

"Disgusting," he says as he looks up. "The pieces are all coming together, making a lot of sense. I thought some of these cases were linked." His blue eyes are deep and caring. "It will come together," he was saying. "But it won't be easy. We need your information, you've got to tell me everything."

"I'll try."

The cramped interrogation room is filled with a bad odor from the unwashed man. Some of the cops can't take it and leave only Parker and Grady to stay behind.

"O.K. Man of a Thousand Faces. We got a positive I.D. on you for kidnap, assault and rape with intent to kill. You admitted injecting Manuela Sebastiane moments before she died with some drug. It's on tape. We also have you starring on videotape killing a cop. Now, Plastic Man, want to put on record what you carry in your mind? You're a dead man any way you look at it."

The filthy man stretched his legs out and pulled an empty chair toward himself with his foot. "Mind if I put my feet up ? My circulation is killing me."

"Good." Parker kicked the empty chair away. "Then we can watch you die and save the taxpayers a lot of time and money."

"Hey," said the vagrant. "What did I do?"

Parker picked up a clipboard but didn't look at it. "You heard me. For starters we have a victim who has fingered you for kidnap and rape, you're on tape killing a police officer and admitted to causing the death of Dr. Manuela Sebastiane and eighteen others,."

The unwashed man threw his head back and winked. "Rape. They always call it rape - after. She loved it, asked me to come in her, got off on it, said I was terrific. Ask her. She had such a great time she couldn't stand it. You know how those broads are. Now she's angry and crying rape. Well at least she gave me a good time. Tell her thanks next time you see her." He ran his tongue over his filthy cracked lips.

Parker lunged for him and Grady pulled him back. The vagrant sat up, interested. "You seem to be emotionally involved, Detective. Perhaps you shouldn't be on this case. Conflict of interest? Are you personally involved? Have you been bought like your partner? Have you fucked her? I know who she is. She's very good..." He smiled, licked his lips.

Parker kept his boiling anger internal. On the outside he was calm, his quiet menacing voice so low only the dirty man could hear him. "We're going to charge you with Murder One - special circumstances, kidnapping, attempted murder, extortion, everything we can possibly cram down your fucking throat. Do you hear me?"

The guy nodded. The smirk faded from his face.

"Are you going to tell us who you're taking the fall for and why? We want names. They can't get to you."

The man's mouth curled, his eyes narrowed. "The people I'm involved with can get to anyone - anywhere - any time. Believe me."

"Names," whispered Parker, coming closer. "Give me names and then you can go take a shower and get nice laundered and ironed prison issue so we can start feeding and housing you for the rest of your life." He came in closer. "Which might be shorter than you want." Parker walked a few steps away and turned back to him. "We'll keep you alive if you want to sing. If not," he shrugged, "it's going out you talked anyway. And if you're right about your friends, they'll get to you no matter where you are."

The unwashed man remained seemingly impassive, however, his eyes exposed busy calculation.

"You have five minutes. Then we put you out into the general prison population." Parker started to gather his things up. "How long you figure your chances of staying alive in there ? Five minutes? Half an hour?" He checked his watch. "It's three o'clock now."

CHAPTER TWENTY-SIX

Three hours into the interrogation the room smelled like an open sewer. Parker, and the two FBI agents had no intention of taking a break, and the defendant had only given them some information but did not seem ready to crack on the important things they want to know.

"I gotta tell you JOHN, you'll be doing us all a favor if you give us names so you can get rid of those clothes and wash off that filth. I can't imagine how you must feel being that close to yourself... You'll be doing yourself a great favor." He looked at the two impeccable FBI men, looking as fresh as they had when they first entered the room. "Us too." Parker could have been cast as an insurance salesman in a Mutual of Omaha commercial. He couldn't have sounded more honest, more down-home wholesome all-American.

The filthy man isn't buying it. He knows Parker is as tough and cold and manipulative beneath that simple act as he is himself. "Give up my life for a bar of soap?" sneered the man. "Think I'm a Jew in Auschwitz?"

Parker thought for the umpteenth time he would like to let go and lose it. Wrap his fingers around the bastard's throat till his palms touched would be first choice. The misery the man has caused, the human lives he has taken or ruined with his traumatic, emotional destruction! Yet Parker forces himself to stay calm. A lot could be riding on this man's information. He will do everything in his power to get him to say as much as possible. "I told you, as soon as you give us the names, we'll have the D.A. in here cutting you a deal." He turns to the Feds. "If that's all right with you gentlemen." The two federal agents blink their assent, a look not wasted on the prisoner.

The man realizes that if he doesn't compromise soon, it's only a matter of time till the FBI will leave the room and the monster will be unleashed from Parker. At least, that's what he would have done if their roles were reversed. Unexpected behavior overpowers an opponent by catching him off guard and thus weakening him.

"How long do I wait for the D.A.?"

"He's here."

"I wash first."

"You gotta be kidding," said Parker. He nods toward the door and it opens almost immediately. Ed Wiseberger, a handsome perfectly groomed, slightly starched politician who has recently been elected D.A. elegantly saunters in. Because of his huge local win he almost immediately started his campaign for Governor. Nodding to the two FBI men he starts to say something but stops as the onslaught of offensive stench permeating the room reaches him. Pulling a monogrammed handkerchief from his pocket, he holds it to his nose and looks at Parker in surprise. Parker shrugs and suppresses a smile. Totally ignoring the prisoner the D.A. addresses himself to Parker. "Uh, is there any way we can take care of this uh, problem before we talk?"

Parker shook his head no, very slowly. The D.A. reads the warning in his eyes and girds himself to sit down opposite the foul man. They size each other up - both costumed for their respective roles, both confident in their ability to outmaneuver and outsmart the other. Born con men - one taking the high road, the other - the lowest.

"O.K. John Doe. What have you got for us?"

"You tell me what you have for me first," countered the prisoner.

"Life without parole," answered the D.A. smoothly, or execution."

"No good." The man's lips twisted in anger.

"Okay, it's Special Circumstances - death penalty in each case unless you talk to us." He pushes his chair back and starts toward the door. A moment's pause, only the clock ticks, as everyone watches the D.A. reach for the handle.

"Congressman Leef," tosses out the prisoner. "Life sentence with chance for parole..."

"You've got to give us more." The D.A. takes his hand away but doesn't move from the door.

"Concurrent terms with chance of parole will give you corporate names as well as government," bargains the prisoner. "Look, I'm a professional, I'm hired to work for those guys. I don't give a shit for their politics. I take their money and do the job. That's it. But I don't want my competition hired to take me out. You give this case any kind of publicity, you won't have to fill the needle because I won't make it out of the cell alive."

"That's right," agreed Weisberger. "You don't give us names we hold you for murder-one - right in the middle of the general prison population."

"My life expectancy would be less than two hours."

The D.A. looks bored and shrugs.

The prisoner hesitates but starts talking the moment he sees Weisberger start to move again. "Okay Mr. District Attorney, come back. Here are the keys to your political future. Remember me when you give your next acceptance speech, because your prize witness is about to rub out your competition. But first - I want to see your deal in writing – officially. You won't put me in the general prison population, I want to represent myself, writing privileges, private television set, access to books, telephone, four hours of exercise, no talk of the death penalty, eligibility for parole, and while you're having that typed up I want a shower."

"You get a shower WITH a bar of soap after you give us what you know. You can start singing after you sign." The D.A. mumbles something into the phone and within seconds an aide appears with an official document. Weisberger scans it a slow and agonizing time, then hands it to Parker who is able to speed read it.

"Well," said Weisberger. "Is it all right with you? I know it sticks in your gut, but..." He hands it to the two Federal agents who scan it together.

Parker bites his lip, angry, then tosses his head - Make the deal - it will be good to see him go stir crazy."

The agents nod in agreement and hand the paper to the prisoner. The man scans the paper, goes back over it weighing every word. The D.A. sits back and cracks his knuckles. Parker is poised on the edge of his chair. The two FBI men remained unflappable, their eyes darting from the prisoner to the D.A. to the detective. No one says a word. Were it not for the incidental noise of the street and the outside hallway, they would have been able to hear each other breathing.

The prisoner puts the paper down and stares at the D.A. The professional politician makes a point of checking out the condition of his manicured nails. The man picks up the pen and Parker leans toward him again, willing him to sign. But once again, he throws the pen back down and picks up the paper to read another clause. "What about parole?" he asks.

"I put 'Best Efforts', that's all I can legally do," mumbles Weisberger, flicking a speck of nothing off his perfectly tailored lapel then checks his gold Cartier watch.

The man's face darkens, his lips twist, his fist opens and shuts. Again he picks up the pen, hesitates, then slowly - ever so slowly - signs a name to the document. The 'fish is caught and the D.A. snatches the paper and leaves the room. An audible sigh of relief runs through it.

Two policemen bring in a video recorder. They set it up quickly and quietly while everyone else fills their coffee cups, take off their jackets and settle in.

"I'll be glad when this is over so I can breathe again," Parker says before reading the prisoner his Miranda rights for the camera. On video and audio-tape the man waives his right to an attorney.

"Shall we start with the television reporter who committed suicide on the evening news?"

The man leans back and smiles, relishing the moment for the dramatic response it will elicit. "Seth MacDonald, Chairman and CEO of Larkin Communications," he says in loud deliberate tones. "He hires me for that hit when I was working for a company developing surveillance and," he can't contain a snicker, "other forms of technology. Good hit, huh? Looked like suicide."

Parker's eyes narrow, his mouth twitches as he writes the name down with three question marks after it. Even the two unflappable FBI agents look around as unease rustles through the shocked room. Seth Macdonald is one of the most powerful media moguls in the country . He just received one of the White House's greatest honors, the Presidential Service Award in a ceremony that was broadcast only two weeks ago.

"What is the name of the company you work for?" asked Parker.

"Anson Industries."

Parker's pencil nearly drops. "Who was your immediate superior?"

"Robert Jordan."

A flush spreads over Parker's face. "You went directly to the CEO?" He used discipline maintaining his composure.

"Yes."

"Will you directly state his position."

"Why? You already said it." He shrugged then looks directly into the camera lens. "Robert Jordan is Chief Executive Officer of Anson Industries."

"What kind of work were you doing?

He leaned back smiling, knowing he had dropped a bombshell. "I told you, security, surveillance..."

"Details, John Doe - your requests run high." Parker said through clenched teeth.

Although the room was hot and airless and the men inside had long since become accustomed to the putrid smell, they sat in rapt attention as the filthy man exposed a sordid tale of uncountable wealth, unaccountable greed, and lust for power that closely matches everything Jenny Webster told Parker.

As the digital clock clicks to 4:30, streaks of dawn filtering through the smudged windows reveals a mountain of Styrofoam cups and soft drink cans. The prisoner's voice drones a tale of such immorality, that the men who listen have trouble believing its real. But nevertheless, they are spellbound in rapt attention as his story unfolds.

"Senators Brume and Hunt and Congressman Leef are at the last meeting," repeats the man, his tone impatient, his throat husky with fatigue, his voice heavy with the drama he's creating.

"Can anyone corroborate that?" asks Parker, his shirtsleeves rolled up, his usually pink face a color similar to cream. "Do you have video or audio tapes?"

"Yes, I have them. But I'm not sure they can be found unless my sentence is commuted."

"Not possible." Parker is quiet and seemingly patient. The FBI men give him an approving nod.

The exhausted man stops. He doesn't want to continue, but the smell and the stress and the time are reaching unbearable proportions. "What the hell - it's my patriotic duty to pull the scum down." Video and tape recorders start to grind in their mechanical way as the man begins to tell his story.

CHAPTER TWENTY-SEVEN

Dawn is quickly turning into daylight as Parker leaned on my doorbell. Announcing himself he ran up the stairs two at a time to get to the door. Sleepily I invite him in.

He opens a bag with two paper cups. "Here's some coffee. I want you to be awake to hear this."

Leading him into the kitchen I ask what could be so important this early in the morning. I don't add that his usually pristine appearance was anything but pulled together.

"The guy talked. He named Robert Jordan, Seth Macdonald, Senators Gerald Brume, Lloyd Hunt and Congressman Erik Leef. Do any of the names besides Jordan's mean anything to you personally?"

"Well sure, besides being well known public figures I interviewed some executives from Larkin Communication, and then of course, you know I had interviewed Jordan the day that..."

"Yes," he interrupted before I'd have to explain. "But if Jordan ordered that, it doesn't seem likely he would let it happen on Anson property. Doesn't make sense."

"Exactly why it was chosen. Reverse logic."

"Perhaps. Go on."

I hesitated. "I could tell you my suspicions about some of the people you mentioned, but it isn't evidence."

"Then tell me about Mannie."

I take a deep breath. "Okay. I've done a lot of thinking and piecing things together. I had Mannie's external hard drive before any of this happened. She had mine. We would copy each other's in case something happened to one of us and our computers were gone. There was a diary, notes, correspondence - you know, private things. Anyway, with that help I put together this scenario: Mannie had alienated the other scientists in her lab because she wasn't a team player. So they decided to make her one."

He looked at me quizzically.

"They needed a human fetus to develop full term outside the body. Mannie objected, thought it was too soon. They could have merged any egg and sperm in a Petri dish, but they decided that Mannie might lighten up if she went through the beginnings of pregnancy - it started as a joke. So they drugged her and impregnated her using a vial of their collective sperm. It was collective so no one would feel personally responsible."

Parker looked genuinely shocked. "That's disgusting."

I shrugged. "People have different perceptions of behavior. Pranks can be very damaging. Anyway, as soon as Mannie conceived, they were going to retrieve the fertilized egg and start the experiment. But something screwed up and they had to wait three and a half months before the artificial womb was ready. Meanwhile, Mannie was unaware anything was happening - except she felt miserable and didn't want anyone to know it. Including me."

Parker pulled the plastic cover off one of the cups and spilled coffee on the counter. I got a paper towel and started to mop it up, but Parker took the towel from me. "Keep talking." He took over the mopping.

"When Mannie found out she was pregnant and what they planned to do, she wouldn't go along with them. They tried to pressure her saying she had reverted to stereotypical behavior and was turning her back on scientific responsibilities. But she remained adamant. So they decided to give her an older operating room drug, Ketamine, that would knock her out so she wouldn't remember anything but would leave her ambulatory. That way they'd get the fetus and would accuse her of having a false pregnancy when she realized she had lost the baby."

He shook his head. "It doesn't sound feasible, too amateur. Couldn't sophisticated scientists find better ways to conceive a baby? I'm sorry Jenny, but it sounds ridiculous."

"I know, but I'm pretty sure that's what happened. It was a mixture of arrogance and cruelty. That man you have in custody - Larry Martin or whatever his name is, worked for Anson and injected her with the drug that caused the accident."

"We know that, he confessed to it on tape."

"Good." My eyes teared up but I was able to hold the tears back. "They did it to retrieve the fetus from Mannie. And for some reason after she was injected Mannie managed to drive away - and then you know what happened..." I shuddered. "A slaughter."

"That's pretty close to the prisoner's story. A police car had parked near them and he couldn't pull her into the van without arousing suspicion. So he let her go."

I slowly shook my head. "Because I left her alone at the restaurant people were maimed and killed." I could no longer control the tears.

"Don't blame yourself for that." He started to touch me to comfort me but drew back.

I let my breath out. "Why didn't they kill me for knowing what happened to Mannie? They must have known she told me."

Parker's eyes narrowed. "Maybe they didn't." He frowned. "You can't blame yourself for any of this."

"Mannie tried to keep as much information from me as possible, but..." I closed my eyes, then opened them a moment later, hopeful. "Do you think her baby could still be alive?"

He smiled gently. "Jenny, I'm sorry. It never had a chance."

"I guess it was a dream then..."

"Mannie was four months pregnant," consoled Parker. "It isn't possible a fetus could survive a trauma like that - nothing could. You have to accept the only possible conclusion. We'll know more after the rest of the tests are concluded."

I reached for my coffee. "I'm sorry if I sound bitter and self-pitying, but I think I have accepted the conclusion."

"I know you have, I'm sorry."

He looked so sweet, so sincere it made more tears fall.

"I'm sorry, I shouldn't have said that."

He took my hand gently, "We could be apologizing to each other for days like this. I know what you've gone through, believe me, and you handled it splendidly." He paused, "but Jenny, tell me, why the conspiracy? Why the elaborate technology? What's really happening?"

My hand is tingling, warm from his contact. He was so kind, so caring. He had said all along that he wanted to get to the root of Mannie's accident and I think he's an ally. I took a deep breath to steady myself. I hope he'll believe this. "Anson Industries is manufacturing human beings - flesh and blood designer humans."

A long pause as he searched my face, looking for a sign I'm kidding.

He tilted his head. "Are you sure?" He whispered as if he didn't want anyone else to hear us.

My eyes met his and I continued. "They're creating different types of genetically based humans generated by Mannie's work creating portable external wombs. As we speak they're setting up manufacturing processes to create them."

"Humans? Flesh and blood?" He looked at me, then off to the side, across the room.

"Have you read "Brave New World", a book by Aldous Huxley?"

He thought for a moment, "Yes, in high school."

"Well, Huxley foresaw a society that was divided into categories, workers with mental limitations but physical abilities to do menial work, managers who were a little brighter to tell them what to do, and the top of the pile - the ruling class."

"Yes, I remember..."

I sat back. "If you're in the wrong class, no matter how hard you try, your genetic implants will never let you get higher - no matter what."

"Right, but that's science fiction."

I look straight at him. "Detective Parker, remember the space shuttle and the space stations that Isaac Asimov wrote about?"

He looked like he hadn't so I went on. "Asimov's fantasies are now very much reality. It is the same with Huxley's *Brave New World*. Except our society has not yet succumbed to that level of mass mind control. But believe me, the people at Anson and other places are working on it and they're not far from achieving it."

Parker stared at me. I could read his mind and he was thinking I looked intelligent and was speaking in a clear and rational way, except the things I was saying are off the grid. I had been warned of this by Elizabeth. He's thinking that perhaps the guys at the station are right and I'm out of kilter, traumatized by the things that happened to me. He had wanted to get to what he came here to talk about, but maybe he's wrong about me. Maybe I'm kind of *out there*,

I interrupted his chain of thought. "Genetic engineering has made the manufacture of different types of humans possible. It's been in development for years and its now ready for commercial application."

Parker leaned toward me looking concerned. "Jenny, I'm not taping this because it sounds - well..."

"Crazy. Unbelievable. Weird. But if you look at it scientifically, it's feasible. Since genetic engineering we've had the power to create and manipulate different kinds of life. Golly. Our scientists have the opportunity to play god. It's natural for them to want to take science further. That reality has been happening for years You can have your favorite pet cloned after its gone. It's what Mary Shelley warned of in the book, Frankenstein."

"Clifton's records say you were hospitalized for..."

"Schizophrenia. That's what they label me to discredit my attempts to expose what they're doing. It's an easy diagnosis with the things I'm saying; mind reading machines, thought producing technology. Classic Schizophrenia. And I told you about the transponder implants they're putting in fetal and babies' brains that first night when I told you about Mannie."

"Yes, but why would anyone need that clumsy technology if they're about to manufacture humans with predetermined genetic abilities?" said Parker. "Why use implants if they can do it from the moment of conception?"

"Because it's going to take at least two or more generations to cover the planet with manufactured human creations. In the meantime they have to gain control of the existing populations. They're starting with the leaders and people in communications, that's why they tried to use me. And who is to say that many of the people hospitalized in mental hospitals with diagnosis of Schizophrenia, really know and understand what is happening to the world as we know it and have tried to warn us. It's a solid state conspiracy."

"I see your point. It's logical." His hand was shaking as he put his cup down. "Uh, Jenny, that brings me to..."

I interrupt because I want him to understand what I'm saying. "Scientists can now add or delete certain areas of genes that decide intelligence, physical and creative abilities. So now, instead of being born on the wrong side of the blanket or the tracks, a human being will have their destiny determined by the whim of a medical technician. Have you noticed how many very young children are amazing concert musicians or performers as well as pre-adolescents who are graduating from universities?"

Parker looked at me somberly. I think I hit home with him.

"That's explosive."

"That's what I'm trying to tell you."

"I thought it was bigger than I possibly imagined when we got that guy's confession - but this goes beyond anything I envisioned. Jenny...." He seemed shaken, undecided. "Are you absolutely sure?"

"It's happening under the corporate guise of Research and Development."

I'm feeling excited. He's trying to believe me, trying to accept what I'm saying. If someone with his intelligence and sensitivity can help me, we can cut off the head of the organization. I'm feeling relief. He's starting to believe me.

Tears start to come again, but this time from gratitude and vindication.

Parker starts to sit down, then changes his mind. He hands me a napkin to wipe the tears from my eyes.

"Uh, Jenny, I have to tell you something."

"Yes?" I look at him and know my eyes are shining, my smile brighter and happier than he has ever seen me.

Parker turns away and busies himself by wiping the edge of the counter top. "This is going to be hard for you."

"Oh, these aren't unhappy tears, I'm very happy. I know the difficulties facing us. I'm a realist. But if we can get those people and prevent what they're doing, if we can divert what could be one of the worst human disasters that has ever happened on this planet. Prevent being taken over by what may be an alien presence. Think of the ramifications, think of how many millions of people we're saving. I'm not sure anyone other than a few will ever know what could have happened to them and that's great, If I wasn't so shy, I'd throw my arms around you and hug you."

Parker blushed. "Jenny, I understand how important this all is..."

"Important?" I interrupted. "It's monumental! Thank God for giving me the strength to survive and find somebody like you to help fight this." I'm practically floating with excitement.

Parker looks uncomfortable.

I become quiet. "I know this won't bring Tim or Mannie back, and maybe my trust for a long time. But incredible good has come from these sacrifices." My voice cracks with the intense emotion I'm feeling. "At last I have someone who will help me save so many people from this conspiracy."

Parker chokes up as well. "Jenny," he clears his throat. "I don't want you to take this the wrong way. I believe you, but there are many people who won't."

"I know. It's all right, I understand. That's why your input is so important. Your credibility will help us to find others in this struggle to keep our psychological and mental independence."

"Yes, except."

"Except what? Do you have doubts?"

"Well, of course I have doubts until I see proof. Doubts go on till the proof comes in. Look, I want to believe you and..." He could barely continue.

"And?" I smiled, waiting.

"Except, well... This is hard."

My smile is fading. "What? Come on."

"Jenny, you've given us a hell of a lot. You're a heroine! The heroine of this whole thing."

I giggled. "Heroine! You're a romantic! Do you know that? I'm not a heroine I'm a victim that survived."

His face is bright red and he moves away from me. "You've uncovered something incredibly big, except." He stares at his feet. "I can't tell you how much we, I, appreciate what you've gone through..." His voice brakes. He's having trouble keeping it together.

Uneasiness is creeping over me. Why is he so uncomfortable? What is he trying to say?

Parker finally looks me in the eye. "You've suffered more than anyone deserves, but..." He clears his voice. "This may be more difficult for you."

"What do you mean?"

"Jenny, I know how you want to be a part of the investigation. But we can't let you. We'll have to be distanced from you. You can't be involved."

"Why not?"

Disbelief shoots through me. "This is my story. Who says I can't? I lived it and it has to be told." My vision begins to cloud.

"You're going to have to keep a very low profile. You should not cover this for the news, go anywhere near it. In fact, I don't think you're going to be able to testify."

"Are you kidding? I'm probably one of the only eyewitnesses you have. They've killed everyone else. I'm totally involved! You may not have a case without me."

He steeled himself. This was hard. "That's a chance we're taking. But we think it's better if you stay away. Believe me Jenny. I know what I'm saying."

"You know what you're saying? I have incredibly important information. I've lived this! I've seen so much- so many things, things that no one would possibly dream of having happened." I could see in the mirror my face was turning pale, almost translucent, drained with anguish. "I can't believe you're throwing me away like this, discarding me like some disposable nonentity. I can only think you don't want to solve this!"

"I'm sorry. It doesn't come from me."

I almost lose my temper and fight to stay calm. "Then where is it coming from?"

"They." He stopped.

"THEY what?" I demanded.

He returned my gaze, his eyes soft and sad. "They think you're crazy."

The words hit like a club - exploding in my head, breaking up and shattering into thousands of little pieces of matter and sound bites. So there it is. Just what Elizabeth warned me of.

"Crazy." I can barely speak. "Do you think I'm crazy?"

"Not me. I told you."

I could barely hear him - pieces of the word were still falling through the air. "Who?" I managed. "Who thinks that?"

"The system. Law enforcement quarters are not secure with this kind of thing."

"What thing? Dealing with mad women like me? I know what you're saying."

"No, Jenny. You're taking this - well, yes, I can understand how you feel - but you have to understand that anything you say will discredit our findings. It sounds crazy. There is no proof of the things you're talking about."

My breathing stops. Water drips from the faucet, the shine from the metal faucet almost hurts my eyes. The detective has gone out of focus, the floor is moving, undulating, imitating the waves of dizziness coursing through my body. Insanity's stain has already cost me almost a year of my life and the man I loved. I had really started to care about Parker and now he was acting like the rest.

I have to fight back. "I could give you leads," I managed. "I know so much about this."

"I'm sorry. This was discussed at the highest levels."

"Highest levels - you've got to be kidding... The lowest thinking at the highest levels."

Jenny, we think it's for the best. That's why I came here. To tell you what was decided."

"Decided." I want to turn away and not be near him anymore, but I force myself to stay in front of him. "You've decided, like Robert Jordan and his cronies deciding what is best for everyone but themselves. Is there any difference between you and Jordan's cabal wielding your power? Who says you're capable - or they are - or even if I am? You people say I'm crazy. What do you think I feel about you when you throw away valuable information? That isn't a sane or intelligent action."

"Look Jenny, I understand your anger."

"I'm not angry. I'm astounded. And disgusted. I've lived this case, lost two people I loved very much because of it. But I never backed off till you guys found the man who can prove everything I said. And you need me to testify against him."

"No, we're going to plea bargain him. Look, you have us wrong. Believe me."

"Plea bargain and you expect me to believe you? How can I? I know where the records are in the hospital, what has been done with all the experiments. Hell, they tried them on me. I remember them! All that pain, all that suffering and you have an eye witness you don't want to use! Incredible!"

Parker stood silently, shaking his head imperceptibly.

"Please." Tears are coming again and I can't control them. "I think you'd better leave."

"Look, Jenny we want your information, we need it. I didn't say that we didn't. All I said was you were going to have to stay low profile. You can't be involved. If you are, it can cause problems."

"Problems because I know the truth born of insanity. I understand you want to use me expediently. It doesn't matter what I've done or can do - just take what you want when you want it. No different than Larry Martin, except this time the rapists leave my clothes on."

Parker stood stiffly, clutching the counter. "No you have it entirely wrong. It's..."

"Sounds like I don't. Sounds like I'm a police department public relations problem. Who would listen to a crazy woman? I don't want to hear any more of this. Just leave."

He scraped his chair back. I don't look up. My heart pounds heavily with hurt and betrayal as I listen to his footsteps leave the kitchen, cross the living room, and the sound of the door as he opens it and goes out. The door clicks shut.

After all I had been through, all I had learned, how could this possibly happen to me? I go over to the counter and start to clean up. Parker had left the morning newspaper. I open it. Robert Jordan's picture stares out from the center of the top of the page. The headline reads that his company Anson Industries had just bought one of the major cable companies creating one of the largest communications networks in the world. "WHAT NEXT?" asks the headline. Beneath it is listed all the different companies and interests Anson has under its umbrella; covering almost all the needs of modern civilization and for world domination.

If I'm kept away from the investigation and can only give them one- dimensional information, democracy and with it, our freedom will be lost. If the police department's public relations don't want me to be seen, that is no problem. But I can't stay home with the doors shut and do nothing. I can't wait for the police to come when they hit a brick wall. No, they need someone to go through those walls, clear the paths, show them the way. I'm trained. This is the destiny of my training.

I close my eyes. A white light swirls in the middle of my forehead. I can feel a buzzing, a vibration in the top of my skull whirling and lifting me up off my body, through the kitchen into the living room, through the front door and down to the sidewalk.

Parker is heading for a car parked a few feet past my apartment building. Shaking ripples up through my body. I can see him so clearly - as clearly as if I'm next to him.

Parker checks out the street. There is stillness, yet he has an unsettling, kind of queasy feeling. He reaches the car and pulls out his key and puts it in the lock. He stops. A cold breeze sweeps over him. He's tired. He needs a shower. Perhaps a half hour nap before he goes back to the police station. He slides into the driver seat, not really seeing anything except the ignition, stifles a yawn and buckles his seat belt.

"A nap's a good idea Detective Parker. Perhaps then you'll think clearly."

He looks up and grabs for the door. He can't believe this. It's my voice. He turns and seems me sitting in the passenger seat of his car.

"How did you get here?" He looks around desperately."

I smile. "Believe me. I know how to help you Detective Parker. I can keep a very low profile, An invisible one."

THE END

EPILOGUE

THE END IS THE BEGINNING

Those who see a vision that is withheld from those lacking the necessary equipment for its comprehension, are regarded as fanciful and unreliable.

When many see the vision its possibility is admitted.

But when humanity itself has awakened and has an open eye, the vision is no longer emphasized but a fact is stated and a law enunciated.

Such has been the history of the past and such will be the process in the future...

~ ANONYMOUS ~

ABOUT THE AUTHOR

Since the age of five when she wrote, produced, directed and starred in her own musical J. has been involved in the entertainment business.

As a theatre major, J. studied in England then worked in television and theatre as an actor and later a TV executive. Writing came while researching a character for a screenplay and J. ended up as a feature writer for the LOS ANGELES TIMES, while starting two magazines, and writing for various publications

Involved in animal welfare, the arts and science, this is J.'s second book of the Jenny Webster series which begins with "Between Body and Soul" and continues to "Solid State Conspiracy".

VISIT AUTHOR WEBSITE AT
WWW.JSILVERSTONE.COM